# EXPOSURE

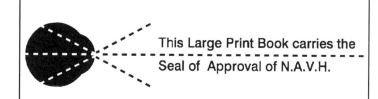

This Large Print Book carries the
Seal of Approval of N.A.V.H.

# Exposure

## Brandilyn Collins

**THORNDIKE PRESS**

*A part of Gale, Cengage Learning*

GALE
CENGAGE Learning

Detroit • New York • San Francisco • New Haven, Conn • Waterville, Maine • London

GALE
CENGAGE Learning

**LIBRARY OF CONGRESS CATALOGING-IN-PUBLICATION DATA**

Collins, Brandilyn.
　　Exposure / by Brandilyn Collins.
　　　　p. cm. — (Thorndike Press large print Christian mystery)
　　　ISBN-13: 978-1-4104-2097-8 (alk. paper)
　　　ISBN-10: 1-4104-2097-3 (alk. paper)
　　　　1. Women journalists—Fiction. 2. Paranoia—Fiction. 3.
Fear—Fiction. 4. Large type books. I. Title.
PS3553.O4747815E92 2009b
813'.54—dc22
　　　　　　　　　　　　　　　　　　　　　　　　　2009030482

Published in 2009 by arrangement with The Zondervan Corporation LLC.

*For my mom,*
*Ruth Seamands,*
*and the denizens of Wilmore*

■ ■ ■ ■

# PART 1

■ ■ ■ ■

Of all the liars in the world, sometimes
the worst are your own fears.

Rudyard Kipling

# ONE

She'd forgotten to turn on the porch lights.

Kaycee Raye pulled into her driveway and slowed her red PT Cruiser. Her gaze bored into the night. The streetlamp across the road behind her dispelled too few shadows. Someone could be out there, watching.

Her gaze cut left to the neighbor's decrepit black barn and its fence in need of paint. The barn hulked sullen and taunting, its bowed slats the perfect hiding place for peering eyes.

Kaycee shuddered.

She looked down Village Circle, running to the left of the barn into the apartment complex of Jessamine Village. All was quiet. Not unusual for nighttime in Wilmore, Kentucky, a small town about twenty minutes south of Lexington.

To the right of Kaycee's house old Mrs. Foley's wide front porch was lit. Kaycee stared into the dimness beyond the lamplight, searching for movement.

A curtain on Mrs. Foley's side living room window edged back. Kaycee tensed. Backlit by a yellow glow, the elderly woman's thin frame hunched behind the glass. Watching.

Kaycee's fingers curled around the steering wheel. *It's only Mrs. Foley, it's only Mrs. Foley.* The woman was harmless. Still, a vise clamped around Kaycee's chest. Since childhood she'd fought the strangling sense of being watched. Talk about Las Vegas odds — what were the chances of her buying a house next to a snoopy old woman?

Kaycee struggled to grasp the coping skills she'd learned over the years. Rational argument. Deep breathing for calm. Willing her muscles to relax. But her lungs only constricted more.

Swallowing hard, she eyed Mrs. Foley's silhouette. Las Vegas odds? Maybe. But fears could come true, even one's *worst* fear. Hadn't that happened to Kaycee's best friend, Mandy Parksley? Mandy had been plagued by the fear that, like her own mother, she would die young and leave her daughter, Hannah, behind. Kaycee insisted that would never come to pass. Mandy was healthy and fit. But at thirty-three she'd suddenly developed a brain tumor — and died within nine months.

Mrs. Foley's head moved slightly, as if she was trying to see inside Kaycee's car. That did it. Time to flush the woman out. Kaycee flicked on the light inside her Cruiser, leaned sideways, and waved with animation. "Hey there, Mrs. Foley!" She forced the words through clenched teeth.

The woman jerked away from the window, her curtain fluttering shut.

Breath returned to Kaycee slowly.

The bulb in her car seemed to brighten, exposing her to the night. Kaycee smacked off the light and glanced around.

*Push back the fear.*

But she couldn't. At Mandy's death a year ago, Kaycee's lifelong coping skills had crumbled. Rational thinking no longer worked. If Mandy's worst fear could happen, why couldn't Kaycee's? Maybe there *were* people out there watching.

How ironic that Mandy had been drawn to her through Kaycee's syndicated newspaper column about overcoming fear. "Who's There?" had millions of readers across the country, all so grateful to Kaycee for helping them fight back. Crazy but courageous Kaycee Raye. If she could overcome her multiple fears, so could they.

In the end, she hadn't been able to help Mandy.

11

If her readers only knew how far down she'd spiraled since then.

Shoulders tight, Kaycee hit the remote button to open her garage and drove inside. As the door closed she slid from her car, gripping her purse. She hurried under the covered walkway to her back entrance, key in hand. Kaycee shoved open the door, her fingers scrabbling around the door frame for the overhead light switch. As the fluorescent light flickered on, she whisked inside, shut the door, and locked it.

Eyes closed, she exhaled.

The weight upon her lifted. In her own home she could relax. Unlike her mother, she didn't peer out windows every minute. How she missed inheriting that habit, she'd never know. Still, all blinds and curtains had to be closed at night. She needed to complete that task. When she'd left to visit Hannah, it had been daylight.

Kaycee's heart squeezed. Every time Kaycee was with Hannah — which was often, after she'd slid into place as surrogate mother — Mandy's death hit her all over again. But this particular visit had been unusually heartrending. It had taken every ounce of fortitude Kaycee could muster to tell the begging, grief-stricken nine-year-old that she couldn't leave her father and new

12

stepmom and come live with her.

Kaycee placed her purse and key on the gray Formica counter at her left — the short bottom of a long-stemmed L of cabinets and sink — and inhaled the comforting smell of home. Tonight it mixed the regular scent of the old house's wood with the chicken baked for supper. For once Kaycee had eaten a regular meal.

As the tension in her shoulders unwound, Kaycee breathed a prayer for Hannah. It wasn't fair to lose your mother at that young age. But to see your father remarry within months, bringing a new mom with a daughter of her own into the house — Kaycee could strangle the man, even as she'd assured Hannah, "You can't leave your dad; he loves you."

"Yeah, like he loved Mom," Hannah sobbed. "She might as well have been a dog that died. Just go out and get another one."

Kaycee sighed. Families were so hard. But so was not having one.

Someday. At thirty, she still had time.

Kaycee stepped away from the counter — and heard a click. A flash lit the room.

Her head snapped up, her gaze cutting to the round table across the wide kitchen. A camera sat upon it.

Where had *that* come from?

13

It had taken a picture. *All by itself.*

She stared at the camera, stunned. It was small and black. Looked like a digital point-and-shoot. She had one of those. Only hers was silver. And bigger. And the last time she saw the thing it was in its case, sitting in the bottom drawer of her desk.

The camera's lens stuck out. Aimed at her. It had taken a picture of *her.*

Kaycee looked around wildly, her paranoia like a thousand skittering insects across her back. Who had done this? Somebody could be watching her by remote through that lens *right now.*

No. The thought was too petrifying. And far-fetched. Someone was just pulling a joke.

But who would do that? And how would they get into her house? She hadn't given a key to anyone.

Kaycee edged toward the table sideways, palms up, as if the camera might explode in her face. Dark imaginings filled her head. Somewhere in a shadowy room sat a man, eyes glued to a monitor, chuckling at her terror as she approached.

Who was he? What group was he a part of? What did they want?

*Kaycee, stop it. There's a rational explanation . . .*

Her thigh grazed the table. The camera sat no higher than that part of her body. Did it have a wide enough lens to include her face when it took the picture?

She extended a trembling arm and knocked the camera ninety degrees. There. Now they couldn't see her.

Shallow-breathing, she leaned over to look down at the black rectangle. Its "on" light glowed golden.

What other pictures had it taken? Had they gone around her house, photographing every room?

*Nobody was here. It's a joke, just a joke.*

Kaycee reached out a tentative hand, drew it back. Reached out again. On the third try she picked up the camera.

She flipped it around and studied its controls on the back. Turned a dial to the "view" mode. A picture of herself filled the screen — with her head cropped off. Kaycee saw only her wiry body, the loose-fitting jeans, and three-quarter-sleeve purple top. So much for a wide lens.

Her finger hesitated over the back arrow button, then pressed.

Onto the screen jumped the close-up gruesome face of a dead man. Eyes half open, dark red holes in his jaw and forehead. Blood matted his hair. Printed in bold in the bottom left corner of the picture, across his neck: WE SEE YOU.

Kaycee dropped the camera and screamed.

# Two

Hannah Parksley slumped on her bed, knees pulled up to her chin. Her eyes burned, her throat ached, and her insides felt empty. Just dead. She should have begged Kaycee harder to go live with her. Hannah knew she wanted to say yes. Kaycee was always there for her. But tonight while Hannah poured out her heart to Kaycee behind the closed door of her bedroom, where was her own father? Out in the den with Gail, his new wife, and Gail's twelve-year-old daughter, Becky. Watching TV.

Fresh tears filled Hannah's eyes. How could she stay in this house another night?

Sniffing, she picked a piece of lint off her pink bedspread and dropped it onto the carpet.

A little over a year ago Hannah's mom would have been putting her to bed right now, even though she was weak from fighting cancer. That was another lifetime.

17

Hannah didn't even know who she was anymore.

Pushing off her bed, she crossed to her dresser and picked up the gold-framed picture of her mom. It had been taken two years ago, when her mother was healthy and normal. When she still had her shiny brown hair and could laugh like in the photo, with her head thrown back and eyes half squinted.

Hannah hugged the frame to her chest. If only she could press her mom inside her heart so she could fill the big hole that ached and ached there.

She heard laughter from the den. The sound wrenched Hannah's insides. Weren't they just one happy family. *Laughing* at a TV show. Like they didn't even care she was in here by herself, crying.

Truth was, they didn't.

She might as well face it: this wasn't going to change. Her mom was never coming back. Looking through the house, except for this bedroom, you'd never know Hannah's mom had even lived here. All pictures of her on the fireplace mantel, in the master bedroom — gone. All her clothes cleaned out. Everything in the house she loved, even the color of the den and kitchen — gone. The walls had been repainted, their old couch traded for a new one. All because Gail thought the colors were "too blue." The plates Hannah's mom had loved, and her silverware — gone. Gail had brought her own.

Hannah set her mom's picture on the dresser and pressed her palm against the glass. She closed her eyes, remembering the feel of her mother's hugs. Her smell. Her voice. Hannah's heart ripped at the memories. She backed away from the picture, pressing fists to her chest. And now she didn't have her father either. He kept telling her they had to "build a new life." She didn't want to build a new life. She just wanted her old one back.

"Can you see me from heaven?" Hannah whispered to the photo. "Please tell God to make Dad send Gail away."

A loud cackle from the den. Gail, laughing.

Hannah's teeth clenched. She stared toward the den, picturing Gail with her bleached blonde hair, the red, red lipstick. Hannah knew the truth about her and Hannah's dad. He'd started hanging around with Gail before Hannah's mom even died. He didn't think Hannah knew that. Well, she *did.*

In the picture, Hannah's mom smiled on.

Had *she* known when she was sick and dying? Had she known she'd already been pushed aside?

The terrible thought swept Hannah into motion. She swiveled toward her closet and threw open the door.

She yanked out her small pink roller suitcase and dragged it to her dresser. Out of a drawer she pulled a couple pair of jeans and three tops. Threw them into the suitcase. Her hands worked feverishly, her breath hitching on little sobs as she opened her top drawer and scraped through underwear and socks. Hannah tossed some of each into the case. Then added her pajamas. She ran to her bed, picked up the small white pillow she'd had since a baby, and pressed it inside. Then stood in the middle of her room, turning in a frantic circle, thinking, *What else, what else?*

Only then did it hit her. She really was running away.

Hannah picked up her mother's picture and placed it on top of her small pillow.

Tears rolling down her cheeks, she zipped the suitcase. She turned it upright and pulled out the handle.

A note. Shouldn't she say something to her dad?

Hannah fumbled in the middle drawer of

her little desk and pulled out a piece of paper and pen. She wrote the first thing that came to her mind and stuffed the note under her pillow. The paper and pen went back in the drawer.

Her eyes roamed to the window. It was dark out there.

She gazed into the night, courage flagging. Where would she go? In her mind's eye she saw herself hurrying down her street and through her neighborhood. At Main she'd turn right and go over the railroad tracks, past the downtown area to South Maple. Kaycee lived at the very end of that street. Of course. Hannah would go to Kaycee's. She'd convince Kaycee to let her stay there.

It would be a long, scary walk.

Hannah gazed at her bed — where she'd cried countless tears — and knew she couldn't sleep there again. If she stayed in this house another night, she would drown. Hannah looked back to the window. She could do this. Didn't Kaycee always write about fighting your fears?

Hannah swiped at her cheeks. No one here would miss her anyway.

She returned to her dresser, grabbed a sweatshirt, and put it on.

Quietly she opened the door to her room. The sound of the TV grew louder. She could hear Becky giggling. Hannah's mouth tightened. Pulling her suitcase into the hall, she closed the door behind her. The carpet hushed her footsteps as she crept toward the kitchen. Every step she took gave her more courage. No changing her mind now. She couldn't bear to face Gail's anger if she was caught.

Reaching the end of the hall Hannah turned into the kitchen. She couldn't get to the front door without being spotted. On the linoleum she slowed, picking up her sneakered feet so they wouldn't squeak. The rubber wheels on her suitcase made no sound.

At the door to the garage Hannah held her breath as she rotated the knob. Holding the door open with her body, she picked her suitcase up over the threshold. Inch by inch she closed the door. She turned the outside knob, brought the door into place, then slowly released the handle.

Hannah wiped her forehead and listened. No sound from the kitchen.

She grabbed the handle on her suitcase and scurried past two cars to the side garage door. Hannah slipped through it quickly.

Fresh air slapped her in the face. It wasn't that chilly, just dark here between her house and the neighbor's. Hannah drew in her shoulders and surveyed the sidewalk out front. Streetlamps would light her way. *Please, please, no one see me.* Especially some policeman driving by. She'd be stopped for sure.

Heart beating in her ears, Hannah clutched her suitcase and ventured into the night.

# THREE

Kaycee jumped back from the table, casting crazed looks all around. A dead man. That mangled, bloodied face . . .

*We see you.*

Her worst fear come true.

Kaycee tore across the kitchen and grabbed her keys. She rammed out the back door and hurtled to her car. With its engine running, she barely waited for the garage door to open before screeching backwards, down her driveway, out onto the street. Gripping the steering wheel, she punched the accelerator and flew down South Maple. She skidded right onto Main and down a block. Kaycee carved out a parking space in front of Casa de José Mexican Restaurant. She jumped from her car, leaving keys in the ignition, and raced across the deserted street toward the white stone building that housed the Wilmore police station. Inside the entrance she veered left past the Ale-8-

One and Pepsi machines and pounded on the locked door to the offices. She pulled back, gasping. Kaycee caught sight of herself in the one-way mirror — her face white, her kinky-curled red hair wilder than ever. Her light blue eyes glazed with shock.

The police station door shoved open to reveal Officer Mark Burnett. Great, of all the policemen it would have to be thirty-five-year-old Mark. Last month he'd accused her of "living off other people's fears" through writing her column. She'd known he was just being defensive. "Who's There?" had apparently struck a nerve about his own private fear. Not that he'd ever admit reading it. But the memory still stung.

"Kaycee." Mark pulled her inside the station. "What is it?"

Her tongue tied. "I . . . there's a camera in my house . . . a dead man."

"A dead man in your house?"

"No, he's in the camera."

"A dead man in a camera?"

"No-no, in a picture."

Mark raised his eyebrows, turning them into their signature spread V. His deep brown eyes narrowed. "Who's the dead man?"

"I've never seen him before. He's all bloodied and . . . *dead!*"

A nonplused expression flitted across Mark's squared face. His lips, usually turned up at the corners, drew in. He knew her too well — all the Wilmore policemen did. In the past year since Mandy's death, Kaycee had run to the police four times, convinced someone was lurking around her house.

Now make that five.

"This time it's for real, Mark. I walked into my house, and the camera was just there — out of nowhere. And it took a picture of me!"

"How'd it do that?"

"I don't know, it just did! And the picture said, 'We see you.'"

"Who sees you?"

"I don't *know!*"

"Okay, okay, calm down."

*Calm down?* "I'm not being crazy. It really happened."

"All right, I hear you." He nudged her back out the door. "I'll go with you to your house. Take a look around."

The thought of going back to that house, even with a policeman . . . "Okay. Thanks."

"Where's your car?" Mark held the outside door open as they stepped onto the sidewalk. Light from a tall black lamppost on their left shone golden on his brown hair.

"Over there." She pointed toward the restaurant and its yellow curb. Mark said nothing about the fact she'd parked close to a fire hydrant.

"You all right to drive yourself? I'll follow you."

"Yeah, I'm . . . good."

He gave her a little smile.

Kaycee crossed the street while he peeled left toward a black-and-white cruiser in the parking lot. Driving back to her house, it was all she could do to keep her eyes on the road. The rearview mirror pulled at her, as did the shadowed yards on her right and left. Somewhere out there people were watching. Not imagined this time. For real.

Kaycee pictured her mother, always looking over her shoulder. Always afraid. Driven to uproot Kaycee and move every few years. The irrational paranoia in Monica Raye had been so great it had oozed its way into her daughter's soul by the time Kaycee was nine. But never had Monica Raye faced any proof that her fears were based in reality.

That picture! The man's bloodied face. It wailed a siren song of violence and utter terror. Of a world breaking apart.

Kaycee blinked. What did *that* mean?

She turned into her driveway and hit the button for the garage door. As it opened,

Mark pulled into the drive behind her.

In silence they walked under the covered way toward the back door. Kaycee could feel the vibes coming off Mark. He didn't believe anyone hid inside the house. After all, she'd cried wolf four times before.

As her shaking hand lifted the house key, Mark stopped her. "When you got here, was this door locked?"

"Yes, and bolted. This key turns the bolt and opens the door, but the regular lock stays in position until I undo it from inside."

Mark looked around. "See anything unusual out here?"

"No."

"All right. Let's go in."

Kaycee slid her key into the lock. As she pushed open the door, panic overwhelmed her. She swallowed hard. "I'll just . . . wait out here."

He moved to go inside.

"Light switch is on your left, remember? And the camera's across the kitchen, on the table." A thought hit her. "Oh, no."

"What?"

"I picked up the camera. I left fingerprints."

"Okay."

The overhead light flicked on. Kaycee's heart cantered into double time. She pressed knuckles to her mouth.

*Fight the fear, fight the fear.*

Mark stepped into the kitchen.

That dead man's face. It throbbed in her memory. The eyelids frozen half open. The gore. Who was he? Who killed him?

*Who* was watching her?

"Where'd you say the camera is?" Mark spoke over his shoulder.

"On the table." She pointed, averting her gaze.

"Don't see it. Is there some other table?"

"No. It's right where you're looking."

"There's nothing there."

She stilled for a moment, then edged over the threshold to his side.

The table was empty.

Anger and fear and violation swelled within her. She stared at the blank spot, one hand thrust in her hair. "It was there, I swear it. It was *there.*"

"Okay, okay."

"Don't talk to me like I'm a two-year-old, Mark. I'm telling you I saw a camera on that table!"

"Maybe you —"

"It took a picture of me." Her voice rose. "I picked it up and saw the picture in its viewer. And then I clicked back one photo — and that's when I saw the dead man. A close-up. And it wasn't just *any* dead man. It was *real* dead. Like holes-in-his-head dead. And words were written right into the picture. They said, 'We see you' . . ."

Kaycee leaned against the counter and covered her eyes with her hand.

Awkward silence rolled off Mark.

"Tell you what." He touched her on the arm. "Let's walk through the house together, all right? Make sure everything's clear."

With unseen eyes watching? No way. She couldn't walk through this house ever again.

Mark surveyed her. "You could stay here and wait if you want."

By *herself?* "No way. I'm coming."

Muscles like taut rubber bands, she trailed him out of the kitchen.

# FOUR

The longest day in Martin Giordano's twenty-nine years had begun with a mouse in the toilet.

"Eeeeee!" his four-year-old daughter, Tammy, shrieked. "Daddy, get it out!"

Martin stood in his pajamas, surveying the gray creature swimming around the stained bowl. What to do? He couldn't flush the thing. What if it backed up the pipes? But he wasn't about to reach his hand in there and pull it out.

Lorraine hovered behind him, one hand to her mouth and the other gripping their little girl's shoulder. Tammy's frightened sobs quickly turned to heavy coughing. "Come on now, shh, shh." Lorraine picked Tammy up and held her tight. "You don't want to make the cough worse. Daddy will take care of the mouse." Carrying Tammy from the bathroom, she looked over her shoulder. "Get my big ladle."

Martin trotted to their cluttered kitchen and grabbed the utensil from its top drawer. Back in the bathroom he closed the door. In one fluid motion he dunked the large metal scoop into the toilet, jerked out the mouse, and flung it into the cracked bathtub. Water flew in all directions. The mouse landed with a wet *thwap.*

Before it could struggle to its feet, Martin beat it to death with the back of the ladle.

Breathing hard, he stared at the tiny body and shuddered. Corpses looked so cold.

With the ladle he scooped up the mouse and threw it in the waste paper basket. Sweat itched under Martin's pajama top as he carried the trash into the kitchen and emptied it into the garbage can. The tainted ladle went into the sink.

From Tammy's bedroom barked the sound of the cough she'd had for months now. The cough that remained undiagnosed, along with the paleness of Tammy's skin and her constant tiredness.

Martin wrapped his fingers around the edge of the old Formica counter and rested his forehead against a cabinet. If only her sickness could be taken care of as easily as fishing a mouse from the toilet. All the money that surrounded him every workday, and he couldn't even afford proper medical care for his only child.

Now, after hours at Atlantic City Trust Bank, Martin still heard that cough in his mind as he fought to reconcile his books. Left elbow pressed against his desk, right leg jiggling, he stared at the digits jumbling in his head. His fingers twitched against the calculator keys. To his right behind the teller counter, Shelley and Olga talked in low tones as they performed the workday's final duties. Martin's gaze slid in their direction. At twenty-four, the same age as Martin's wife, soft-spoken Shelley stood tall and thin, a willow tree next to Olga's stump of a figure. Olga was in her fifties, a no-nonsense, diligent worker who gushed constantly about her "blessed grandbabies."

Guilt twinged in Martin's stomach.

"Tammy's too sick to go to preschool again," Lorraine had told him as he left for work. "I'll just keep her home with me."

"Home" was a dingy two-bedroom apartment in an old building opposite two rows of storage units running parallel to each other. The living room window overlooked the units and their surrounding concrete. The view from the kitchen window on the opposite side was a rundown industrial street. Next door to the apartment lay the cramped office for the rentals, where Lorraine spent her days. The rental place ran the width of a block. It was gray and depressing, but the apartment came free along with a meager weekly paycheck for Lorraine's management of the storage units. They could have lived in a much better place if it weren't for Tammy's sickness. Seemed like every other dollar went for doctor visits and cough syrup.

Martin glanced at the clock on the bank's wall. His leg jiggled higher.

A faint sound from the rear door of the long bank made Martin's head jerk. He stilled, listening. Both doors had been locked when the bank closed. Another noise, a metallic click. Martin swiveled in his chair. The door yanked open.

Four men wearing black ski masks over their heads burst inside, the first two with guns drawn. The second pair each carried four large duffel bags.

Martin jumped to his feet.

"Stay where you are!" The man in the lead pointed a gun at his chest. "Hands in the air."

"You too." The second gunman aimed at Shelley and Olga. His voice sounded like stirred gravel. "Get your hands up now."

Shelley's thin arms rose, shaking. Her gray eyes bugged, her mouth hanging open. Olga stacked both hands on top of her head. Her lips pressed, a defiant expression on her rectangular face.

"Back up against the wall."

The women obeyed.

Martin's heart rammed against his chest. His eyes cut from his coworkers to the gunmen. The leader was tall and lithe, the second very short but stocky. Even though the man was fully clothed, Martin could tell he was all muscle. The third and fourth were moving so fast he could hardly tell their sizes. All four wore black from head to toe, including gloves. The cutouts on the ski masks were small, barely showing their eyes, noses, and mouths.

The two carrying duffel bags threw them on the floor near the vault and hustled back outside. They quickly returned, each carrying four more bags.

"Come out front." Man Number Two kept his gun on Shelley and Olga. "Hands stay up. Hurry."

The leader ran to Martin, Man Number Three beside him. The third man whipped a pistol from his pants pocket. Martin flinched.

*Lorraine. Tammy.*

"Where are the keys to the vault?" the leader demanded.

"In my long desk drawer."

"Stand back."

Martin stepped aside while the leader grabbed at the drawer. Man Number Three kept his gun on Martin's face. In that horrific second Martin pictured his head blown away.

He glanced at the two women as Olga shoved through the teller's swing door with her thigh. Shelley followed. They stopped in front of the counter five feet from Man Number Two.

"Over there. Move it." The robber gestured with his chin toward the rear of the bank. Both women scurried toward the vault. One of the men herded them to stand off to one side. At their feet lay the empty duffel bags.

The leader yanked Martin's keys from the drawer and tossed them over. Martin's arm jerked up to catch them.

"Open the vault."

Martin swallowed. He looked at Shelley and Olga as they huddled, white-faced, staring down the barrels of two guns. "Don't hurt them."

"Go."

Martin headed to the vault. With fumbling fingers he inserted the key and cranked the heavy door open. Shelley and Olga crowded nearby, the younger woman's breath like muffled gasps.

"Inside." The leader pushed him. "You two, go with him."

Shelley let out a wail.

Martin's heart dropped to his toes. "I can't go in there! I've got claustrophobia!"

"Shut up and go."

Martin and the women slunk inside, the first two men behind them. In the center of the vault stood two large metal carts with Plexiglas tops, crammed with money. The bills were pressed down, stacked, and bound according to denomination.

The second two men hustled in the duffel bags.

Air squeezed into Martin's lungs, thick and heavy. The walls bent in, so close. Sweat trickled down his forehead.

"Look at all that cash!" Number Three peered into one of the carts.

Those carts held far more money than normal for a bank. Three casinos on the Atlantic City strip sent their daily take into Trust Bank. Three other banks also sent their daily deposits.

"How'd you get in here?" Martin heard himself ask. *Keep talking. Keep calm.* "That door was locked."

The leader stabbed him with a look. "We

can pick a lock, so what?" He grabbed Shelley's arm. She yelped. "Get on your knees by the cart. You too." He gestured toward Olga and Martin.

Man Number Four unzipped a duffel bag and withdrew a flathead screwdriver and hammer.

"You can't lock us in here." Olga sank to her knees. "I'm supposed to visit my grandkids. If I don't show up, they'll know something's wrong."

"I said you'll be fine," the leader snapped.

Martin got down beside Shelley. His mouth was open now, sucking in air. His clothes stuck to his skin.

Man Number Three yanked pieces of rope from a duffel bag. With rough movements he tied Shelley's hands to a leg on the first rectangular cart. She lowered her head and cried.

"It'll be . . . okay," Martin whispered. He could barely breathe. "It'll . . . be okay."

Number Three bound Olga to the leg next to Shelley. He tied Martin to one at the other end.

"Look down and close your eyes," the leader said.

Martin did as he was told. He heard the sound of hammering, metal against metal as one of the men pried open the padlocked compartments of the cart. The legs jerked this way and that, pulling at his arms, his shoulders. The smell of dust and perspiration swirled around him, and his heart swelled against his ribs. This wasn't over yet. What if they shut him and the two women in this vault? Martin thought of his words to Shelley. *It'll be okay.* Maybe it wouldn't. He and his coworkers might all be killed.

He thought of Lorraine in their run-down apartment. She was probably reading to Tammy. Such a good mom. She deserved so much better.

*Tammy, your daddy loves you.*

The pounding stopped on the cart to which they were tied. Feet squeaked against the floor. The noise began again as they broke into the second cart. All that clanking and smashing. The sounds rattled in Martin's brain. His teeth set on edge.

Zippers opened. Martin cast a look upward. Each of the four men was throwing bound stacks of money into the bags by denomination. Guns protruded from their pockets.

The leader shook a bag. "Pack 'em tight."

"Did we bring enough bags?" another one asked.

"Just pack 'em down."

Martin lowered his head. The sounds continued around him, the rustle of clothes, the soft plop of bill stacks tossed upon one another. Ten minutes. The men couldn't have been in the bank longer than that, but it seemed a lifetime. A drop of sweat rolled off his jaw onto the floor.

Shelley sniffed. Olga had not made a sound.

"How much you think's in here?" one of the robbers asked, his words breathless.

"He oughtta know." The leader's clipped voice. A knee dug into Martin's shoulder. "How much?"

For a moment rebellion burned. A lie formed on Martin's tongue, then melted away. "Almost seven million."

"Seven million!" one of them crowed.

Claustrophobia welled up Martin's throat. He forced himself to examine the binding around his hands. He tried to pull his wrists apart — and they moved a fraction of an inch. How long before he could work his way out of the rope?

"Come on, come on," one of the men hissed.

Martin's heart constricted. He gazed toward the door of the vault. Beyond it he could see the length of the bank, the glass front door at the other end. Through that lay the outside world. His family. *Air.*

"This one's full," Number Two said. A zipper closed. "Who's got room for more hundreds?"

"Here." The leader's voice.

The cart jiggled, the soft sound of gloves scraping bottom.

"That's it."

*Zzzip.* Multiple bags closed. All but the leader ran out of the vault, carrying two duffels each, leaving nine full ones behind. Martin figured each bag had to weigh around thirty-five pounds. One duffel on the vault floor remained empty. The leader stayed in the vault, keeping his eye on Martin and the women. As if they could go anywhere.

The three men soon returned, lugging out six more bags total. Two of them ran back a third time and picked up the rest, including the empty one. Their footfalls scuffed across the bank floor, then faded.

At the vault's door the leader turned, gun drawn. He pointed it at Martin's head. Martin went cold.

"Have a nice evening."

The man swiveled and disappeared.

Martin's body sagged. Shelley burst into sobs.

"Shh, wait." Martin listened for the open-

41

ing of the rear door. He heard nothing but the whoosh of blood in his ears.

"They're gone." Olga twisted her hands in her rope.

Martin tried to think. His head was about to explode. He needed to *breathe.* "Let's get this cart out of the vault. Shelley?"

"Yeah, okay." Her voice shook.

"I'll get in front." Martin shuffled around, the women moving in the same direction, until his end of the cart pointed outward. Martin's back was now to the door, nothing but the closing-in walls of the vault in his line of vision. He dragged in air. "Okay. I'll back up. Follow me."

As a team, they performed an awkward knee ballet, inching the cart along. When he passed the vault door, Martin turned his head to the side and gulped deep breaths.

"You okay?" Olga's face shone with perspiration.

"Yeah."

Another minute and the entire cart stood outside the vault. Martin's insides still shook. But he could breathe.

He twisted his arm to view his watch. The robbers had been gone maybe five minutes. "Try to untie yourself."

Dry-throated, Martin fought against his rope. Shelley struggled fitfully with hers, sniffing and swallowing hard enough to make her throat click. Olga made no sound.

Within minutes Martin's skin burned.

Slowly his rope loosened. He pushed his thumb beneath the topknot and worked it. When he could turn one wrist perpendicular to another, he picked at the ties with the first two fingers on his right hand.

After twenty minutes his left hand wriggled free. He slipped out of the rope completely. Ignoring the pain in his wrists, he moved to untie Shelley, then Olga. His fumbling fingers had gone numb.

His nerves felt like raw meat. Nico hadn't told him he'd be shackled in the vault. Martin wouldn't sleep for weeks.

But they'd pulled it off.

Martin and Shelley pushed to their feet. Olga's legs were stiff. She sat down on the floor and massaged her muscles. Martin stumbled toward the nearest bank alarm.

As he reached out his hand to set it off, he checked his watch. Nico and his three cohorts had been gone for almost thirty minutes.

Plenty of time for a clean getaway.

# FIVE

Pulse fluttering, Kaycee followed Officer Mark Burnett as he checked the rooms in her house. He looked carefully, making sure all windows were locked. Every footfall felt like a step toward Kaycee's grave. Around this corner, maybe the next, the people watching her would be waiting.

First Mark went through the open arched entry into the dining room, where he bent down to look under the table. Then under the matching arch into the large living room at the front of the house. Kaycee hung close, her spine rigid and brittle. She tingled with the sense of eyes watching from the dark outside. Before they left a room she closed all curtains and shades within it.

"We forgot the back bathroom and utility area." She pointed with her chin toward the living room's second arch, leading back to the kitchen.

"We'll circle around."

They crossed back into the kitchen, the offending bare table on their left, pantry on their right. Past the pantry and down the hall. Kaycee remained there while Mark checked the half bath on their left, then the utility room. "All clear," he announced.

In the hall to the right was the door to Kaycee's office, where she wrote her newspaper columns — thanks to Mandy Parksley. Four years ago Kaycee read Mandy some excerpts from her diary about struggling with the paranoia of being watched. Mandy knew someone at the *Jessamine Journal,* a local weekly paper, and made a phone call. "You've got something here, Kaycee," she urged. "And that knack of yours for seeing a fear in others, even when they won't admit it. The way you saw through mine. You can help people."

It turned out that the only way Kaycee could publicly write about her fears was to inject a sort of self-deprecating humor. The technique was a hit. Within six months Kaycee's local "Who's There?" had gone national.

Kaycee pressed against the wall as Mark checked under her desk, which sat in front of a window facing Mrs. Foley's house. His gaze roved around her filing cabinet, a table, an old stuffed armchair that used to belong

45

to her mother.

The office led into the den at the house's front corner. Not much furniture to check behind there. A couch, a TV, some tables and lamps. Most of Kaycee's house was furnished sparsely. Five years ago the down payment alone had taken everything she had. Since then she'd added what pieces she could.

From the den they climbed the stairs and turned left. The upstairs area only covered the middle part of the house, leaving down-stairs "wings." Mark searched through the two bedrooms and the adjoining bath in the middle. He checked in the closets, under the beds, and behind the shower curtain. Kaycee hung back, feeling awkward and vulnerable as he looked through her private spaces.

*We see you.*

How would she ever sleep here tonight?

Back in the hall, Mark gave her a nod. "Everything's clear."

Kaycee didn't know whether to laugh or cry.

They descended the stairs in silence.

Mark unlocked the front door and walked outside. Kaycee turned on the porch lights and followed. Her white-columned porch wrapped partially around the side of the

46

house, ending at the set-back dining room. From that part of the porch a sliding door to the right led into the living room, and a second one at the end led to the dining area. Mark inspected the locks on both doors. They were secure.

Back inside, Kaycee relocked and bolted the front door. She faced Mark in her living room, arms crossed. The worn hardwood floors and the comfy sofa in her peripheral vision didn't feel so homey now. The walls pulsed with unseen threat.

"That camera was *here,* Mark. Somebody put it in my house."

He nodded. "You want to make a statement? I'll add it to the file."

"Bet that file's getting pretty thick." Kaycee couldn't keep the defensiveness from her tone.

Mark looked at a loss for words — almost as if he wanted to believe she wasn't crazy but couldn't find the evidence.

Kaycee's heart panged. She shifted on her feet. "So what do we do now?"

"I'll be on patrol all night. You can have my cell phone number. And I'll drive by here often."

"And what if whoever brought that camera comes back between drives?"

"Call me and I'll come —"

"I could be dead by the time you get here."

Mark pulled in a long breath. "Kaycee, I'll do whatever I can to keep you safe. I *am* taking this seriously."

"Really? Or are you thinking, 'Sure, sure, this is just crazy Kaycee.' "

"I don't think you're crazy. Maybe sometimes your fears make you see things . . ."

"I *told* you that camera was here."

Mark held up a hand. "Okay."

For a moment they faced off, his hurtful words from last month echoing in her head. Even if they had revealed more about his own issues than hers, they still hurt. Kaycee swallowed. "And I am *not* making this up just to give me fodder for my next column."

"I never said anything like that."

"Close to it . . . last month at the birthday party for Chief Davis. You told me all my column does is stir up other people's fears, and I don't really want to overcome my own, because then what would I do for a living?"

"If I said that, I didn't mean it."

"You did say it. You know you did."

Mark looked away, forehead creasing. Kaycee continued to eye him. Why couldn't he just admit he had fears like everybody else? His were written all over him. Ever since his fiancée broke their engagement

48

and moved away three years ago, he'd kept his distance from women, clearly scared to death of being hurt again. But no, he had to put on this act like he didn't need anybody.

Mark swung his gaze back to her. "I'm sorry, Kaycee. I'd had a bad day. I don't really think that about you."

Kaycee's eyes burned. She didn't care what most people said about her — Kaycee Raye's whole life was laid out in "Who's There?" But this man was different.

She lifted a shoulder. "Never mind. It's okay."

Silence ticked by. Mark cleared his throat. "Maybe you shouldn't stay alone tonight. Is there somewhere else you can sleep? A friend's house?"

Kaycee glanced at her watch. Going on ten o'clock. Not too late to call Tricia. Kaycee certainly didn't want to stay in this house. The very thought of turning out the light, trying to sleep . . .

A terrifying thought flared. "Mark, the words on that photo said, 'We see you,' " Kaycee blurted. "Could somebody have hooked up video cameras in here?"

Great, now he really *would* think she was crazy.

He spread his hands. "I searched all over the house."

"You were looking for people."

"You want me to look again — for cameras?"

"Well, if I'm in a starring role, at least I should know about it."

"Was that a yes?"

She nodded tightly.

Again they walked through every room. Mark searched corners, window sills, within the leaves of plants — anywhere a tiny video camera might be hidden. He found nothing. By the time he finished, Kaycee's nerves sizzled.

Mark stood in her kitchen, hands on his hips. "So how about that friend's house?"

Kaycee crossed her arms. How she wanted to leave. The darkness beat giant wings against her windows. But there was *nothing* in this house. No intruder. No lens. If she stayed with someone she'd be giving in. How would she ever regain the strength she'd had before Mandy's death if she caved in to her fears?

"Kaycee, you don't have to fight this one," Mark said, as if reading her thoughts.

That one sentence, coming from Mark, was all it took. Any resolve Kaycee could find within herself melted away. "Maybe I'll just . . . call somebody."

"Good. I'll escort you wherever you go.

Tomorrow you can come down to the station and fill out a report. And if you want an officer to come back into the house with you, whoever's on duty will do that."

"Okay."

Soaked in defeat, Kaycee picked up the phone and dialed the familiar number. Tricia Goodwin answered on the second ring. "Of course you can come," she said. "What happened?"

"Tell you when I get there. Don't freak when a policeman pulls up behind me."

Mark waited in the living room while Kaycee threw some clothes and toiletries into a small bag upstairs. The dead man's face throbbed in her mind.

They left through the back door. Kaycee locked the bolt and walked alongside Mark to her car, throwing glances into the dense and hovering darkness.

Mark followed her to Tricia's small wooden house near Asbury Seminary. As Kaycee trudged up the front sidewalk, her thoughts spun back to the first "Who's There?" column she'd written four years ago. "Soaked Up" — the story of how her paranoia began at the age of nine. Never as she penned those words could she have imagined this night.

*We see you.*

51

Only as Tricia opened the door did Kaycee realize the terrible mistake she'd made in running to her friend. What was to keep *them* from following her here?

# SOAKED UP

When did I first notice the fear in my mother? Don't remember. You might as well ask when I first noticed I had toenails.

My father was killed in a car accident when I was a baby. My mother never remarried. No doubt because she'd make any man crazy. Every night she'd double check the locks on our windows and doors. In public she always glanced over her shoulder. And when she drove, she constantly looked in the rearview mirror as if some monster was chasing us. Made me feel all jittery. Like maybe there *were* monsters back there . . .

Children are sponges. By the time I reached nine I'd soaked up her habit quite nicely and

53

was looking over my shoulder as well. In the car it wasn't fair. My mom had the rearview mirror; I had to turn around. No subtlety in that. Mom acted like she didn't notice. But I knew she did. And it seemed to make her sad.

I took to humor to cheer her up.

"Knock-knock."

"Who's there?"

"Kaycee."

"Kaycee who?"

" 'Kay, see what you've done?"

"What have I done?"

"Fallen for my dumb joke."

My mom died a little over a year ago. I can't help but wonder if her constant fear of being watched caused the heart attack that cut short her life. Not a pleasant thought, seeing as how I'm managing to carry on her tradition.

In fact my mother's fears now pale in comparison to mine. I've managed to branch out. None of my new fears make any more sense than the paranoia. Bees (no, I'm not allergic). The dentist's drill. (The mere *sound* of that thing!) Heights. Claustrophobia — especially dark, closed spaces. (Oh man, just thinking about that one. It's second only to the fear of being watched.) Plummeting downhill, as in roller coasters.

Since the age of nine I've fought the fears. With that much experience under my belt, I have found ways to cope.

How about you? Not that I expect you to be plagued with as many fears as I have. But everyone is afraid of something. Better to get those fears out in the open where we can fight them. Because whatever they are, they too often guide our choices. They hold us back.

Not to mention they form our worst nightmares.

Think about it; torturing me would be easy. Just put me on a roller coaster in a dark, closed cage filled with bumblebees and a madly drilling dentist.

Hang on a sec. I'm starting to hyperventilate . . .

# Six

Minutes from home, Hannah almost turned back. The darkness made her insides feel like jelly. The streetlamps weren't very far apart, but it still seemed so dim between them. Maybe it wouldn't seem so dark if she were with somebody, but by herself . . . And lots of houses didn't have porch lights on. Hannah tried to tell herself that was good — neighbors wouldn't be so likely to see her. But the farther she went, the heavier her fear grew. Now she could hardly breathe.

At the end of her street — Brookwood Lane — Hannah stopped. She was shivering, but her palm felt moist, clamped around the handle of her suitcase. She dried her hand on her jeans.

The night was so very big.

She stood at the corner of East Margaret Street. Once she turned right she'd go to Butler Boulevard and turn left. Then it was a long way down even just to Main. Hannah thought of that right turn on Main, heading up toward the railroad tracks, and shivered.

Behind her a dog barked. Hannah jumped, then swiveled, searching the yards. She couldn't see it, but it sounded like a big one. What if it came after her?

She veered onto East Margaret and broke into a run. At the next block her suitcase bumped down the curb, its wheels too loud against the pavement. Reaching the other side of the street, she barely slowed, and the wheels caught on the curb. Her suitcase jerked her back, and the handle bit into her palm. Pain tore through her shoulder. Hannah gasped and dropped the handle. Her bag twisted and fell on its side.

Hannah hunched over, cradling her right arm. Tears stung her eyes. This was stupid. Kaycee's house was too far away. Why did she ever think she could get there in the dark?

Her shoulder hurt. And her palm. Hannah massaged them both.

She had to go back home.

Wiping tears away, she righted her suitcase. She turned it halfway around, then stopped. She couldn't go back. All the house doors were locked. She'd have to ring the bell. Gail and her dad would be so *mad.*

Hannah would be in big trouble. Probably couldn't play with any of her friends for weeks. Or see Kaycee. She'd sit in her room day after day, listening while her "family" went on with their happy lives.

Why hadn't she unlocked the garage door?

Some distance down, a car turned off Butler and drove toward Hannah.

She swung her suitcase back around and trotted for the closest house, pretending like she lived there. Its yard was dark. She turned up its sidewalk, then slowed, stealing glances at the car. As it passed, she picked up her suitcase and stepped onto the porch. Hannah held her breath.

The car drove on.

She waited until it was a few blocks up before turning around.

Back on the main sidewalk, she took a deep breath. No going back now. If she could just get past the railroad tracks, she wouldn't be that far from Kaycee's. And when she got there, Kaycee would realize how very sad she was at home. Surely Kaycee would say she could stay.

Fisting her fingers around the suitcase handle, Hannah walked as fast as she could. At Butler she turned left.

The sidewalk was narrow with lots of cracks. On the other side of the street lay a large field full of weeds. In the middle stood a bunch of trees. They looked so frightening in the dark. Hannah kept glancing at them, wondering who might be hiding there. Each block took forever. Hannah had to take them one at a time, telling herself, *Just one more, just one more.*

When she finally reached Main, her whole body trembled.

She crossed Main to the sidewalk and turned right to head up toward the tracks. This part of town felt old and spooky, with small houses close to the road on the other side. The street lamps on her side lit the way with puddles of light. Hannah walked faster between each lamp. Every tree branch seemed to bend toward her like in a scary cartoon, ready to snatch her up.

Two cars passed. Hannah's muscles knotted as she waited for the cars to slow and ask her what she was doing out by herself at night. But they drove on by.

Maybe they hadn't seen her. Maybe they didn't care.

Maybe one of them would come back and kidnap her.

Hannah moved faster.

The sidewalk ended in gravel, making it hard to pull her suitcase. Hannah trudged over the rocks and reached the railroad tracks. She could swear she'd been walking for hours. Her nerves snapped with every step, and her ankles shook. Picking up her suitcase to step over the tracks, Hannah looked right and left for trains, even though the signals lay silent. About forty trains passed through town every day. Hannah could hear them from her house. So could Kaycee.

In each direction the tracks faded to blackness.

Hannah crossed over as fast as she could and put down her suitcase. She glanced at the police station, then veered left past the red boxcar that was the Rail-Side Museum, and onto Rice Street.

The darkness deepened. There were street lights, but one up ahead wasn't working. After the Rail-Side Museum on her left were a couple of old white trailers that nobody lived in. The tracks ran parallel to the road. On her right was the Jessamine Christian Health Care clinic. Her doctor had an office there. Hannah's suitcase wheels sounded so loud in the stillness. Her heart beat hard against her ribs, her breaths shallow and fast. She shouldn't have come this way. Better to take a chance on the Main Street lights —

A whistle sounded far behind her.

*Train.* Hannah froze. The warning went off, clanging the air like a hundred bells in her ears. A rumble began, growing louder. Hannah shrank away from the tracks, hardly able to bear the noise. She'd seen trains pass plenty of times during the day, but now, out here alone at night . . .

The clanging screeched, and the rumble turned into a roar. The whistle blew and blew. Hannah bent over, hands clapped to her ears and eyes squeezed shut. The train came screaming, wind funneling around her body.

*I'm going to die.*

An eternity passed, and still the train rushed by like some hungry monster. Hannah couldn't *stand* it. Yanking up her suitcase handle, she ran as fast as she could up the road, her mouth gulping air. As the caboose passed, she hit the road's curve to the right, where it turned into Walters Lane.

Just one more long street and she'd be at Kaycee's house.

Tears filled her eyes as she ran on, the dark world turning blurry. *Just go, just go, just go.* She passed the Bethel Pointe homes on her left and the gray Potters Inn B&B house on her right, thinking, *Almost there, almost there.* Hannah focused her mind on Kaycee's pretty face, how she would hug

Hannah and pull her inside to a warm, lighted home.

Past the Potters Inn was a small field. Somebody grew corn there in the summer. A house came up on Hannah's left. She blinked against tears as she neared a large bush. She ran harder — and her foot scuffed over something in the street. She flew forward, the suitcase falling from her grasp. Hannah went down on both knees and her left palm. Pavement scraped her skin like a razor, right through her jeans. Hannah yelled out. She curled into a ball, crying at the pain, unable to move.

Something rushed from behind the bush. Hannah's head jerked toward it. She looked up to see a figure towering against the night sky.

Her mouth opened to scream, but something hard clamped against it.

The figure snatched her up in silence.

# SEVEN

Lorraine Giordano peeked through the curtains of the apartment's living room window, hoping to see Martin. She'd heard a car engine. Behind her Tammy sat on the sofa, watching a tape of *Snow White* and hugging her ever-present stuffed bear — a present from her daddy. Lorraine's roving gaze took in the lighted concrete lot and the off-white siding of the two long storage unit buildings that ran parallel to each other and perpendicular to the apartment.

Martin's car was nowhere in sight.

The sound was coming from a blue van backing up toward number seven, a newly rented unit close to the middle of building one. Fifteen units, each ten feet square, formed that building. The opposite units in building two measured ten feet wide by fifteen deep. The front edge of that second building sat directly across from the window where Lorraine stood. She gazed diagonally toward unit seven. The van had entered from the north entrance off Starling Street — the same direction from which Martin would come. A man jumped from the passenger side and ran over to open the storage unit. He was very short for a man, but stocky. Dressed in black. It was hard to see his features from this distance, but Lorraine didn't think he was the one who'd signed the rental contract for the unit. That man wasn't so short. His name was Peter Johns, owner of a tire shop. He'd paid the down payment and first month's rent in cash.

This man was sure in a hurry.

Lorraine's gaze moved beyond him to the north entrance, seeking Martin's car. She glanced back at the van as the door to the storage unit rolled up. The van jerked in reverse until its rear backed into the unit. From the far side of the van the driver slid out. Lorraine caught a glimpse of him at an angle over the hood before he disappeared behind the vehicle. The guy looked as tall as the other one was short. He was wearing a black shirt.

She searched the street beyond the north entrance again. No Martin. Letting the curtain fall closed, she turned from the window.

"Is it Daddy?" Tammy pushed back a

strand of long hair. Her little eyebrows slanted up, her rosebud mouth pursed. The skin beneath her eyes looked blue, almost translucent. She'd not had a good day.

"No. But he'll be here soon."

Lorraine glanced at the clock. Where *was* Martin? He should have been home an hour ago.

The phone rang. Lorraine snatched up the receiver from a worn end table. "AC Storage." Her boss had told her and Martin they could use the business line for personal use, as long as they paid for long distance. It saved them money, but it did mean having to answer customer's calls day or night.

"Hi, it's me." Martin's voice sounded tight, his words clipped.

"Where are you? What's wrong?"

Lorraine heard an intake of breath. "The bank was robbed tonight."

"Oh!"

"It's okay, it's okay. Nobody got hurt."

"Not at all?"

"No, really. I was there, and two women. We're all fine."

"Is it Daddy?" Hope lit Tammy's face.

"Yes, honey, he's coming home." Lorraine threw her a fake smile, then headed for the bedroom, the phone smashed against her ear. She could hardly think what question

65

to ask next. "Are you *sure* you're all right?"

"I'm okay. Just shook up."

"What happened?"

"Four men picked the lock on the back door. They rushed in so fast, none of us could sound the alarm."

"Did they take a lot of money?"

"Everything in the daily carts in the vault. Almost seven million."

*The vault.* Martin would have been forced to open it, and he was claustrophobic. "Did they make you go inside?"

"Yeah."

*Oh, no.* "They pulled a gun on you?"

He hesitated. "Lorraine, I'm okay."

"*Did* they?"

"Yes, but —"

"Martin!" Lorraine's hand pressed against her cheek. "Could you see their faces? Can you identify them?"

"They were wearing masks. All I know is the first guy was tall and thin, and the second was real short but muscular. I don't even remember what the other two looked like, except they all wore solid black."

Men with masks. And guns. Rage shot through Lorraine. What those criminals had put her husband through! How would he ever feel safe at his desk again?

"Martin —"

66

"Look, I can't talk right now. The police just got here, and I have to give them my statement."

Lorraine sank down on the bed. He was trying to keep her from worrying, but what he'd endured had to have been terrifying. "Okay. Just . . . get home as soon as you can."

"I will."

"Martin. I love you."

"I love you too."

The line clicked. Lorraine lowered the phone and stared at the thin brown carpet. A gun aimed at her husband. Martin, who worked so hard trying to support his family. Who'd held her for hours when her mother died, who couldn't wait to rock their newborn. Who'd moved "his girls" here to Atlantic City with dreams of buying a house with a fenced backyard where Tammy could play. Martin, *her* Martin could have been killed. He *could have been killed!*

Lorraine started to shake.

She had dreams of her own, and Martin was in the center of all of them. Lorraine wanted a big family — something she'd never had. Now both her parents were dead, and she had no siblings. She wanted four, maybe five kids. The old Ford van she'd driven to Atlantic City full of moving boxes in the back still only had its front two seats — one for her, one for Tammy. How big and empty it seemed. When the three of them drove somewhere as a family, they used Martin's car. Lorraine dreamed of needing a new van *full* of seats, every one taken. That nice house with the picket fence — she wanted it ringing with kids' noise and laughter. Friends coming over to play, slumber parties, and afternoons of baking cookies. Martin was a good father. She could see him on the floor with the kids, reading them stories, wrestling with his sons . . .

Lorraine's dreams were built on hope. And on Martin. She would be nothing without Martin.

And some greedy, scum-of-the-earth criminals had held a gun to his head.

"Mommy!" Tammy called from the living room.

Lorraine closed her eyes and took a long, deep breath. "Coming, sweetie!"

Rising from the bed, she pushed down her fear and anger. As she headed up the hall she managed to paste a smile on her face. "Guess what, Tammy? Daddy will be home soon!"

# EIGHT

Kaycee slumped on Tricia's couch, one leg stretched out on the cushions. Her elbow dug into the back, her head resting on a fist. Exhaustion and anxiety warred in her nerves. Not to mention concern over her own sanity. She'd told Tricia everything, wanting, *needing* empathy. But the further Kaycee got into her story, the less plausible it sounded.

Still — that dead man's face. The gore smeared in his hair, his half-open eyes. *We see you.* The picture wouldn't go away. It floated in Kaycee's brain like a photo on ocean waves, first bobbing on a crest, then pulled under only to resurface.

Now after midnight she and Tricia sat, each deep in thought, trying to find an explanation for the inexplicable. Tricia was in her rocker-recliner, the footrest popped up. Her ample frame, some forty pounds overweight, filled most of the chair. In jeans and a sweatshirt, no makeup, she looked tired, her plump lips drawn down, her eyes at slow blink. Tricia worked as an administrative assistant to the dean of students at Asbury College — which meant reporting to work first thing in the morning. She should have been in bed long ago.

Kaycee rubbed her forehead. "I'm losing my mind, Tricia. This is the fifth time since Mandy's death I've called the police to my house. Before it was just thinking I'd seen a shadow or something. But I swear this camera was real." Kaycee squeezed her eyes shut. "Tomorrow the chief of police will be coming around to cart me to the loony bin."

Tricia shifted in her chair. "I have a theory. Just hear me out, okay?"

"Okay."

Tricia looked away, as if gathering her thoughts. "We both know you've been really struggling since Mandy's death. Long before she got sick you'd gotten your paranoia under control, and your 'Who's There?' column was helping people with their own fears. Well, it still is. But in this past year you've been fighting this whole your-worst-fear-really-can-come-true thing."

"Yeah, and tonight it has."

"That's just my point. At least you think it has. It's like since Mandy died your mind has been conjuring up your *own* worst fear, culminating in actually 'seeing' the camera. You of all people know how fears can color our perceptions."

"But I *saw* that dead man's pic— !"

"Just hold on." Tricia raised both hands, palms spread. "Three weeks ago you wrote a column about one of your readers who's scared of having her picture taken, remember? You titled it 'Exposure.' The mere sight of a camera drives the woman into a frenzy. With that in the back of your mind, added to your heightened fear these days of being watched, your brain came up with tonight's scenario. Kaycee, think about what you 'saw.' A picture of somebody dead — think *Mandy* — and the most frightening words of your life printed on the photo — *We see you.*"

"Then why didn't I see Mandy in the picture?"

Tricia shook her head. "You couldn't have handled that. So your mind came up with . . . someone else."

Tricia's words drifted through Kaycee slowly, pebbles through thick oil. They made some sense, but . . . "Tricia, if I didn't see that camera, if I didn't hold it in my hand and see a picture of myself *and* that dead man, then I really am going crazy. Even my

71

mother never did anything like this."

Tricia let out a long sigh. "Kaycee." Her voice was gentle. "You were already upset over your visit with Hannah. Like you've told me, you hate what's happening to her, but you know you can't interfere. She *has* to make her new family work, because that's her reality. So it doesn't make you crazy that in the midst of all you were dealing with tonight, you thought you saw that camera." Tricia fell silent for a moment. "I mean, consider the alternative. Do you *want* to believe someone got into your house without breaking a window, set up some high-tech camera, waited until you ran out of the house, took away the camera and disappeared — all without leaving a trace? Do you *really* want to believe that?"

*No.*

Kaycee's throat tightened. She swiveled to press both feet against the floor and thrust her head in her hands. Tricia was right. Her mind had just crumbled for a moment. Kaycee imagined herself walking into her kitchen that evening. The flash that lit the room — could that have been car headlights through the dining room windows? She wasn't used to a sight like that; usually her curtains were closed after dark.

Tricia's phone rang. Kaycee barely registered the sound.

"Who in the world could that be at this hour?" Tricia's chair creaked as she leaned over to pick up the receiver on a nearby table. "Hello?"

Kaycee stared at the carpet between her feet. The camera *was* all in her mind. It had to be. If it was real, how could she ever feel safe in her beloved home again? How could she ever fight her way back to the strength she'd had before Mandy's death?

"You've got the wrong number," Tricia said into the phone. "There's no Belinda here." She dropped the receiver back into its cradle with an irritated *tsk.* "Some people."

Silence.

"Kaycee, you okay?"

Kaycee raised her head. She felt sick. "I think I better go back into therapy."

"Maybe you should. And how about praying?"

Back to one of Tricia's favorite topics. "You know I've already done that. It didn't keep Mandy alive. And it hasn't helped me in the last year — not at all."

Kaycee had started going to church when she moved to Wilmore five years ago, shortly after her mother died. But Mandy's illness and her own downward spiral had soured her on God. He could have saved Mandy's life if he wanted to. And he could whisk away Kaycee's fears. But he hadn't done either of those things.

Empathy creased Tricia's forehead. "Kaycee, I can't tell you why God chose to let Mandy die. But I do know he'll help you fight your fear. You have to *keep* praying. Ten, twenty, thirty times a day if you need to."

Kaycee shrugged. She didn't want to fight it thirty times a day. She just wanted it gone.

"You know he helps me fight my own," Tricia said quietly.

*But your fear can't begin to compare to mine.*

Kaycee winced. She knew better. One thing she'd learned from writing her column — everyone seemed to think his or her own fear was the worst. People understood those with the same fear, but thought others who struggled with different ones rather silly — "Why can't they just get over it?" As for Tricia, she was thirty-seven, a born mother with no solid prospects for a husband in sight and her biological clock ticking away. That, Kaycee knew, was a real fear many women faced.

Tricia shoved down the footrest of her chair and leaned forward. "Kaycee. *Do* you think you could have imagined the camera?"

Kaycee's finger traced a circle on her jeans. "I don't know. Yes." There. She'd said it. "Because . . . it's like you said — the alternative's a whole lot worse. Tomorrow I need to go home and finish my column for this week. I have to work in my office, live in my house. This town's my life, and I'm *not* moving!" Her jaw flexed at the bitter memory of her mother forcing her to move constantly as a child. No more of that, ever again. Kaycee had first heard of Wilmore, Kentucky and its friendly, quiet atmosphere soon after her mother's death. Its very name stirred something within her. Kaycee wanted to choose her own place to live — and settle for good. She visited Wilmore to check it out, and the town had felt so right. So comforting. Like coming home.

Tricia rose and padded over to the couch to sit beside Kaycee. "It's okay," she whispered. "It's going to be okay."

Kaycee's fingers curled into the couch. She leaned against Tricia, eyes burning and tiredness seeping through her bones.

Only then did it register — the name Tricia had spoken into the phone some minutes ago.

*Belinda.*

It hit Kaycee like a punch in the gut.

# NINE

Martin drove home from the police station, his limbs in knots. The questions the two detectives asked! And while a tape recorder was running. Was it just his guilty conscience, or did they suspect him already? He'd been nervous, shaken. But what victim wouldn't be after staring down the barrel of a gun? He'd told the detectives of his claustrophobia, how he'd had to force himself to remain calm in the vault. The memory of those moments still hung over Martin like a suffocating cloud.

"I hear you." Detective Forturo tapped his pen against the table. "I got a brother who's claustrophobic. He would've gone nuts." Forturo was huge and bald, a wattle of ruddy skin at his neck. And so thorough. He must have been on the force for decades. Every time their gazes met Martin had to will himself not to look away.

*"You'll do this right, won't you?"* Nico's dirty

brown eyes had bored into Martin at their last meeting. The man was so cold. Martin had seen enough of the Mafia as a kid in New York City to know its members lived by their own code of honor. But Nico's honor went no further than the Lucchese family. *"Wouldn't want anything to happen to you, with your sick little girl and all."*

Nico's threat echoed in Martin's brain as he watched the detectives' tape recorder turn. If it weren't for Tammy he never would have done this.

Besides, he'd *had* to do it. Once he started talking to Nico, once he began to hear the plan, there was no backing out. He'd be dead by now.

The detectives wanted to know every detail, beginning with how the robbers got into the bank. Martin shook his head. "Everything happened so fast. But I did ask them how they got in because I'd locked those doors myself. The leader told me they picked the lock."

Surprised flicked across Detective Petra's face. He looked ten years younger than Forturo, a muscled, solid block of a man with shaggy brown hair. "He answered your question?"

Ice slid through Martin's veins. He managed a shrug. "Not really. They were working on getting the vault open, and he mumbled some disgusted comment like, 'So we can pick a lock.' "

The detectives wanted descriptions of the four men, what they were wearing, down to the make of shoes. The brand of duffel bags they carried. Martin honestly couldn't remember any of that. "Maybe Shelley or Olga can tell you more."

Forturo jotted a note. "Hope so. And we'll look at the tapes from your security cameras."

The two women were somewhere else in the station, also being questioned. Martin tried to imagine their answers. Surely they'd say good things about him. He'd gotten them out of the vault and untied them. He'd kept his cool.

The detectives moved on to ask about his home life, his friends. How long had his family lived in Atlantic City and what had brought them here? What did he do after hours? Who did he hang out with?

Did they suspect his connections?

Much of what Martin told them was the truth. He and his wife and daughter had left New York City six months ago. At twenty-eight he'd wanted to leave the mean streets of NYC and move to some new town big enough to provide opportunity and decent medical care for Tammy. They didn't socialize much. Lorraine was in the rental office most of the day, right next to their small apartment. Many times Tammy had to stay home from preschool with her. As for Martin, he worked at the bank and came home.

Except for the times he'd spent at a certain bar after work. The bar where he'd met Nico. But Martin kept that to himself.

After an hour and a half of questioning, the detectives said he could go home. But Martin hadn't seen the last of being interviewed. No, tonight had only been the beginning. The FBI would be heading up this investigation, Forturo told him, and agents were already on the way from their Newark office, about two hours' drive away. They'd meet with the detectives to go over the information gleaned tonight, but tomorrow they'd want to see Martin personally.

His fingers tightened on the wheel. Why hadn't he thought about all this ahead of time? What made him think he could fool all these professionals?

A good night's sleep, that's all he needed. He was just too tense tonight. No time to calm down.

Forturo had towered over Martin as they stood. "Thanks for all your help, Mr. Giordano. Sorry you had to go through this."

"Sure. Thanks."

He walked to his eleven-year-old Pontiac in the station parking lot, rehashing his answers. *I did it right. Didn't I?*

In the car his thoughts had turned to the money.

His cut was one hundred thousand. A pittance, given the take. But to Martin it amounted to a gold mine. One hundred thousand could buy Tammy all the tests she needed. The care and medicine, if they discovered some hard-to-cure disease. They could make a down payment on a house — in a year. He couldn't go throwing around money anytime soon.

All Martin had to do now was keep it from Lorraine. How he'd explain the money he didn't know. A long lost rich uncle died? He'd think of something. For now he'd hide it. Somewhere.

Tomorrow he would get the cash.

Martin turned into the lighted storage lot and parked his Pontiac next to Lorraine's old van. As he rounded the corner toward the apartment, the door flew open. Lorraine ran out, their daughter in her arms. "Daddy's home, Tammy!" Feigned brightness coated the terror in his wife's voice. "Daddy's home!"

Martin wrapped them both in a desperate hug and hung on tight.

# TEN

Darkness surrounds Kaycee, smothering, chewing. She senses walls around her, closing in. Something mashes her arms to her chest. Both legs prickle with sleep. Kaycee struggles to cry out, but her mouth won't move. She fights for oxygen, but the air is stale and thick as cheese. Panic swells her throat shut. Fingers — her own? — claw her lungs. Breathe. *Breathe!*

Someone shoves her from behind. Kaycee's limbs wrench free, and she scrabbles through blackness, churning, churning. Light seeps toward her, then drenches her body. Her blinded eyes squeeze shut.

The world stops. Time hangs in the hall of her mind, a fat quivering drop, then zips from sight in ragged ribbons.

Running footsteps. A wail. Someone falls to her knees, and Kaycee feels the motion in her own body. Through this unknown person's eyes she sees two red-black holes in a man's pallid face. Puddled blood by his head on a dark yellow floor. Its sweet-iron smell cloys the air. The someone screams, and Kaycee's throat rips. She scrambles away and tumbles off a cliff edge into nothingness —

A violent spasm jerked Kaycee awake.

Her eyes flew open to a dark bedroom — not her own. Her heart pummeled her ribs, each breath an uneven staccato. Heaviness pressed her into the bed, her skin slick with sweat.

*Tricia's guestroom.*

Someone was there, watching Kaycee. She could *feel* it.

For a moment she couldn't move.

With a small cry she threw back the bed-covers, rolled to her side, and fumbled for the switch on the nightstand lamp. Blessed golden light spilled into the room. She sat up, casting wild glances into all four corners. She saw beige walls, a framed print of mallards in flight. White dresser. Her overnight bag on the floor.

No one was there.

*A dream. Just a dream.* Kaycee ran a hand through her hair and willed her breathing to calm.

The small digital clock on the nightstand read ten minutes after three.

She flopped back down against her pillow, air whooshing from her mouth. Her pulse wouldn't slow. That dream! It had been so real. Even now she could feel the darkness, hear the scream, see the two bullet holes in that dead man's head. Smell the blood . . .

It was the same man she'd seen in the camera. But that picture had been a close-up. No view of the dark yellow floor, the spilled blood.

Through whose eyes had she seen these things in the dream? Whose scream did she feel in her own throat?

Kaycee gripped the bedcovers. No one, that's who. Her mind had just gone wild in sleep, adding its own imaginings to the picture she thought she'd seen. That photo hadn't even been real. Nor the camera.

And *no one* was watching her.

Kaycee's thoughts snagged on her still rapid heartbeat, then abruptly spun to Tricia's windows. Were they all locked?

*Stop it, Kaycee.*

But the fear only grew.

She slid from bed onto shaky legs. Edging to the door, she opened it with caution. Stuck her head out. A nightlight tinted the hall in yellow-green. Kaycee glanced at the closed door on her left. She didn't want to wake Tricia. Ghostlike, Kaycee stepped over her threshold and glided down the hall into the TV room. She turned on a lamp. Pulse skittering, she eyed the sliding door onto the backyard patio. Its lever was down in the locked position, but the curtains were pulled back, the night a sucking black void that would swallow her whole.

Kaycee could feel unseen eyes upon her, watching through the glass.

She hurried over and yanked the curtains closed.

*Belinda.* The name tumbled through her mind. She'd fallen asleep with that name on her lips. Why did it haunt her so? She didn't know anyone by that name. Never had.

*Belinda . . .*

The sensations of the dream shuddered anew over Kaycee's skin. She pulled both arms across her chest. Her gaze fell upon a window near the corner of the room, and she hurried to it. With trembling hand she nudged back its curtains to check the lock, then let them fall shut. A thin crack of night pulsed between the two halves of fabric. Kaycee pulled one side firmly over the other.

As if chased, she fled into the kitchen and flicked on its overhead light. Checked its windows and rolled down the shades. Then she flung herself into the living room where she and Tricia had sat. Here the curtains were already closed. She'd insisted upon that as soon as she arrived. Kaycee felt the lock on every window and on the front door.

Done. Dry-mouthed, Kaycee hunched before the door, feet cold against the tile and fingers gripped beneath her chin.

So much for fighting the fear.

She wandered to the couch and sank upon it, drawing her pajama-clad knees to her chest. *Why* couldn't she get this fear under control again? Even her mother had never been this crazy. She hadn't called police to their house or seen some camera that went off by itself.

Kaycee's mouth twisted. Maybe, but her mother had given in to her fears in worse ways. What about all that moving they'd done? Even now Kaycee felt a stab of pain just thinking about it. Easy enough for Monica Raye to move, with no roots of her own. Her parents had died by the time Kaycee was two, and she, like Kaycee, had no siblings. But in town after town Kaycee would make friends just to be torn from them. No matter how she begged to stay put, her mother never listened. Monica Raye's secretarial skills were highly portable. She refused to see that her daughter was not.

Kaycee pictured her mother on the Christmas Eve three years before her heart attack. Kaycee had graduated from college the previous year and was still struggling to get her fear of being watched under control. To that day they'd never spoken openly about their common paranoia.

"Kaycee, I'm so sorry," her mom said. Blinking lights from the Christmas tree played across her face.

"Sorry for what?"

Her mom absently rubbed the ragged scar on her left forearm — the remnant of some childhood accident. "For passing it on to you. I wish . . ." Her voice tightened. "I wish I hadn't."

Kaycee stared at her. What made her broach this forbidden subject now? "It's okay."

But of course — it wasn't. What it had cost Kaycee as a child. What it cost her even then.

"I tried to make a better life for you, Kaycee. I hope you'll believe that."

Kaycee's chest constricted. Did her mother see through hcr that well? Did she see that as much as Kaycee loved her, the seed of blame had long ago taken root and grown in her daughter's heart?

"Mom, really. It's okay."

Her mother started to say more, then

turned away.

Kaycee leaned her head back against Tricia's couch. So much left unsaid. You think you have plenty of time, then suddenly — you don't. Three years later Monica Raye was dead. If only they'd fought their fear together over the years. Maybe they could have helped each other. Now, Kaycee thought, this paranoia would destroy her.

Kaycee shivered, suddenly cold. She pushed off the couch and hustled back into Tricia's guest bedroom, leaving the lights on behind her. Unseen eyes seemed to follow her every move. She closed her door and locked it. Jumped into bed and pulled up the covers. She could not bring herself to turn off the lamp.

Her gaze roamed to the drawn curtains of the window to her right. They were out there. Watching.

Kaycee squeezed her eyes shut. *No.*

The dream washed over her once again. Darkness . . . screams. Running feet . . . the dead man's face. Puddled blood on a dark yellow floor.

Kaycee buried her face in the pillow and prayed for morning.

■ ■ ■ ■

# PART 2

■ ■ ■ ■

Fear is only as deep as the mind allows.
                                    Japanese proverb

# ELEVEN

Man, those eggs looked good.

Thirty-two-year-old Joel "Nico" Nicorelli sat down to breakfast with the underboss of the Lucchese family. As always when he came in to Vince "Bear" Terelli, Nico held his face just right — half *Sure, boss* and half confidence in the respect due himself. He hadn't been made a captain for nothing.

And he didn't plan on staying there.

In La Cosa Nostra, Nico had worked his way from the bottom up. First he'd been a lowly street worker, helping to run the Lucchese family's rackets and loan sharking. After a few years he'd moved up to soldier, becoming a "made" member and taking the solemn oath of Omerta — swearing absolute loyalty to the family. As a soldier he'd done real good, always gunning for the next level. Three years ago he'd made captain, reporting directly to the underboss. Not many higher than Nico now.

Only Bear, plus his counterpart, the *consigliere*. Both those guys reported to the family patriarch, the boss.

Bear trusted nobody. Made the man too cautious. When Nico made underboss, the family's power would go way up. No dreaming, just fact. Nico could outplay Bear any day.

Light drenched Bear's sunroom, the Atlantic Ocean curling on the beach in the distance. The table was set with silver and china. Bear knew how to live it up good. To his right lay the morning paper, top half of the front page up. Nico knew he'd read the lead article. Nico had read it himself, three times. The numbers still boomed in his head. Six million, nine hundred seventy-three thousand, five hundred and seventy-two dollars. Total weight of the cash — five hundred thirty-two pounds. Largest take from a bank vault in U.S. history.

And *he* — Joel "Nico" Nicorelli — had done it.

Nico's stomach growled as Bear's wife, Marie, poured coffee. Nico hadn't eaten since yesterday afternoon. At the gurgling sound Marie gave him a smile.

Bear grunted low in his throat — the sound that had earned him his nickname. Everybody in La Cosa Nostra, from the street workers to the boss, had a nickname. It was your personal identity, what with all the Tonys and Franks. And it was part protection. The fewer people who knew your real name, the better.

"Good thing Martha made extra." Martha had been the Terellis' cook for years.

Nico tilted his head. His mouth watered, but he couldn't eat till the boss said so. Marie set down the silver urn and left.

Bear turned his flat brown eyes on Nico. His black-gray brows hung low and bushy. He had a long face with a scar running up his left jaw to his ear. Got it years ago in some fight. The other guy got whacked.

One thing about Bear. When he called you to come in, you never wanted to see him rub that scar.

"So." Bear guzzled his coffee. "Tell me."

Already, the undertone. Just 'cause some G-men didn't do what they'd expected. The Feds were the Feds.

"Went good." Nico rested his wrists on the table. "Fifteen duffel bags. The van was packed."

Bear flapped his fingers at a small pitcher of cream — *take it.* Nico poured some in his coffee. No invitation to eat yet.

The underboss lifted the steaming platter of eggs and ham and gave himself a large helping. "Money's in the storage unit." It wasn't a question. He set the platter down and started cutting the ham into perfect squares. The man was weird with his food.

Nico nodded. "In twelve boxes by denomination. Lids taped down."

The storage unit had been Nico's idea. In the past week G-men had come down on some of the family's businesses, wanting to see the books. Tax evasion, they said. Yeah, yeah, the old standby when they wanted to put on the heat and couldn't get the family on anything else. But the timing was bad. The robbery was a go. What to do with the money until things calmed down? Bear wanted to delay. Stupid. Nico kept his head on straight. Let's do it right under their noses, he said. With G-men already leaning on them, the Feds wouldn't finger the family for the heist. Plus, those guys would be pulled away and put on the robbery since they were already in town, and the closest FBI office was two hours away in Newark. Something else — Giordano's wife managed storage rentals. What a joint to stash the money — and Giordano wouldn't even know about it. The Feds wouldn't look for the cash so close to one of the bank employees — at least not right away. If they did get the bright idea — not likely — by then the money would be long gone.

Nico had sent one of his associates to AC Storage to rent the unit. Eddy used a fake ID and address and paid in cash. There'd be nothing to prove that empty unit was tied to the Lucchese family.

"And the getaway?" Bear put eggs and a piece of ham on his fork and shoved them in his mouth. Every bite would be exactly the same.

"We had a second van at the auto-wrecking shop. Me and Stump took the money from the duffels and put it in the boxes there. I loaded one duffel with Giordano's cut in twenties. Don't want the guy flashing big bills. Then we drove to the storage. Sammy and Paul crushed the van. Took the license plate off first."

Bear gestured with his chin toward the newspaper. "Almost seven million. A record."

"Yeah." Some praise. But Nico kept a poker face. Most bank heists got you peanuts. He wouldn't have bothered if he didn't know about Trust Bank's huge daily deposits. That's what made him seek out Giordano in the first place. Still, even he hadn't expected seven million.

The underboss took another precise bite. "A record means a lotta heat."

"We'll handle it."

"Hope so. Now we got double the G-men." Bear shot Nico a hard look.

Here it came.

For some unknown reason the agents leaning on them apparently pulled out of town yesterday afternoon. Probably itching to go home to their wives for the night. Nico had heard this just a couple hours ago. A friend of his — a paid informant — on the Atlantic City police force told him the cops had to wait two hours last night for the Feds to show. Meanwhile this morning one of Nico's soldiers said the old G-men were back sniffing around. Red-faced for sure. Cut out for twelve hours and see what happens. Now some higher up was sure to hammer them over it, and they'd take it out on the family.

Nico lifted a shoulder. "They're spinnin' circles. They got nothin'."

Bear's eyes locked on Nico. "I put Slim on it. He says give him twenty-four hours and we can swallow the money."

Nico kept his mouth shut. Bear knew he'd cold-cocked him. Slim, another captain. Always trying to muscle by Nico. Not this time. So the Feds went right instead of left. Figuring out how to launder the money wasn't nothin' like bringing it in. Nico was the earner.

Bear ran his tongue over his teeth — a signal he'd made his point and was moving on. But this wouldn't be the end of it, Nico knew. Everything had to go down perfect from here. Bear picked up his mug and swigged coffee. "How about Giordano?"

Nico tapped the rim of his empty plate. Anger mashed around in his gut. Bear was starving him on purpose. "He came through last night. But he worries me."

"Oh?"

"Guy was sweatin' bullets."

"You said he came through."

"He did. Last night he did it up right. His nerves just made him look more the part."

"So what's the problem?" Bear waved at the food. "Eat, eat."

Now that it was half cold. Nico reached for the platter. "He was *too* nervous. He blabbered. Asked me how we'd gotten into the bank when the doors were locked." Nico took his first bite of ham and eggs. The velvety, salty flavor exploded in his mouth.

"Sounds like a decent question, comin' from a guy who's supposed to look like he might get popped any minute."

"Maybe. But what's he gonna do if the Feds lean on him day after day?"

Bear's coffee mug stopped at his lips.

"Think he'll talk?"

"I don't know."

A sigh rattled Bear's throat. He set down his coffee cup. "Why didn't you take care of this last night?"

Nico bit back a smirk. "And have a murder attached to the heist?"

Bear grunted. He stared at his plate for a minute, then pushed more food onto his fork. "You told me Giordano was solid. You vouched for the guy." Bear's tone threatened.

"Giordano's perfect. Got a sick kid who needs a bunch of medical tests. That's reason enough to keep his mouth shut. Besides, without him I wouldn't have known about the bank's security system. What kind of locks on the doors. How many employees would be there after closing." Nico kept his voice even. This was not the big deal Bear was trying to make of it, even on top of the Fed problem. Everything was under control. "I'm just tellin' you he was more nervous than I figured. I'll take care of him."

"Take care of him now, Nico. Seven million's a lot of money."

That *he'd* brought in. "Sure."

Bear wiped his lips with a napkin and stared out the window at the ocean. "What's with this guy? Got a good job. Health insurance. Then he gets involved in somethin' like this." Bear shook his head. "A man gets greedy . . ."

Nico said nothing.

The underboss went back to eating. "The kid — boy or girl?"

"Girl."

"How old?"

"Just turned four."

Bear shook his head again. He had a four-year-old granddaughter. Nico knew he was crazy about the kid.

"And you got Giordano's cut. A hundred thousand."

"It's in a closet in my house."

"Make sure it gets put back."

Nico clamped his jaws down. Seven million dollars, and the man was worried about a lousy hundred grand. Nico gestured with his hand — *yeah, sure.*

The underboss sniffed. "You shouldn't have brought him in, Nico. Now we got problems."

"I said I'll take care of it."

"How you know it's not too late? What if he talked last night?"

"Nobody beat down my door this morning." Nico shifted in his chair. "He didn't talk 'cause of the kid."

Bear pressed his hands flat on the table

and leaned back. "I don't want him found. And I want you to do this personally."

Nico's anger rose. Any of his soldiers could have done the burn. That's what they were there for. This was Bear's way of rubbing his face in it. So much for pulling off a record heist.

"Sure."

Bear's fork poked up another bite of egg and ham. "The little girl — she lives with her mother?"

"Yeah."

"And the mother knows nothin' about this."

"No."

"How you know? A man doesn't just find a hundred thousand dollars on his way to take a leak."

"I warned him. Giordano knows he needs to sit on the money for now. If he tells his wife, so what? Guy's in too deep. But now — don't matter. He won't get the chance."

He wouldn't even get the cash.

Bear chewed, then swigged coffee. "Never underestimate the vengeance of a woman. If she knows, then her husband goes missin' — she'll sing to anybody who'll listen."

Nico shrugged. "If she knows, I'll whack her too."

# TWELVE

Kaycee awoke to the smell of blood.

Her eyes popped open. Her chugging brain took in the walls of Tricia's guestroom, the framed print of flying mallards. White dresser.

No blood.

Kaycee let out a breath and rubbed a hand across her forehead. Her face and chest were hot. Deep in her mind the dream played on — the running feet and screams, the dead man on a dark yellow floor. She tried in vain to shake off the senses.

Her body felt heavy. She'd gotten little sleep.

Kaycee checked the digital clock on the nightstand. Six-fifty-five.

Tricia's doorbell rang.

Rising up on one elbow, Kaycee frowned. The doorbell — at this hour?

She slipped from bed and crossed the room. As she pulled the door open she heard Tricia's muted footsteps in the tiled entryway, the sound of a lock clicking open. Kaycee trotted down the short hall. She reached the foyer as Tricia, wrapped in a robe, opened the front door. Mark Burnett stood on the porch, still in uniform. His face looked grim.

Kaycee ran a hand over her bed-head curls. They had to be sticking out like Pippi Longstocking's braids.

"Tricia, Kaycee." He made eye contact with them both. "Can I talk to you for a minute?"

"Sure." Tricia stood back and held out her arm, ushering him inside. As he stepped onto the tile, she shut the door behind him.

Mark looked to Kaycee. "We got a call this morning from Ryan Parksley. Hannah's missing. She wasn't in her room when her stepmother went to wake her for school. Bed wasn't slept in."

Tricia gasped. Kaycee's mouth creaked open, but no words came to her tongue.

"They think she ran away. Her suitcase is missing, plus a baby pillow from her bed. Also a picture of her mom that she keeps on the dresser."

"Oh." Kaycee's voice blurted, thin and bleak. "I was at her house last night. She begged me to let her come live with me.

She's so unhappy at home . . ."

Mark nodded. "Mr. Parksley said you'd been there. You were the first person he thought to call, but of course you weren't home. He and Mrs. Parksley phoned all Hannah's friends they could think of. No one knows where she is."

Kaycee's gaze bounced to Tricia, who stood round-eyed, fingers pressed to her lips. Suddenly, worries about some non-existent dead man and a dream seemed so insignificant. "Did you check around my house?" Kaycee asked. "Maybe she slept on the porch?" It would have been cold and so frightening. Kaycee couldn't bear the thought of Hannah waiting for her, alone and crying.

"Yeah. She's not there. Any idea where else she might go?"

"How about the black barn next door?"

"Checked that too."

Kaycee stared at the floor, replaying conversations she'd had with Hannah. Other than the friends the girl's parents would know to call, she could think of no one. She shook her head. "I don't know what else to tell you."

Mark nodded. "Chief Davis is on it, and Deputy Chief Norrel. I'm supposed to be going off duty, but I'll stay till we find her."

"I'll help you. What should I do first? Report to the police station? Drive around the streets and look?"

The last question chilled her. What did she expect to find, Hannah's body lying beside the road?

"It'll be all right, Kaycee. We'll find her." Mark's brown eyes looked deep into hers, as if he saw her fear. "Best thing you can do is call Ryan Parksley and go over the names of those friends. See if he missed somebody."

"Okay. I need to go home first. I have a list of her closest friends and their phone numbers." A month ago they'd all had a slumber party at Kaycee's house, and she'd talked to each parent beforehand.

"Good. You should get home as soon as you can. Hannah may turn up there yet. She could be hiding out somewhere, afraid of getting in trouble."

The words spit fire at Kaycee. Hannah, waiting in desperation for her, while she'd run off to Tricia's because of her own weakness. Why hadn't she stayed put last night? She should have been strong, should have fought the fear.

Kaycee pulled in a breath. "Okay. You have my home phone number in your files. Plus I'll give you my cell. I want to know the minute you learn anything. And I'll keep in touch with the station."

Tricia fetched paper and pen. Kaycee scratched out her cell number and thrust the paper into Mark's hands. Briefly, he gripped her fingers. "We'll find her, Kaycee."

She nodded, throat tight, then swiveled toward the guestroom to dress.

# Thirteen

Cold anger coiled in Nico's gut as he drove away from Bear's mansion. The ham and eggs sat like mud in his stomach. Good food couldn't make up for the threats. Or comparing him to Slim. Nico had to fix one issue he'd "created," Bear said, while Slim fixed the second. Two too many mistakes. Too much clean-up.

For three years as captain Nico had kept his soldiers in line, made sure his street rackets ran like well-oiled machines. Anybody tried to muscle in, he got taken care of. He'd never made a wrong move. Always proved his loyalty to the family. Had consistently been an earner. Now look at him. This job was the biggest single take the family'd ever seen. And he'd planned it from start to finish.

Some thanks he got.

"Anything goes wrong here, it's on you." Bear had leaned over his emptied plate, piercing Nico with a look that said more than the words.

*Yeah, yeah.*

Nico swerved into the driveway of his two-story house and turned off the engine. He slid out and slammed the door. A phone call to Giordano and a change of cars, and he'd be on his way.

Just as well Bear told him to do this himself, Nico thought as he stalked into his empty house. After the breakfast he'd had, his fingers were itching to pull a trigger.

# FOURTEEN

Kaycee left Tricia's house on trembling legs.

Hannah's features hung foremost in her mind — the sad gray eyes, the sweet round face framed by light brown hair with bangs. Kaycee could almost see Hannah out there somewhere, begging for her to help.

As Kaycee traipsed down the sidewalk the weight of unseen eyes pressed upon her.

Looking in all directions, she slid into her PT Cruiser. Her fingers pressed like claws against the steering wheel.

Minutes later Kaycee pulled into her own driveway — and the full terror of last night flooded back. In her mind she saw the flash go off in her kitchen, saw the dead man's photo in her hands. *We see you.* Her white wood house, once so inviting with its wraparound porch and columns, now loomed like some bleached monster.

Kaycee's gaze cruised the front and side yards. No Hannah.

The dimness inside her garage hung threatening and heavy as the automatic door closed. The one light in the ceiling wasn't enough to dispel the shadows in her head. Clutching her overnight bag and purse, Kaycee stepped out of the garage and walked around to the back. No Hannah. Kaycee gazed across her backyard, the two oak trees, the small shed in the far corner.

Had the police looked there?

She tossed her belongings on the ground and cut across the lawn toward the shed. Kaycee never used the thing, couldn't remember looking inside it since she moved in. As she reached the middle of her yard, an unspeakable thought rose in her mind. What if Hannah *was* in there — dead?

A small moan pushed from her. Kaycee raced across the grass and drew up at the shed, hands clasped against her neck. Seconds passed before she found the courage to open the door.

It squeaked on unused hinges. The smell of mold and dirt filtered out. Steeling herself, Kaycee looked inside.

Empty.

Relief overwhelmed her. She pulled back and let go of the handle. The door banged shut.

She walked around to the rear of the shed.

No Hannah.

Back near the garage, Kaycee picked up her purse and overnight bag, chiding herself. How could she possibly think Hannah would come this far at night? Surely there were a dozen friends in her own neighborhood she could have run to.

*But she never made it, did she?*

Kaycee couldn't allow herself to dwell on that thought. She needed to get in her house and call Ryan Parksley right away. And she didn't need the distraction of worrying about some camera and a dead man.

With resolve she thrust her key into its lock. She pushed open the door, intending to barrel inside — and a new wave of fright washed over her. Kaycee stopped, peering inside her kitchen like some orphan come to beg. No camera on the table. Nothing out of place.

Heart scudding, she slipped into the house.

The door closed behind Kaycee with finality, as if she'd just entered a tomb.

She dropped her overnight case on the floor, her purse and keys on the counter. The room was too dark. Kaycee flung open the window blinds.

*We see you.*

The unknown "they" watched as she

walked down the short hall off the kitchen. The feeling shivered her skin, but she pushed on. She needed to get to the list of Hannah's friends in her desk drawer — the ones she'd called for the slumber party. She could imagine Ryan Parksley, beside himself, needing to hear from her.

Kaycee slowed at the doorway to her office and surveyed the room.

Everything looked normal.

She walked to her desk and shuffled through papers from the bottom tier of a metal inbox. *There.* A list of eight friends. Kaycee sank into her chair and picked up the phone beside her computer.

As she punched in the Parksley's number, Kaycee remembered she had to finish her newspaper column today. She'd been about to start it last night when Hannah called, asking her to come over right away. The deadline was noon.

How in the world could she possibly think to write?

Ryan answered on the first ring. He sounded like a man on a tight wire. Kaycee read him the names. He'd already called every one.

She closed her eyes, not knowing what to say.

"She'd come to you first, Kaycee."

"I . . . wasn't here."

"I know."

"And it's so far. Hannah would be scared to death in the dark. I'm thinking she must have a new friend somewhere . . ."

But who? Hannah confided in Kaycee about everything, and she'd never mentioned a new friend.

Ryan breathed over the line. Kaycee could feel his despair. "It's my fault," he said. "Since her mother died, we've hardly been able to talk."

Anger twinged within Kaycee. He and Hannah couldn't talk? Maybe because he'd shoved the memory of her mother aside in no time and rushed out to get married again. He should have been man enough to face his own grieving. Now he'd caused his daughter double the pain.

"Is there anything she told you, Kaycee? Any place she mentioned where she might go?"

Kaycee racked her brain. Trouble was, Hannah hadn't wanted to be anywhere but with her. And Kaycee had told her no. If she'd only said yes — just for the night. This wasn't Ryan's fault, it was *hers.* "I can't think of anything. I wish I could."

"Yeah." The defeat in his voice was palpable. "Okay, well. Keep in touch if you think of something."

"I will. I'll be looking for her, Ryan. She's somewhere close, probably just scared to come out of hiding now."

"Right. I think so too."

Of course he did. It was the best solace they had at the moment.

Kaycee hung up the phone, pressed her face in her hands, and prayed.

When she straightened, she focused dull eyes on the wall clock. Seven-forty-five. Had she really woken up only fifty minutes ago? It seemed like hours. Tiredness seeped through her. She needed a shower and coffee. She longed to go out and look for Hannah but knew she should stay in the house. Mark Burnett was right. Officers were searching the streets. She could only remain here and hope Hannah would show up.

Her column. She'd better finish it while she had the chance.

*If* she could write at all.

With a deep sigh, Kaycee flicked on the computer and pushed to her feet. She headed into the kitchen, anxiety over Hannah clawing at her back and the sensation of being watched tingling her veins. By rote she made coffee and poured it with cream into a stainless-steel mug. She pressed down the lid.

Snatches of lines she should write stole into her mind. It was the second of a humorous two-parter about a recent foray to the dentist. Part one had told the sordid tale of dragging herself into the dreaded dentist's office because a tooth was bothering her — only to learn she needed two crowns and two large fillings. The only way she'd survive? Drugs, administered by the dentist. Kaycee had decided not to tell him she couldn't function on such medication.

Toting her coffee, Kaycee circled the long way around to her office, stopping first to open curtains in the dining room, the living room, and den. At each window she peered outside, praying to catch sight of Hannah, afraid she would see *them.* Whoever they were.

Kaycee returned to her desk and sat down. Staring at the fiery sunset picture on her desktop, she searched within herself for the concentration to write. Her eyes soon pulled to the phone. *Please, somebody, call. Tell me Hannah's safe.*

Coffee mug to her lips, Kaycee reluctantly reached for the mouse. At her touch the desktop picture blipped off — to a photo of the dead man with half-open eyes. Blood spilled from his head in a sickening puddle. And he lay on a dark yellow floor.

# FIFTEEN

Martin was knotting his tie before the bedroom mirror when the phone rang out in the living room. He barely registered it. His head felt like mush, and his insides still trembled. He hadn't slept all night, going over and over his interview with the police. Had he tripped up anywhere?

Lorraine's voice filtered from Tammy's room. She was trying to get their daughter up for preschool. The rundown school, as inexpensive as they could find, was sponsored by a church. Even so it pinched their budget. But Lorraine had insisted Tammy needed the "socializing" even if she couldn't go every day.

Soon they could send her to a much better school.

Martin finished the knot and pushed it upward. Nico was supposed to send one of his men over with the money today. Martin still didn't know where he'd hide it. He sure couldn't stick it in their account at Trust Bank.

The phone rang again. This time the sound drilled through Martin's head. *Nico?*

He dashed for the living room and snatched up the receiver. "AC Storage."

"Martin." Nico's voice.

"Yeah."

"I'm comin' to see you. Ten minutes."

*Ten minutes!* Martin threw a look down the hall toward Tammy's bedroom. He turned toward the wall, lowering his voice. "My family's still here."

"Your wife know anything?"

"Of course not."

"You sure?"

"Yes!"

"Good. Get 'em out."

"It's not that easy. My daughter's slow getting dressed."

"You'll think of something."

Martin pressed a hand to his forehead. "I just don't know how to do that."

"You want your money or not?"

"Yeah, but —"

"See you in ten minutes. Unlock your front door to let me know they're gone, or you lose the money. *Don't* cross me, Giordano."

The line clicked.

Martin slammed down the phone. What was he supposed to tell Lorraine?

"Who was that?"

He whirled around. Lorraine stood at the top of the hall, Tammy's hairbrush in her hands. Lorraine's own long strawberry blonde hair wasn't even combed, and she still wore her pajamas. This would never work.

"I — nobody."

"What do you mean, nobody?"

"Wrong number."

Lorraine gave him a look. "What's wrong with you? You've been acting strange since you woke up."

Martin's eyes flicked to the kitchen wall clock. *Nine minutes.* "I *was* held up at gunpoint last night, in case you forgot."

Her face softened. "Of course I didn't forget, honey." Lorraine followed his glance to the clock, then refocused on him, puzzled.

He stared at her. "Why don't you go get dressed?"

"I'm working on it."

"Well, work faster."

She cocked her head. "Okay, what's going on. Who was on the phone?"

"Just get dressed. *Please.* You and Tammy need to leave."

"Tammy's still in bed, sick again. She's not going anywhere today."

Martin felt the blood drain from his face. "You have to take her."

"Why?"

"Because . . . because she's missing too many days."

"But she's sick."

Panic ballooned in Martin's chest. "She'll feel better. Just take her!"

"Martin, what is *wrong* with you?"

He looked at her, helpless, a dozen lies trailing through his head. His wife was too smart and independent. She wasn't going to just let him push her out the door.

"Please, Lorraine, just trust me." He looked at the clock. *Seven minutes.* "I need you out of here."

She drew herself up, her expression firming. Defiance shone in her eyes. "I'm not going anywhere until you tell me what's going on."

"I — I can't."

*"Why?"*

"Because it's . . ." He thrust a hand into his hair. A hundred thousand dollars. For Tammy. For them. In six minutes they were going to lose a *hundred thousand dollars.* "Please, Lorraine, just *go.*"

Her jaw flexed. "No."

In seconds Martin closed the gap between them. He pushed his face in hers. "Get out of here. Now."

She glared back. "I *told* you — I'm not taking Tammy out today."

"You have to!"

"No, I don't!"

"Lorraine —" He swung away, head swiveling left and right. His brain could hardly focus. "Where are your car keys?"

"Martin, I'm not —"

He grabbed her arms. "*Where* are your car keys?"

"Get off me!" She flung him away. The hairbrush fell to the floor.

"Mommy!" Tammy's voice cut through Martin's senses. He jerked his head toward the hallway. She stood outside her door, teddy bear trailing in her hand.

"Tammy, go back to bed!" he snapped. Instant tears welled in her eyes.

"*Don't* you yell at her." Lorraine turned and bent down, putting her hands on her knees. "Tammy, honey, go back to bed."

"But Daddy's —"

Lorraine scooted down the hall toward her. "Go on now. I'll be with you in a sec." She nudged Tammy back into her room.

Martin's eyes raked to the clock. Less than five minutes. He slapped both hands to his head. Too late, this wouldn't work. He'd go outside, wait for Nico in the parking lot —

And watch the man drive right on by. One thing Nico had insisted on from day one: follow instructions perfectly or all bets are off.

Surely Nico would come back and hand him the money later. He'd have to pay up or Martin might give him over to the cops.

Right, and give himself up in the process? Nico knew he wouldn't do that. Besides, if he did, he wouldn't live to see nightfall. And what about Lorraine and Tammy?

*"Don't cross me, Martin."* If he didn't do this right, they could all be killed.

Lorraine closed Tammy's door and stalked back to him, arms folded. "You better talk to me."

Martin's wild gaze fell to the kitchen table by the window — and Lorraine's purse. He yanked it up and thrust it into her arms, crazy words spilling from his mouth. "Listen to me. Grab Tammy and drive away from here *right now.* Stay gone for half an hour. A man's coming over, and if he finds you here we're going to lose a lot of money. Go!"

She gawked at him. "What money?"

*"Leave."* Martin pushed her hard. Lorraine stumbled sideways two steps, shock creasing her forehead, then righted herself. She

twisted back to stare at Martin.

"Is this about the bank robbery?"

Martin felt his face crumble. "Please, Lorraine."

Her eyes widened. "It isn't, right? Tell me it isn't."

"It isn't."

"Then why don't I believe you?"

He licked his lips. "I . . . I just want Tammy to get well."

Lorraine processed the words. She looked at him from the corner of her eye, as if afraid to hear what was coming next. "I want her to get well too, Martin."

Desperation flooded his veins. "Lorraine, *go*. This man's part of the mob. If he finds you here, he'll kill us all."

"The mob? As in *Mafia?*" Color drained from Lorraine's cheeks. Martin could read her thoughts. The Mafia were in movies, not real life. Not *their* life. "What have you done?"

"Just get Tammy out of here!"

Mouth open, she ogled Martin, fear and confusion wrenching her expression. He knew she'd never leave him alone in trouble. But the thought of Tammy being hurt . . .

She snatched up Tammy's hairbrush and ran down the hall.

Martin dropped his head in his hands. A

second . . . two ticked by. He was going to explode. Suddenly he remembered Nico's instruction about the door. He hurried over and unlocked it.

From outside drifted the sound of a car. Heart in his throat, Martin jumped to a window and peered through the curtains.

Nico had arrived.

# Sixteen

At the sight of the horrific picture, Kaycee rocked back in her chair. The coffee mug smacked against her mouth, sloshing hot liquid across her lips. "Aah!" She dropped the mug and shoved her rolling chair away from the desk. The mug landed with a *crack,* spewing coffee on the hardwood floor.

Robotlike, she bent over and righted it.

Kaycee stared at the monitor, lips throbbing.

Same dead man. But this shot wasn't a close-up. It showed the body down to the chest, the man's arms splayed out. In bold letters across the bottom of the picture ran one word.

*Exposure.*

A strangled sound seeped from Kaycee's throat. That dark yellow floor. It was the same one from her dream. And the spilled blood looked just the same.

How did they know her *dream?*

*We see you. Exposure.*

On her desktop the dead man flashed away. The crimson-yellow sunset re-appeared.

Kaycee's heartbeat sounded in her ears.

A loud bang burst from the street. Kaycee yelped. She jerked to her right, peered through the den and out a front window.

A truck. Just an old truck. Backfiring. Kaycee pressed a hand to her racing heart. She was about to throw up.

Her mouth and chin burned. Leaving the spilled coffee, she jumped up and ran to the kitchen. She yanked open the freezer door and grabbed three ice cubes. With fumbling fingers she threw them into a plastic zip bag and pressed the coldness against her skin.

Kaycee leaned weakly against the counter. Her mind couldn't process what had just happened. How could somebody do that to her computer? Why? Who *were* these people? What did they want?

*Exposure.* Like the title of her column about the woman afraid of cameras . . .

The phone rang.

*Hannah.*

Kaycee threw the ice bag in the sink and snatched up the receiver, not stopping to check the incoming ID. "Hello?"

"Kaycee, this is Chief Davis."

The police chief — a kind and patient man in his mid-fifties, with little hair left and a lean, angular face. "Did you find Hannah?"

"No. We went through her house. No sign of forced entry. Her parents report no strange phone calls. And Hannah doesn't have access to Internet that they don't know about. Has she ever been on the Internet at your house?"

His words were clipped, but he sounded so calm. Kaycee knew that was part of his job, but how could he sound so *calm?*

"No. She's never been on my computer at all. Hannah doesn't even talk about My-Space or anything like that."

"Okay, good. I'm calling to give you a heads-up. In searching her room we found a note beneath her pillow. Her father says it's Hannah's handwriting."

"What did it say?"

"Let me read it to you. I've got it bagged up here."

Kaycee's lips throbbed.

" 'I've run away. Don't look for me. I'll come back when I'm ready. Dad, why did you marry Gail? You act like you've forgotten Mom. And me. I asked Kaycee if I could live with her, but she said no. So I'm leaving.' "

*She said no.* Heat shot through Kaycee's limbs. She couldn't bear to imagine it — Hannah walking out into the night because of *her*. If she'd just let the girl stay with her for a few days . . .

"Kaycee?"

"I — yeah." She could hardly breathe. What had happened to Hannah? She apparently hadn't tried to come here after all. So where did she go? They should have found her by now. A beautiful little girl out alone after dark.

"Listen to me, Kaycee, this is not your fault."

"Uh-huh."

"It isn't. Don't go there. Believe me, Ryan Parksley is feeling enough guilt for the both of you. I've left an officer to stay with them and help them get through this." Kaycee heard muted voices in the background. "But guilt won't help Hannah right now. We need everyone involved to focus on any possibilities of where she might have gone."

"I just can't think of any place else. I talked to Ryan about her friends who spent the night here. He'd called them all."

"We're already starting to interview each of those girls. Maybe one of them knows something."

"What else can you do?" Kaycee couldn't

imagine where to look first, if Hannah's friends proved to be no help.

"I've called in everyone on our force — that's eleven officers total. We're giving this our full attention. I've got officers going door to door in Hannah's neighborhood, and we'll come through yours. Her room has been sealed. We're putting her information out on NCIC — the National Crime Information Center. It will start being disseminated regionally, then on throughout the country."

Kaycee's nerves prickled. Her mouth wouldn't stop stinging. This didn't sound right. NCIC, checking the house for forced entry, sealing Hannah's room . . . "But that sounds so . . . I mean, she ran away. She's somewhere close."

"Most likely so." The chief's voice remained even. Kaycee knew he was trying to console her. In the worst of circumstances, or talking to the craziest of people, the chief was known to employ what he called his "velvet touch." No matter what was said — or had to be said — he remained calm and respectful. "But we always work on a worst-case scenario. We have to."

Sealed. As in crime scene. Abduction. A shudder ran down Kaycee's back. She couldn't consider the possibility. She couldn't.

Papers rustled. "Now while I've got you — I have a report on my desk about Officer Burnett being called to your house last night. I've only had time to glance at it. You thought someone had broken in. Something about a camera —"

"It's nothing." Kaycee pictured the dead man on her computer, the dark yellow floor.

"You obviously didn't think that last night."

"Chief, really, forget it. It's just like before — I got scared over nothing. Just find Hannah. I want to help look for her. What can I do?"

"Nothing right now. Ryan Parksley wants to be doing something too. The hardest thing is simply to wait. But if Hannah ran away as we expect, she could return anytime. I've asked Mr. Parksley to stay home in case she comes back. And it's just as possible — perhaps even more — that Hannah will call *you.* So the best thing you can do for now is stay by the phone."

"I can't help knock on doors? Do something?"

"The Parksleys' neighbors are already calling to volunteer their help. This is Wilmore. You know how fast news travels."

Yes, she did. Every person called would

phone ten more.

"But they don't know Hannah like I do."

"I understand." The chief's tone remained gentle. "You are special to Hannah. That's why we think she may try to contact you. At least for the next couple hours, the best thing you can do is stay there. If she calls, you need to persuade her to tell you where she is."

Kaycee's chin dropped. "Okay." But it wasn't. Hanging around her house didn't feel productive at all.

"Thanks, Kaycee. I — yes?" The last word muffled, as if Chief Davis had turned from his receiver. "Be right there." His voice cleared. "Kaycee, let me know the minute you hear or think of anything. And we'll keep in touch with you."

"Okay, Chief — thanks for telling me about the note."

"No problem."

The line clicked in her ear.

Mind whirling, Kaycee set the phone on the counter and picked up the ice bag from the sink, pressing it to her mouth and chin. She stumbled to the kitchen table, sank into a chair. *Hannah, where are you?* Kaycee stared at the center of the table — and her thoughts flipped to the camera sitting there the previous night. She *hadn't* imagined it.

Unless she now wanted to believe she'd imagined the picture on her desktop too.

The horrific realization sank into her being.

But how did they know about the yellow floor in her dream? How were they doing this?

No. This couldn't be. Maybe that desktop photo *was* all in her mind. With the dream still echoing in her head, she'd subconsciously conjured the picture with details to match.

But deep in her heart she knew she hadn't. She'd *seen* that picture on her computer. It was real.

*Exposure. We see you.*

The skin on Kaycee's back crawled. She twisted to look behind her.

Nothing. Just a silent house. It roared in her ears.

But someone *had* been here last night. They'd put that camera on this very table. And they'd hacked into her computer to flash a second picture on her desktop. They *were* watching.

Her worst fear come true.

Panic burst in Kaycee's chest. She had to tell Chief Davis!

Kaycee threw down the ice bag and shoved back her chair. She jumped to her feet and

130

made for the phone —

*Wait.*

She jerked to a stop, hands hanging in the air. She couldn't do this, not now. Call the chief and pull some officer from looking for Hannah so he could come here and look around? And what would he find anyway? The camera was gone. The photo on her computer had vanished into cyberspace. Mark had checked the whole house last night and found nothing.

No way could she take police attention away from Hannah for another dead-end search. Besides, they'd just think she was seeing things again.

A tremble started in Kaycee's gut. She stumbled to the table and sat again, thinking of her mother. What would Monica Raye have done in a situation like this?

Gone stark raving mad, that's what.

"God." Kaycee tipped her face toward the heavens. "Please help me. And bring Hannah home safe. *Now.*" The minute Hannah was found, Kaycee would call Chief Davis about all this. He'd get to the bottom of it. Somehow. He'd make it stop. Maybe he'd call in a tech, and they'd take apart her computer, find out who'd hacked into it . . .

*If* he believed her at all.

For now Kaycee had to fight her fear

alone. Just for a little while. Hannah was more important. Surely she'd turn up soon.

Minutes ticked by. Kaycee couldn't get up. She could only continue begging God to protect Hannah and herself, careening from one nightmare to the other.

Kaycee's bleary focus happened to graze the microwave clock. Eight-thirty.

*My column.*

Imminent responsibility rushed in. Kaycee lowered her head in her hands. She had three and a half hours to finish her work. This was the newspaper business. Her deadline could not be missed.

A deadline that could only be met by sitting at her computer. What if the dead man's picture jumped onto the screen again?

A new thought spun into her mind. Kaycee's breath hitched. What if the camera and photos were the work of some sick readers of her column? People preying on her worst fear. She'd never said where she lived in any of her columns. But with the Internet, plus the fact that she'd initially started writing for the *Jessamine Journal* in nearby Nicholasville, anyone who really wanted to find her could do it.

The idea bloomed within her. This had to be it. Some crazy "Who's There?" readers were sneaking in and out of her house, hack-

ing into her computer. So smart, so obsessed
—

Could they have taken Hannah?

Kaycee stilled. Her insides went utterly cold.

But why would they? What would they want with a nine-year-old?

"No," Kaycee said aloud. That was another dead end. Nobody had taken Hannah. The police didn't think so, even if they did have to pursue a "worst-case scenario." Hannah's note proved she'd run away.

In fact, she'd probably done it for attention from her dad. Her note practically said so.

The twelve o'clock deadline ticked in Kaycee's head. Time was running out.

She forced herself to her feet. She had to write the column and get it out of the way. If Hannah hadn't been found by the time she was done, she'd insist on going out to help look.

And if those crazy people were out there watching as she searched, if they were watching this very minute through some hidden lens Mark never found — so be it. She'd beat them and her fear. She *would*.

Kaycee hadn't gone two steps before terror nearly drove her to the floor.

# Seventeen

Lorraine had just scooped Tammy from bed when she heard Martin running down the hall. He carved to a stop in Tammy's doorway, breathing hard.

"He's here."

Lorraine froze.

Tammy blinked from her to Daddy. "Who's here? Where're we going?"

Multiple sensations hit Lorraine at once. The warmth of Tammy's body in her arms, the little-girl smell of shampoo and sleepiness. The abject terror on Martin's face. What was happening here?

A car door slammed outside.

Lorraine clutched Tammy to her chest. "What should I do?"

Martin's gaze bounced around the room. He bounded toward the closet and yanked open the door. "Hide in here." He swept clothes aside on the hanging rod.

Tammy wailed. Lorraine pressed fingers

over her mouth. "Shh-shh. It's a game; you have to be quiet." Ducking down, she shoved herself and Tammy inside, all the way to the deep back. She crouched on shoes and toys, their edges biting into her bare feet, and held Tammy tight.

Martin pushed the clothes back in place to hide them. "Don't move till I come get you." He banged the door shut. The closet went black.

"Mommyyy!" Tammy twisted in her arms.

"Shh." Lorraine's heart rammed against her ribs. The darkness closed in on her. Her leg muscles already burned, Tammy's weight dragging at her shoulders. "You have to be quiet."

"I'm scared!"

"Hush!" Lorraine pressed the little girl's face against her thudding chest. Tammy squirmed and fought, fear driving her limbs. Lorraine held on tighter as Martin's words echoed in her mind: *He'll kill us all.*

Tammy bucked her head back and started to sob loudly. Lorraine did the only thing she could — what just minutes ago she'd have considered child abuse. She clapped a hand over her daughter's mouth and dug her fingers into the tender cheeks.

# EIGHTEEN

Kaycee edged inside her office and saw two things at once — the "flying boxes" of her monitor's screensaver and a pool of coffee on her hardwood floor. She approached her desk and reached for the mouse as if it were a cobra. With the barest brush of fingers, she pushed it. The flying boxes disappeared.

Her sunset desktop filled the screen.

Kaycee let out a breath and turned back to the kitchen for a wet dish towel, carrying the coffee mug. She cleaned up the spilled liquid, laid the dirty towel and mug in one side of the sink, and washed her hands.

As she reentered her office a realization hit. When she got home she'd never checked upstairs.

She stopped in her tracks. They could be up there. Right now. All this time she'd been in the house, *all this time,* and they could be lurking up there.

Slowly Kaycee's head turned in the direction of the stairs. She swallowed hard, trying to convince herself to just settle down and write.

*We see you.*

They were upstairs. She knew it.

No. This was just more paranoia. She wouldn't give in.

Kaycee walked to her desk chair and placed a hand on its back, willing herself to sit. But her body wouldn't obey. The upper level hovered in her mind like a preying monster.

She looked back toward the stairs.

Maybe she should call the police after all.

*No, Kaycee.* They were all out looking for Hannah.

Kaycee licked her lips, aware of her own breathing, the feel of her feet against the floor. She lifted her hand from the chair. All she had to do was check, prove to herself no one was up there.

Fight the fear.

Weighted with dread, Kaycee turned and forced herself toward the staircase.

# NINETEEN

Nico turned off Huff Street into AC Storage. He swung left and drove up to the office and Giordano's apartment on his left. His gaze raked to the right — across the concrete and to the two long storage buildings. No one in sight.

He cut the engine on the old Chevy.

Nico kept this car hidden in his garage for jobs like this. It wasn't registered with the DMV, and the plates were stolen long ago.

Where was Giordano's car?

Nico gazed straight ahead, past the apartment. Must be in a parking space around the corner.

He pulled his Beretta 92 semi-automatic from the glove compartment.

The plan was simple. Nico had done it a dozen times. Get his hit into the car with some story — in this case the promise of handing over the money. Nico would tell Giordano to lie down in the backseat, since it wouldn't do for the two of them to be seen together. Then he'd drive him to a back room of one of the family's businesses and put a bullet in his head. The body would be boated some distance out into the ocean, weighted, and dumped.

Nico got out of his car. He stuck the Beretta in the waistband of his pants and strode toward Giordano's apartment. He'd just check around the corner first, make sure he saw only one car there.

As he passed the door it opened. "Nico." Giordano stepped back and waved him to come in.

Nico hesitated, then followed him inside. He shut the door.

Giordano stood frozen in his cluttered living room, looking shell-shocked. Everything about him — his expression, the way he stood, his heavy breathing — told Nico the guy had to go. If the cops got suspicious and came down on him, he'd cave.

"Get in the car. We're goin' for a ride."

Giordano's eyes widened. "Why?"

"You want your money, don't you?"

"But you were supposed to bring it."

"You think I'm gonna drive around with a hundred grand in my pocket?"

Giordano's fingers curled toward his palms. "How am I getting back here?"

"I'll bring you."

"Then you'll still be driving around with the money."

Nico stomped over and thrust his face in Giordano's. "What are you, some smart guy? Get in the car!"

Giordano shrank back. "Okay, just . . . okay." His nervous gaze flitted around the apartment.

"What're you lookin' for?"

"Nothing."

Nico stood aside and stuck out an arm — *go*. He didn't want to have to get ugly and draw his gun. Not here. Giordano eyed him, then started toward the door.

From down the hall came a squeak and muted thump. Giordano hesitated midstep, his back muscles tensing. Then he jerked forward.

Nico slapped him in the shoulder. "What was that?"

"Nothing. Let's go." Giordano kept moving.

Nico raked his gaze down the hall. The first door on the right was closed. And he'd never checked around the corner for the second car. "Your wife and kid still here?"

"No!" Giordano whirled around, face flushed.

"I think they are." If they'd looked out a

window and seen him . . .

"No, it's just a mouse. We get 'em all the time. I pulled one out of the toilet yesterday."

"Pretty big mouse."

Giordano swallowed hard. "Let's just go, okay? Do what you said, no problem with me."

"We got real problems if you didn't do what I told you."

"I did!" Giordano's arms thrust outward and hung there. Sweat popped out on his forehead. "I told my wife to leave — she left."

Nico turned toward the hall. "Let's check."

"No!" Like a madman Giordano rushed forward. He grabbed one of Nico's arms and pulled. Nico cursed and pushed him back. Giordano stumbled into a coffee table and flailed his arms for balance.

Nico kept walking.

Behind him Giordano roared. Nico heard running feet. He swiveled around as Giordano rammed a head-butt off-center in his chest. Nico flew backward and crashed into a wall. Giordano leapt for him, but he scrambled to his feet and out of the way.

"Ungh." Giordano landed hard on the

floor. In an instant he shoved up and twisted around.

Rage shot through Nico. He whipped the Beretta from his waistband. "Stop!"

Giordano stilled.

"Get your hands up."

The man's arms floated upward. Giordano blinked as if in a daze. "Don't kill me. Please."

Nico's eyes narrowed. When he gave this guy cement shoes, he'd be *laughing.* "Back up out of the hall. Now."

Giordano moved backward, his arms shaking. Nico pressed him on until they both stood in the living room.

"When I tell you to, you're gonna turn and walk out that door. You're gonna get in the backseat of my car and lie down. Got it?" Nico's voice was cold steel. Everything in him wanted to beat Giordano senseless right now. Forget driving the idiot to a family business. Nico was putting a bullet between his eyes the minute he lay down in the car. Then Nico would come back inside and finish off the wife and kid, and whoever else was in that room. Four old grandparents and the puppy too.

"Giordano, you hear me?"

"Yeah."

"Don't move."

Keeping his eyes on his target, Nico sidled toward the living room window. He drew back a frayed sheer curtain with his left hand and threw a glance outside. All clear.

From the corner of his eye he saw Giordano launch like a rocket.

Nico jerked and his finger pulled the trigger. *Crack, crack.* Holes torched in Giordano's left jaw and right forehead. The man's body recoiled, and he stumbled backward. Both arms flew up.

He thudded to the floor, face down.

Curses burst from Nico. He shoved his pistol in the waistband of his pants and ran to Giordano. Yanked his shoulder to flip him over. Giordano's eyes were at half mast, his breath a rattle in his throat. Blood pumped from his head and down his temple.

Fury flooded Nico. "Get up!" He kicked Giordano, then wrenched his arm, dragging him over the carpet. Blood smeared in his wake. "Get up!" When Giordano's head hit the hall floor, Nico came to his senses. The guy wasn't going anywhere. Nico threw the man's limp arm down and straightened, glaring at him.

Giordano twitched — and his breathing stopped. The blood stopped spurting.

Nico ran a hand down his face. Good, real good. Now he'd have to load a deadweight body in the car in broad daylight.

The sound of a loud engine filtered from outside. Nico ran back to the window and edged away the sheers. A man climbed down from a pickup truck and walked over to open his storage unit in the first building. As Nico watched, a van turned into the parking lot and headed for a unit in the second building.

*Too late.*

He pulled back from the window, thoughts racing. Any minute now more renters were likely to show up. No way could he take the chance on waiting for them to clear.

He turned away, his gaze cutting to Giordano. Blood from the corpse had run onto the hall floor.

Beyond Giordano through the kitchen window, Nico caught a glimpse of black and white on Huff Street.

A police car. Slowing down.

For a stoplight? Or to turn into AC Storage? Maybe some cop coming to pick Giordano up — take him to the station where the Feds could question him?

Nico sprang for the apartment exit. He flung open the door, twisted the cheap lock into place, and slipped through, closing it behind him. Glanced around. The two renters were out of sight in their units. He couldn't see the black-and-white. If the cop turned in, it would be in seconds.

He ran to his car, pulling the Beretta from his waistband, and jumped inside. Threw the pistol under his seat. He surged on the engine and veered right, up between the two storage buildings, toward the north entrance, forcing himself not to go too fast. As he passed each renter's car, he flung a look in its direction. One man glanced around, then went back to his boxes. Nico checked his rearview mirror. No black-and-white near Giordano's apartment. But too late to go back now.

Nico hit Starling Street and turned left.

His shoulders felt like steel. In seconds it had all gone wrong. And he was gonna pay. Bear would eat him alive for leaving Giordano for the cops to find.

Nico smacked the steering wheel and cursed.

# TWENTY

At the bottom of the stairs Kaycee peered upward, shoulders lifted, one hand on the banister. She stopped to listen.

No sound from the second floor.

With a deep breath, she mounted the first step.

Certain places on the staircase always creaked, Kaycee knew that. Even so, when the third step groaned beneath her foot, a shiver scuttled across the back of her neck. Her beloved house, her haven for the past five years shape-shifted as she climbed. The walls closed in, the air thickened.

Kaycee reached the sixth step.

She told herself nothing was up there. In two minutes she'd be feeling like an idiot. If she were a child watching her mother mount the stairs with such horror, she'd be disgusted.

But hey, *this* fear wasn't irrational. She'd just seen a dead man on her monitor.

At the ninth stair Kaycee smelled blood.

The sudden odor flooded her, carrying sound with it — the multiple screams and rush of footsteps from her dream. Only Kaycee wasn't asleep. The noise banged through the house, her head, so very real.

*I'm just imagining this. I'm just . . .*

She bent low, a darkness she'd never known closing in. Her fingers curled around the worn banister, fighting to keep her steady. For a long minute she could only drag in air.

*We see you.*

Eyes bored into her back. She whirled around, knowing they hulked behind her — and nearly lost her balance.

No one below.

Slowly the sounds and smell faded until only the rumor of them remained.

Kaycee turned forward again. She scanned the landing above her, looking for she knew not what.

Her fingers cramped as she pried them from the banister.

Five more stairs.

The eleventh creaked louder than the third, as breath-catching as nails on a chalkboard. Kaycee's shoulders jerked. She leaned to her right, looking up and around the corner into the hall. Her narrowed eyes searched the carpet for footprints, drag marks. Anything. She saw nothing.

One last stair and she reached the landing. She paused, head cocked, gaze raking across what length of hallway she could see. Her mind still throbbed with memories of the footsteps, the screams and smell. But they didn't come back.

At the door to the hallway, Kaycee looked toward the dim guest bedroom a short distance on her right. Through its open door she spotted the foot of the bed, its yellow spread smooth to the floor, and one of the windows. The curtains were closed. Grasping her upper arms, she moved down the hall and into the room. She took in the whole bed, the maple dresser and nightstand, framed carousel prints on the walls. The second window's curtains were also drawn. Kaycee pulled back all the window dressings, letting light into the room.

She thought of Mark the night before, checking all closed-off spaces. Heart knocking, she approached the closet. She fisted her hand around the knob and pulled back the door.

Coats and extra clothes hung as she'd left them. Boxes on the shelves. Kaycee shut the door quickly.

Before she could think twice she sank to

her knees, bent down, and lifted the covers to check beneath the bed. Nothing there.

Gaining courage, she retraced her steps up the hall, past the doorway to the stair landing. Turned right into the bathroom. This one was easy. The shower curtain remained pushed all the way back, as Mark had left it. The tub stood empty.

By the time she reached her bedroom, Kaycee wanted this torture to be over. She stepped inside and took it all in with a glance. Her gold comforter and pillows, the two old dressers that once belonged to her mother. She walked around to the other side of the bed, then knelt down to check beneath it. All clear. Finally only her closet remained. Her courage faltered as she approached it, and she hated that.

She didn't want to live with fear *any more.*

Jaw tight, she flung back the closet door — to the sight of her clothes hanging as she'd left them. The floor, the shelf were undisturbed.

Cold relief washed over Kaycee. She closed the door, backed up, and sank upon her bed. Hand to her forehead, she willed her heart to slow. Minutes passed. She couldn't move.

Her column. Time was ticking.

Kaycee struggled to gather pieces of her

strength off the floor.

Slowly, jaw set with determination, she rose and walked toward the stairs. As Kaycee descended, her ankles still trembled.

Back in her office she sat at her desk and gazed at the sunset picture on her desktop. Hannah's face rose in her mind. Kaycee breathed another prayer for the girl, then clicked into a new Word document. Headed the new column: "World's Worst Dental Patient, Part 2." Kaycee's eyes fell on the time at the bottom right corner of her monitor. Almost nine. She'd left the Parksleys' house shortly after nine last night.

Hannah hadn't been seen in twelve hours.

Kaycee gazed at the page waiting to be filled, trying to focus.

Her search through the upstairs rooms wedged back into her thoughts. They'd planned it this way, hadn't they? She wasn't supposed to find anything she could take to the police. It would have been far better if they *had* left something behind. Something tangible. Now she still had no proof they'd even been here . . .

Kaycee swiveled around to look over her right shoulder, then her left. She scanned the office walls, the ceiling. They could have returned last night after Mark checked the house and hidden a video camera. They

150

could be watching right now.

*Exposure.*

But they wanted more than just to watch. They wanted to drive her crazy. And these were high-tech people. Maybe they knew about the dark yellow floor in her dream because they *caused* her to have that dream in the first place. Somehow they'd pushed thoughts into her brain — sights, smells, and sounds. Maybe through hypnosis. Or through something like the subliminal advertising once used in movie theaters — when a split-second flash of buttery popcorn on the screen, too fast for the eyes to register, would send droves of customers to the concession stand.

But why keep showing her pictures of that dead man? Who was he?

Kaycee stared sightlessly at the computer screen. Her mind swirled until it numbed . . .

She blinked. Awareness returned. She took in the white page, the bold heading of the new column. She had to write it. Now.

Kaycee pulled in a deep breath. Placed her fingers on the keys. *Come on, Kaycee Raye. You've done enough of these. Drag up some humor and write this thing.*

Through sheer will, she began to type.

# WORLD'S WORST DENTAL PATIENT — PART 2

I have a new outlook on drugs.

Remember before my Death by Drilling appointment the dentist gave me a pill to take at home? To start the sedation "process."

"Take it at seven a.m.," he said, "and we'll see you at eight."

D-Day arrives. I pop the pill and settle on the couch to wait for my demise. Turn on the TV to keep me company.

First fifteen minutes I feel fine. Next fifteen minutes, the same. At seven fifty-five, my designated driver, Tricia, will arrive to ferry me the whole two blocks to the dentist's deadly domain.

Suddenly, I am feeling . . . strange.

Out the front window I see Tricia's car pull up to the curb. She toots her horn.

I get up and head for the door. The wall moves — right in front of me. I bounce off and shake my head hard.

Outside, the porch has turned into a shifting sea. I stumble down my three steps like a drunken sailor. Tricia helps me into her car. "You okay?"

"Yeeahhh." I bare all my teeth in a smile.

As we pull up to the dentist's office, Miss Chipper receptionist is out the door before I can even fall from Tricia's car. "Hiiiiey, good *morning*!" She takes my arm to guide me inside. Dratted doorway moves on me. I crash into it twice.

Doc's waiting for me inside, a concerned expression on his face. The fish in his large aquarium give me goggle-eyed glances.

"Hey, fishies, hey, Doc! Let's party!"

At least that's what I try to

153

say. It comes out more like, ". . . heeeey, Dooocc, lesssss paarrrrteeeee."

I remember moving to the chair. The chair that normally wigs me out just to look at it. Now I don't care. I plop right down. "Lessss doooo thiissss thin-ngggg."

Doc gives me more drugs. Whoooo-hawwww. They're crystals under my tongue. Taste like Sweet'N Low. He let's me sit so I can . . . drift . . .

He comes back. Asks me if I'm ready. "Nuhhh-uuhh. Hittt meeee with sommmme mooorrrre."

"You sure? You look pretty wasted."

"Doonn wannaa feeeeel nuthinnnn, Dooooc."

He processes this. My being out cold is clearly in his best interest. "Okay."

I have this vague recollection of asking for a third hit.

After that I'm ready, all right. For anything. All fear gone. You hear me — *all fear.* In the *dentist's* chair. *Man, I can take on the world!*

As long as I don't need to stand up to do it.

I feel the needle go into my cheek for numbing. I don't care. Another needle. (Remember, I needed a lot of work.) I don't care.

The Big D comes at me. By this time I should have a heartbeat of 500, sweat pouring off me. But now? I don't care.

The drill goes on. The fun begins in my mouth.

I start to hum.

My next clear memory is Doc telling me I need to wake up so I can tell him if the temporary crowns feel okay. All of a sudden, I'm coming out of the drug haze. Just like that.

Wow. This is *crazy.* "What time's it?"

"Almost twelve."

*Twelve! Four hours* in that chair?!

Tricia leaves work to come get me. Doc's assistant holds my arm as I get out of the chair. I say I'm fine. Except that a wall shifts on me — just a little. Which makes me giggle. "Doc, yurr bread's the best thing since sliced drugs."

Tricia guides me out the door. To life, liberty, and the pursuit of happiness. I am so relieved, I could cry.

For one glorious morning — in the dentist's chair of all places — I discovered what it felt like to be fearless. I can't begin to tell you how freeing that was. Like floating. Like I could do anything. *Anything.*

I'm going to get that freedom back. Somehow. Without drugs.

With that kind of power I could spit in the face of my worst fear come true.

# Twenty-One

Lorraine huddled in the black closet, clutching Tammy to her chest. Her arms had nearly gone numb from battling the little girl, and her leg muscles shook. Tammy now hung limp and sweating, her breath in a shallow pant. Terror squeezed Lorraine's lungs. The sounds she'd heard from the living room and hall rattled in her head. Voices, running, someone crashing into a wall. Then a noise — twice — muted through two closed doors and all the clothes. Like a metallic *smack*.

*Gunshots?* Shock raced through her veins.

No, couldn't be. They were arguing, and one of them knocked a chair over. Something like that.

Finally — silence.

She cocked her head, trying to listen above the whoosh of blood in her ears. Was that voices she heard? Calmer now, quiet. Or was she just imagining them?

*"Stay here until I come get you."* Lorraine clung to Martin's words. He would come any minute now. Any minute.

Lorraine waited.

If only she'd thought to bring Tammy's stuffed bear in with them. It would have been such a comfort for Tammy.

Dread mushroomed in Lorraine's chest, and Tammy grew heavier and heavier. The air gelled, too stale to breathe. She had no idea how much time had passed. Ten minutes? Thirty? Four times she started to push up, but each time caution overcame her. What if Martin and that man were still in the living room? What if she or Martin or Tammy paid some great price for her own impatience?

Lorraine waited until she could wait no longer. Until she'd convinced herself that far too much time had passed in silence. The man had to be long gone.

But where was Martin?

Deep within her, dark voices whispered of a nightmare too terrible to imagine. She closed her heart, refusing to listen.

"Tammy." Her dry throat could barely form words. "We're going out now. I need you to be quiet. Can you do that?"

Tammy whimpered and nodded. Guilt swept through Lorraine. What she'd put her daughter through. Tammy would have night-mares for weeks.

Lorraine lowered the little girl to the floor. Her own leg muscles were too weak to crab-walk out, carrying the weight of a four-year-old. Tammy cried and grabbed fistfuls of her shirt. "No, no."

"I'm right here. I'll keep a hand on you. We'll go out together."

Gripping Tammy's arm, Lorraine crawled over shoes and toys, urging her daughter along. She ducked under hanging clothes, the bottoms of shirts and pants sweeping over her head. She could smell her own sweat, her half-asleep feet prickling.

She lifted a hand, feeling for the door. When it hit wood, she ran her fingers upward, seeking the knob. The door opened, flooding in light and fresh air. Lorraine blinked and sucked in a greedy breath, oxygen burning in her lungs.

Together they crawled out of the closet.

Lorraine tried to stand, but her stiff legs wouldn't obey. She sank down hard on the carpet. Then listened.

No sound of men talking. Or movement.

The dark voices whispered in her head.

Grimacing, she pushed to her feet. "Tammy, stay here for a minute."

"No!"

"Stay *here*."

Lorraine made her way toward the door. Tammy sprang up and wrapped a little hand around her leg. Lorraine tried to unwind the fingers, but they dug into her skin. Tears bit her eyes. How was she supposed to do this?

She listened again but heard nothing. Martin must have gone somewhere with the man. It would be safe to go out there with Tammy. It had to be. The little girl wasn't about to stay behind.

"Come on." Lorraine reached down. "I'll hold your hand."

Tammy let go of her leg and hung on to her fingers.

At the bedroom door Lorraine gripped the handle and slowly, carefully turned. Somewhere along the way her hands started to tremble. She eased the door open an inch and pressed her ear to the crack.

No sound.

Pushing hair away from her face, she opened the door further. Lorraine nudged ahead of Tammy, leaned her head out the doorway, and looked toward the living room.

Martin sprawled on his back at the edge of the hall, both arms flung out. Blood streaked his face and covered his hair, puddling beneath his head.

Lorraine's mind flew into a thousand pieces. She rushed forward, leaving Tammy behind. At her husband's side she fell to her knees. A black, bloody hole gaped in Martin's jaw, a second in his forehead. She gripped his shoulders, shaking, shaking. "Martin. *Martin!*" His head lolled in rhythm with her yanks, the eyelids half open and unmoving. Beneath them lay nothing but cold frosted glass.

"Daddyyyy!" Tammy ran up the hall and threw herself down next to Martin's head, smearing blood on her pink pajama pants, her arms. The sight was too horrific to bear. Lorraine shoved up and wrenched Tammy away. The little girl kicked and screamed, loud, long shrieks that sizzled in Lorraine's brain.

She craned her head toward Martin. He didn't move.

*No, no, no, no, no.*

The world tilted. It was falling through space and Lorraine had to get off. Clutching Tammy in her arms, she tried to run, but her legs wouldn't move. An unseen force shoved at the small of her back. She stumbled past Martin onto the carpet, through the living room. The front door bulged and contracted as if sucked by a giant wind. An eternity passed before Lorraine reached it. Tammy wailed in her ear as she fumbled for the knob, her seizuring fingers unable to turn it. Three times her hand slipped off, the voices in her head shrieking accusations. She'd known, she'd heard, and she'd *sat in the closet, too afraid to come out.*

Lorraine's palm gripped the handle. She flung the door back and burst out into the fresh and sunny April day, screaming.

# Twenty-Two

By the time Kaycee finished her column at eleven-thirty her nerves hummed. Half her consciousness had fixed upon the phone, praying for a call about Hannah. And the weight of watching eyes never lessened.

As she saved the column, Kaycee steeled herself. She eyed the monitor, anger kicking around in her belly. If the dead man showed up again, she wanted proof. Kaycee pulled her camera from the bottom desk drawer and turned it on. She held it in her left hand, a finger on the button — and closed Word.

The fiery sunset appeared.

Kaycee exhaled and put down the camera. But she left it on. It would turn off by itself in a few minutes.

She pulled up her email program, groaning at all the new messages. Reader mail. Most of it would be positive — *Thank you for opening your soul to me in such a humor-*

*ous yet poignant way. Thank you for helping me face my own fears. You are so courageous.*

Yeah, right.

Kaycee emailed the new column to her syndicate, then turned off the computer. There. No more chances of a dead man on the screen.

She replaced her camera in the bottom drawer.

Motion outside the window caught her eye. Kaycee saw Mrs. Foley weeding the flower bed in her side yard. She wore faded orange sweatpants and a bright green T-shirt, a yellow bandana holding gray frazzled hair out of her eyes.

*"I asked Kaycee if I could live with her, but she said no. So I'm leaving."*

Kaycee stared at Mrs. Foley. Once Hannah had run off into the night, wouldn't the darkness have petrified her? Maybe she'd tried to run here after all . . .

Kaycee jumped up and headed for the front door. Outside she crossed her porch toward Mrs. Foley's house.

Watching eyes followed.

She whirled around, gaze flicking left and right. Every part of her body tingled. She saw the black barn across the way, the emptiness of her own street. A slight breeze ruffled the yellow flowers of a forsythia bush in a neighbor's yard. Everything looked so peaceful on a beautiful spring day.

She knew better. They were there, somewhere.

Hands fisting, Kaycee turned back toward Mrs. Foley and stepped off the side of her porch. She crossed over to her neighbor's lawn. "Mrs. Foley?"

The elderly woman shuffled around on her knees. The back of one bony hand wiped against her chin. With beady eyes, a large nose, and hollow cheeks, she looked like a suspicious Muppet.

Kaycee ran a hand through her kinky hair. Mrs. Foley's stare always made her feel like some exasperating child. "You know Hannah Parksley, the nine-year-old girl who comes over here a lot? She's missing. I wonder if you saw her around my house last night."

Mrs. Foley blinked twice. "How would I know who's around your house?"

No reaction that a child was missing. What was wrong with this woman?

"I was just wondering if you happened to look out the window . . ."

"Don't go peering out my windows at night. I have better things to do."

"I *saw* you looking out your window last

night when I drove in."

Mrs. Foley sniffed. "You must be mistaken."

Uh-huh. She'd no doubt watched Mark Burnett's police car come and go as well. Probably knew exactly how long he'd been in Kaycee's house.

"Mrs. Foley, Hannah is missing. The police think she may have tried to make it over here. If you saw her or anybody else around my house last night, they really need to know."

"I *told* you I saw nothing. As for the child, I'm sure she'll turn up. They usually do."

With the raised chin of put-upon royalty, Mrs. Foley turned her back on Kaycee and resumed weeding.

Kaycee's jaw clenched as she retraced her steps across the porch. Witchy old woman, rattling around in that big house of hers. Probably had corpses in the basement.

Back inside her office Kaycee called the police station. Hannah should have been found by now. What if someone had kidnapped her after she ran away? What if they'd hurt her? If she'd been kidnapped, every hour that passed decreased the odds of her safe return. Kaycee pressed thumb and fingers to her temples. She couldn't think about that. It was too terrible.

On the fourth ring Emma Wooley, the police station's administrative secretary, answered. The chief was out, but Mark Burnett hopped on the phone. "Kaycee, you hear something?"

The sound of his voice rustled through Kaycee like warm wind. "No. But I've stayed home long enough now. I want to help look for Hannah."

"What did Chief tell you to do?"

"He said stay here for at least a couple hours. That's passed. Hannah's not going to show up here now. With everybody looking for her, she's not walking the street in broad daylight. And she's got my cell phone number."

Mark sighed. "Okay. Come down. A friend of the Parksleys has printed up flyers. He and some other neighbors are taking them around. Maybe you can help."

"Thanks, be there soon." Kaycee's stomach growled. She hadn't eaten all morning.

"Hey." Mark's voice gentled. "How about you? You okay?"

Kaycee's throat swelled. The softness in his tone betrayed his thoughts. He really did seem to be sorry for what he'd said at Chief Davis's party. For a moment, she so wanted to tell him about her dream, the picture on her desktop . . .

Kaycee stared at her dark monitor. "I'm fine, Mark. Let's just find Hannah."

She hung up and hurried to her kitchen to pick up her overnight bag, still sitting by the door. Carrying it, she climbed the stairs to change her clothes. Kaycee felt eyes follow her every move, but she steeled herself against the fear. This was no time to give in. Hannah was still out there somewhere, and Kaycee was going to find her.

# TWENTY-THREE

Lorraine slumped in an uncomfortable metal chair at the police station, Tammy on her lap. Her daughter was half asleep, worn out from crying and terror. The heat from her little body made Lorraine's chest feel sweat-slicked and clammy. They sat in a small, grim room with one table, a couple more chairs. A round-faced, beefy detective with a badge that read Jim Tuckney had been questioning her for over an hour. He'd stepped out to talk to somebody. How long he'd been gone — it didn't matter. Didn't matter when she left here or where she went. She and Tammy had no life to go back to.

Her mind played the tape of Martin's body on the floor. All that blood. Vaguely Lorraine remembered screaming outside her apartment, two men running out of different storage units. One of them called 911. He said he'd glanced up when a car drove out of the storage lot, but all he remembered was an old white sedan. He hadn't seen the driver's face.

Lorraine and Tammy were still in their bloodied pajamas when the police arrived. Lorraine could not recall getting dressed.

Electricity had sparked through the police station as Lorraine was ushered to the interview room. She heard snatches of talk about last night's robbery: seven million dollars . . . the FBI . . . no suspects . . . stupid reporters demanding information.

*Seven million dollars.* She couldn't even imagine that much money.

Lorraine had a tiny bit of money in a savings account. She would have to use it for a cheap hotel tonight. Yellow crime-scene tape already cordoned off the apartment by the time the detective drove her and Tammy away. She'd been told she couldn't go back until this evening. Fine timing. What was she supposed to do, step over her husband's blood on the floor to put her daughter to bed?

*How* could Martin be dead?

Emotions were a strange thing. Lorraine had gone from wild crying to frightening calm. In between she'd tried to appear as normal as possible for Tammy's sake. Her little girl refused to be separated from her.

Like it or not, the detective had resigned himself to letting her stay on Lorraine's lap while they talked.

"Who do you think might have done this?" he asked.

Lorraine's mind flashed to Martin, standing nervously before her in their apartment.

*"Please tell me this isn't about the bank robbery."*

*"It isn't."*

*"Then why don't I believe you?"*

Lorraine shook her head. "I have no idea."

Could the detective see the questions in her eyes? The confusion and guilt? In the closet she'd heard gunshots but convinced herself she hadn't. She couldn't afford to deny reality again. Martin, her loyal, law-abiding Martin, had gotten himself mixed up in something. Even when he came home last night, hadn't he acted a little odd? Lorraine figured it was shock. But now that she thought about it, he hadn't seemed shocked *enough.*

Or was she remembering all wrong?

"Know of any enemies he had?" the detective pressed.

Lorraine stared dully at a deep scratch in the wooden table. "Martin doesn't have any enemies. He's such a good man." She couldn't bring herself to speak in the past tense.

*"This guy's in the mob . . ."*

A member of the Mafia had killed her husband in cold blood. And what might that man do to her and Tammy if she talked?

How had Martin met *anybody* in the Mafia?

Detective Tuckney shifted in his chair, and the legs creaked. "How did your husband act last night when he came home after the bank robbery?"

Lorraine kept a poker face. The detective *was* reading her thoughts. "He was real shook up. The minute he saw me and Tammy he just hugged and hugged us —" Lorraine's throat closed. She lowered her chin and blinked back tears.

*"I just want Tammy to get well."*

Detective Tuckney gave her a moment. "You don't think the two could have been related?"

"How? Why would those bank robbers even know where we lived?"

He spread his hands.

"And if they wanted to kill him, why didn't they do it last night? Why would they — why would *anybody* come to our apartment in broad daylight and . . ." Lorraine looked away, her mouth pulling. She swallowed hard and her chest jerked. Tammy stirred in her arms.

*Tall and thin, real short and stocky.* The descriptions blipped into her brain. Martin had said that's what two of the bank robbers looked like. Just like the men she'd seen last night in such a hurry, jumping from a truck to open unit seven. A *newly rented* unit . . .

And one of them had been wearing all black — like the robbers. The driver had at least been wearing a black shirt. She hadn't seen him from the waist down.

Lorraine's eyelids flickered.

"Look, can I just go now? I don't know what else to tell you. I just don't . . . I don't know anything right now."

Detective Tuckney gave a reluctant nod. "I appreciate your time. You have someplace to go for awhile? We'll want to know where to get hold of you."

Before the interview Detective Tuckney had called Nate Houger, Lorraine's landlord and boss who lived in New York, and told him what had happened. The AC Storage office would have to be closed for the day, the detective told him. Sitting next to her apartment, the office was also taped off as part of the crime scene. Lorraine asked Mr. Houger for a second day off, and he said okay. She couldn't imagine returning to work — answering the phone, posting payments — as if nothing in her life had changed.

"There's a motel about a mile from our place," she said. "I'll stay there."

"Okay." Tuckney had pushed back from the table and stood. "Let me go check on something. Be right back."

And now Lorraine waited.

Those two men last night at the storage unit . . . She calculated the time. It would have been soon after the bank was robbed. While Martin was being questioned by police.

But that was crazy. Why would they put the money *there?*

Why not? Maybe it was the perfect place. If Martin had been pulled into the crime, and his wife just happened to manage storage rentals . . .

*Seven million dollars.*

*"I just want Tammy to get well."*

Detective Tuckney returned. For a searing second Lorraine considered telling him everything. Her argument with Martin, the Mafia man at the apartment, the two men at the storage unit. Whoever did this to Martin, Lorraine wanted to see him *fry.*

But a member of the Mafia? She had a

young daughter to protect. A little girl now without a daddy. What would Tammy do if she lost her mother too? And how could Lorraine imply anything to the police that would connect Martin to the robbery? He was dead, and now she wanted to drag his reputation through the mud? It would be all over the newspapers. People would accuse him of being some awful criminal, people who never even knew him.

The words dribbled down Lorraine's throat.

"All right." Detective Tuckney placed his hands low on his hips. "I'll take you back to your car at the storage place. If you want I can go into the apartment and get a few items for you and your daughter before you go to the motel."

Lorraine shuddered at the thought of strangers examining Martin's body.

"No. It's okay."

They drove to the apartment in silence. Tammy fell asleep in the backseat, head lolling. For once Lorraine was glad for her daughter's tiring sickness. If only she could sleep through this herself. If only she could sleep through the rest of her life.

Beyond the crime-scene tape at her apartment, the media had gathered. Lorraine saw two news vans and other cars. Five reporters hurried toward the detective's vehicle, TV and still cameras raising up. Lorraine hunched over and buried her face in her arms.

"Sorry about this. I'll deal with them." Detective Tuckney slid out.

Lorraine heard him asking the reporters to "Get back, please — I'll answer what questions I can over there." Multiple voices — men and women — shouted questions at him.

Something banged against the backseat window behind her. Lorraine jerked around to see a still camera aimed through the glass at her sleeping daughter. Instant rage rocketed up her spine.

"No!" She leapt from the car and rushed the reporter. "Get away!"

He whirled toward her and aimed his camera. It clicked twice.

"Stop, whoa!" Detective Tuckney ran around the front of the car and grabbed her arm. A uniformed officer appeared, pushing the reporter back.

"Mrs. Giordano, I heard you were at home at the time of the murder," one reporter called. "Did you see the suspect?"

"Mommy!" Tammy's wail filtered from the car.

Lorraine wrenched from the detective's

grasp and flung Tammy's door open. Her fingers shook as she unbuckled the seatbelt and pushed her daughter over. She crawled into the car and slammed the door. Wrapping her arms around Tammy, she hid her little girl's face in her chest. "It's okay, it's okay." Together they rocked and cried.

Lorraine would not get out of Detective Tuckney's car again with the reporters around. He drove them to the motel, a policeman behind them in her car. No reporters followed. No need — they'd already gotten their dramatic shots.

In the motel room it took some time to calm Tammy down. Lorraine berated herself for losing control. It had only scared her daughter. She couldn't let that happen again.

As Tammy finally slept Lorraine lay beside her, exhausted and heartbroken, staring at the stained ceiling.

*"Please tell me this isn't about the bank robbery."*

*"It isn't."*

*"Then why don't I believe you?"*

# TWENTY-FOUR

As Kaycee headed out her back door, the phone rang. The sound jangled her nerves. Not even outside yet, and she was trembling.

*Hannah.*

She lunged for the receiver and checked the ID. It was Tricia's number at work. Her shoulders slumped. She pressed Talk. "Hi, Tricia."

"Have they found her yet?"

"No. Not a sign. Not a clue. Except they found a note she left in her bedroom. She ran away because of her dad and stepmom and everything. She mentioned me. I wouldn't let her come live with me —" Kaycee's voice cracked on the last word.

"Hey, hey, stop. Don't go blaming yourself for this."

Sure, no problem.

Tricia blew out a breath. "What about her

friends? She must have gone to one of them."

"No one knows a thing."

Silence spun out. Kaycee envisioned minutes, hours, days of the same hovering lack of words.

*Please, God, send her home.*

"Kaycee, hang in there. They'll find her."

"I know. I'm . . . fine."

"You don't sound fine."

"I'll manage."

"How are you doing there in your house? See anything else strange?"

"Yes. But I can't worry about that right now." Right. Like the fear of being watched wasn't doubling the panic within her.

"What did you see?"

"You know the camera and the picture of that dead man? Turns out they were real after all. The same dead guy blipped onto my computer screen this morning, then went away. So far he hasn't come back."

"Kaycee! Are you sure?"

"Tricia, I saw him. That makes twice now. And he'll show up again. I think some lunatic 'Who's There?' readers are trying to drive me crazy."

"Why would they do that?"

"I have no idea."

More silence. Dread rolled around in Kaycee's gut. Double the panic or not, if it weren't for Hannah, she'd be on the floor right now, catatonic.

Her thoughts skipped to the column she'd just written — that final trip to the dentist and what it had taught her. She needed that power now.

Kaycee glanced out toward the backyard. The day was sunny and warm. Utterly terrifying.

"Did you tell the police about this?" Tricia asked.

"No way. They're all looking for Hannah. When she's found, I'll tell them."

"Yeah. Okay." Tricia sounded too easily convinced. As if she didn't believe in the second photo any more than she believed in the first.

"Tricia?"

"Huh?"

"If something happens to me before Hannah's found, tell Chief Davis everything. About the first picture and the second. And last night at your house I dreamed about it. It's like I was in someone else's body, seeing the dead man and all the blood. I heard screams and footsteps. And the floor under the dead man was dark yellow. Then guess what — the picture I saw this morning on my desktop? The dead man was lying on

180

that very same floor. The one I saw in my *dream.*"

Tricia hesitated. "Really."

"Really. Somehow I think they made me have that dream. Maybe they pushed the sights and sounds into my head, sort of like subliminal advertising. Then they sent a second photo onto my computer this morning, matching the details."

Absolute deadness over the line.

Kaycee's lips firmed. Okay, Tricia wasn't buying any of this. Kaycee could picture that cynical expression of hers, one side of her mouth pulled up, neck arched back. And the raised left eyebrow.

"Tricia, I need to go now. I'm leaving to look for Hannah." Before Tricia could reply, Kaycee clicked off the line.

She hung up the phone and closed her eyes. So she couldn't talk to her best friend about this anymore. Fine. She didn't need Tricia anyway. She just had to find Hannah.

Raising her chin, purse over her shoulder, Kaycee stepped out into the menacing day.

# Twenty-Five

Nico got the call to come in just before noon.

He was pacing the floor in his den in a rage. He'd swept liquor glasses and bottles to the carpet, kicked over the coffee table. Over and over in his mind ran that split second when he pulled the trigger — twice. Why couldn't Giordano have just done what he was told? Nico should have kept his cool, fought the man, pistol-whipped him. Anything to keep him alive and get him into the car. Now cops were crawling all over that place.

Good thing Bear didn't want the money out of there today. That one fact just might keep Nico alive.

He should have gone to the underboss and reported what happened right away. But he was too furious. Not a good frame of mind to be in when you met with Bear. Instead Nico burst through his own front door, shouting curses. In time he calmed down enough to send an associate to drive through AC Storage. Rizzo reported five police cars, some unmarked, and crime-scene tape around the apartment.

You could be sure the police had questioned those two renters Nico had driven by. They wouldn't trace his unregistered Chevy. And he knew the one man who glanced up couldn't have seen much of his face. But would Bear believe that?

After the associate reported, Nico got a call from Dom, one of his soldiers. Dom had heard from his friends on the police force that the homicide detectives were suspicious. Martin Giordano gets held up by a gun at night and shot to death the next morning? A little too convenient. The detectives were talking to the G-men investigating the robbery. Talk had even turned to whether the mob was involved. Did Giordano have any connections? Dom had insisted to his friend the Lucchese family had nothing to do with the heist.

"The cops can't link Giordano to me," Nico told Dom — not that he had to answer to any of his soldiers. "No way."

"Sure, sure."

"You hear anything about what the wife's tellin' the cops?"

"She ain't tellin' 'em nothin'. Said she was lyin' on the bed with her little girl when she heard the shots. Then she was afraid to come out of the bedroom. She and the kid hid in the closet."

So she hadn't seen him. Or if she had, she wasn't talking. "Thanks, man."

"You bet."

Nico hung up the phone and started pacing, trying to get his head on straight. You didn't mess up with this much cash on the line and pay nothing. But he could still take care of things. Once the money was out of that rental, there'd be no way at all to prove a connection between him and Giordano.

He'd be okay with Bear. He'd be okay. As long as the boss didn't start playing with the scar on his face. Nico had seen him do that maybe a dozen times. Every time somebody wound up whacked. A few times Nico had been sent to do the job.

The phone rang again. Nico knew who it was before he picked up.

"I want to see you," Bear growled. The line clicked.

At the underboss's house Nico did the only thing he could. He stuffed his rage at Giordano down in his gut and tried to play it cool.

"What'd you do?" Bear planted himself behind the massive cherry wood desk in his office. His arms were folded, the gray brows meeting over his eyes like one long thundercloud. On the wall behind him spread a leopard skin. Nico had never asked where he got it.

"He came at me, I had to shoot."

"What, you can't control your own guy?"

"My gun was out and he jumped me. I was still going to put him in the car and clean up, but I saw a cop car out the window and thought they were coming to question Giordano. I had to get outta there."

"So now our money's parked at a crime scene."

Nico shook his head. "Don't worry, the cops'll be outta there tomorr—"

"Don't tell me what to worry about!" Bear smacked his palm on the desk. He pointed a thick finger at Nico. "I wondered about this guy from the beginning, but you vouched for him. Then you come back to me whinin' he's no good and how you're gonna take care of it. I tell you how to do that. But you don't listen."

Nico clenched his jaw. Bear wasn't hearing a thing he said. One mistake in all his years. *One* time —

"You got something to say, Nico?"

"I tried to do what you said. Sometimes things happen."

"No. No. Things don't just 'happen.' *You* did this. That short temper of yours — that's what did it."

Nico bit back his answer.

Bear glared at him. "What about the wife and kid? How'd you expect to get Giordano outta there without them seeing you?"

"He told me they were gone."

"And you just believed him."

"He had too much money ridin' on it to cross me."

"Apparently he didn't get the message."

Nico said nothing.

Bear knocked his knuckles against the desk. "The wife — can she finger you?"

"Never saw me. She was busy with the kid."

"You hope so."

"That's what she told the cops."

Bear's hard eyes drilled into Nico. He slid a hand to his face. One finger traced the scar along his jaw line.

Nico went cold.

"Listen to me good, Nico. I don't want you thinkin' with that mule head of yours. I just want you to do what I tell you. Got it?"

"Yeah."

"When you leave here, go home. *Stay*

there. Tell your friends on the force to keep their ears out for any more word from the detectives on the case. We gotta be sure that crime scene opens up by tonight. When you hear it's clear, call me. I want the money outta there long before dawn. Go at one a.m."

"Where you want me to take it?" Nico tried to keep his eyes from that trailing finger.

"I'll let you know. Right now I don't care if we have to bury it in my backyard. I just want it out of there."

"Okay."

"Nothin' goes wrong. Nothin'. We get the money. The cops and G-men stay clueless about the robbery *and* Giordano."

"It's done. I guarantee you. It's done."

Bear dropped his hand, but his gaze was cold. "You done a lot for the family, Nico. I'm givin' you this chance to make things right. You understand?"

Nico swallowed. "Yeah. I understand."

"Go."

As Nico left the room he could feel Bear's eyes shooting daggers at his back.

# TWENTY-SIX

Kaycee closed her kitchen door and tested the lock.

They were out there somewhere. Watching.

Weight descended upon her, as if the sky bulged down. The staring eyes lasered holes in her back. She spun around and cast wild looks over the yard.

Her gaze fell on the storage shed. Had Hannah crept in there sometime this morning, now too afraid to show herself? Kids could be like that. They did stupid things when they were scared.

Like adults.

She headed over to the shed, hearing the grass swish under her feet, feeling the sun on her head. Her chin lifted, and she drew in a long exploring breath through her nose. No smell of blood. That sense hadn't returned since she'd been on the stairs . . .

At the shed Kaycee pulled back the creaky

door. Its musty, dirt-drenched odor leaked out.

Empty.

She let the door fall shut and headed for the garage. Twice she stopped to look behind her.

The small garage was dim. Kaycee hit the button to open the roll-up door. Eyes flicking in all directions, she passed around the front of her PT Cruiser and got in. She pulled the car key out of her purse and tossed the handbag on the passenger seat. Buckled her seatbelt.

Backing out the driveway, she reached for the remote button clipped to her visor to shut the garage door. Her fingers slid over the top of the visor — and hit a slick edge. *What was that?* Kaycee snatched her hand away and braked. The visor snapped down.

A photo slipped out and into her lap. A five-by-seven of the dead man on the dark yellow floor. One side of the picture was smeared with red.

"Ah!" Kaycee flung it away. She thrust the car into park and fumbled with her seatbelt. Shoved open her door and threw herself out on the gravel. One foot slid out from under her. Her legs scissored until the foot took hold. Kaycee righted herself and swiveled toward the car, panting.

For a long moment she stared at the picture on the passenger seat floor. It lay face up and vivid. The dead man looked so real. Any minute now he'd sit up, right out of that photo.

Her right fingers felt sticky. She jerked up her hand and saw red.

Kaycee moaned. In her peripheral vision she saw more red on the door where she'd touched the handle. She jumped away.

Slowly Kaycee's fingers raised to her nose. They smelled like blood.

Something inside Kaycee snapped. She bolted around the car to the house.

At the back door she grabbed the knob and twisted, knowing it was locked, knowing the key was in her purse in that violated car. Knowing they were here, so close, watching and laughing. They wanted her to think she was *mad.*

But now she had evidence. Something to take to the police.

Tears burned her eyes. She swiveled around and stumbled two steps toward the yard. Threw back her head and shouted, "Where are you?" Kaycee's throat closed up and her muscles went stiff. "What do you want from me?"

Mocking silence.

She strode across the grass and turned in

complete circles, looking, shouting. "Come *out* here! What do you *want?*"

Motion from next door caught her eye. Kaycee wrenched around and saw Mrs. Foley, gaping at her like she was nuts. Kaycee's mind bleached white. "Is it *you?*" she screamed. "Are you doing this to me?" She stomped toward the old woman. "Why are you doing this? *Why?*"

Mrs. Foley whirled and disappeared into her house. The door slammed. A lock clicked.

Kaycee pulled up short, breathing hard. She blinked through hot tears, logic slowly returning to her mind. What on earth was she *doing?*

Grimacing, she peered at her blurred right hand. The red was smeared all over.

That blood she'd smelled while climbing the stairs. Maybe it wasn't from her dream at all. Maybe it was *this* blood now, on her fingers.

How had she known this would happen?

Was it from the dead man?

Helplessness and panic whirled inside Kaycee. What was happening? Who was doing this to her? They were taking over everything. Her house, her car, her *life.*

Her gaze cut to her car in the driveway. Its engine was still running, the driver's door open.

*Hannah.* She had to go find Hannah.

Kaycee's fingers curled inward. Okay. Whoever these people were, they'd made a big mistake this time. That photo and blood were evidence. Just wait till the police got hold of it.

Mouth firming, Kaycee bent over to swipe her bloody fingers against the grass. Taking a deep breath, she walked toward the car.

She closed the driver's door. At the passenger side she peered through the window. The photo hadn't moved. Somehow, she'd thought it might.

Screams rose in her mind. Footsteps and running. A door opening to bright sun . . .

Wait. That detail wasn't in her dream. She'd seen a bright light but not a door opening. Where had this come from?

Kaycee pressed both hands against the car, leaned in and breathed.

Slowly the sounds and sights in her head faded. Kaycee pushed hair off her hot cheeks and gathered what courage she could find.

It took all she had to open the car door.

Her purse sat on the seat, her house key inside. Kaycee forced her gaze to the horrifying picture. She needed to put it in a plastic zip bag for protection. But she

192

couldn't leave it here while she returned to the house. She didn't dare. By the time she got back out here, it could be gone.

Kaycee drew the key from her purse and stuck it in her pocket. Gingerly, as if it were made of flesh-eating acid, she picked up the picture by a corner that wasn't stained with blood. Holding it out in front of her like the tail of a dead mouse, she made her way to the back door.

Their eyes watched.

The blood on the doorknob glistened as she inserted her key.

Inside the kitchen she laid the photo on the counter and snatched a large plastic bag from a drawer. She slid the photo into the bag. As she closed it, blood smeared inside the plastic. She lowered her eyes and swallowed hard, steadying herself.

Quickly, she washed the residue of blood off her hand.

She picked up the bagged picture and carried it to the car. Set it on top of the Cruiser while she checked her seat. She didn't want to sit in blood. She saw none there, but the inside handle of her door remained smeared. She'd clean it up later.

Kaycee checked the visor. No blood there either. She pushed it up.

With two fingers she slid the bagged

picture off the roof of the car, then got behind the wheel. Kaycee laid the photo on the passenger seat near her purse. She tried not to look at it, but it pulled at her eyes. Her gaze sidled to the picture.

She stilled, staring. Her eyes widened. Slowly she picked up the photo and brought it toward her face.

It had faded completely to black.

# TWENTY-SEVEN

Fear nearly paralyzed Kaycee as she pulled out of her driveway. The photo-that-no-longer-was lay upside down on the floor of her passenger seat. The only thing left was a black rectangle and some smeared blood.

How to prove to police it had been a picture of the dead man?

Sure, she could tell her story, just like she'd told Tricia. Tell them about her dream, the photo on her desktop, and now this bagged one. She could tell them about smelling blood as she climbed her stairs. Hearing screams and footsteps. That would work, all right. Chief Davis would sign her into the mental ward on one of those mandatory seventy-two-hour mini-vacations.

But there was still blood on that faded photo. They couldn't discount that.

*Hannah.* Even now Kaycee didn't want to pull one officer off of searching for the runaway. Kaycee would hand over this evidence — what remained of it — and help in the search for Hannah. Once she was found Kaycee could tell Chief Davis everything. They'd deal with it then.

Kaycee's mind chanted a mantra that her young friend was safe. Anything else was too horrible to consider. But hours were passing. Hannah should have called by now.

Kaycee reversed left onto South Maple and pushed the Cruiser into drive.

She rolled past the old homes on her street, focusing on the scenery she knew so well. Anything to keep her mind from thinking. Large bare-limbed trees dominated the green front lawns after the April rains. Here and there bright yellow forsythia bushes bloomed. On the right houses gave way to the long white building of Crouse Concrete.

*Wait.*

Kaycee slowed and gazed at the building. It ran long with a flat roof, the left side of the building a number of feet higher than the right. Three extra tall garage doors faced the street. The only windows were in two layers on the left side. The building looked quiet as usual. She wasn't even sure if it was used much anymore.

What if Hannah was in there?

Kaycee turned into the cracked parking lot.

As she got out of the car Kaycee felt eyes upon her. Her tormentors were watching. She knew it.

Kaycee turned in a complete circle, gaze darting. She saw no one.

Drawing both arms across her chest, she walked to the door and tried to open it. Locked.

Kaycee cupped her hands around her eyes and looked through a window. It was so dim inside she could hardly see. Was it an office or a much bigger room? She saw no movement.

She stepped back, every part of her body tingling. Go look around back — that's what she should do. This place was so close to her house. Hannah might have crept back there to hide.

Kaycee looked to the right and over the roof. A thick copse of trees thrust bare-limbed branches into the sky. All those trees behind the building — where *they* could be hiding.

She couldn't do it. She couldn't go back there alone.

Didn't matter, she rationalized. Hannah wouldn't be there anyway. Even if she'd come here in the night, she wouldn't have hidden back there this long. Besides, the police had been searching this neighborhood. Surely they'd already looked.

Kaycee bit her lip. All the same, she should check.

A shudder ran down her spine. She pictured the dead man's face — on her own computer. Remembered the smell of blood on her own staircase. *We see you.* If her house wasn't even safe . . .

Abruptly Kaycee turned toward the Cruiser.

She slid into the driver's seat, sick to her stomach. So much for fighting the fear. She couldn't even bring herself to search behind a building for a lost child.

Kaycee lowered her forehead to the steering wheel and closed her eyes. A storm kicked up within her, swirling. All the years of fighting her destructive fears, all the columns and vows to herself. Just an hour ago she'd finished writing the final part of the dentist story. Such determination she'd ended on, such hope. Now look at her. No better. Good for nothing.

Defeat washed over her in cold, briny waves.

*Pray against the fear.* Tricia's mantra. *You've got to keep praying.*

Kaycee pushed back from the wheel as if

her head weighed a hundred pounds. Dully she stared at the white building. Truth was, she didn't want prayer. She wanted a magic wand.

*God, just bring Hannah back safe, and I promise I'll talk to you all day long.*

Kaycee's cell phone rang. She jumped, then fished it out of her purse. The ID read Wilmore Police. Her heart leapt.

"Hi, it's Kaycee."

"It's Mark. You coming to the station?"

"On my way. Did you find Hannah?"

"No." His voice sounded grim. "But we have some new information."

# Twenty-Eight

On the motel bed Lorraine lay propped on one elbow, watching her daughter. Tammy was sleeping on her back, a fist beneath her chin. Her little-girl snores were quiet and feathery. It had taken her some time to fall asleep. She'd been crying for her stuffed bear. Lorraine reached out and touched Tammy's hair. How to tell her that she would never see her daddy again?

Fresh grief hit Lorraine like an avalanche. Its icy weight snatched the breath from her lungs. She flipped onto her stomach, buried her head in a pillow, and sobbed. The bed shook. Lorraine didn't want to wake Tammy. She clutched the pillow to her chest and rolled off to the floor.

So many things to mourn. She sobbed for Tammy's future without a father. For their days stretching on and on. Lorraine would not make it through this afternoon, this minute. How could she possibly live through a week, a month, a year? She cried for Tammy's first day of elementary school — without a father to kiss good-bye. For her graduations and someday, a wedding. Lorraine cried for no medical insurance, an empty bed at night. For the face she would never see again, the voice she would never hear. For the still body and the half open, glazed eyes, and Tammy smeared with her daddy's blood. For the *senselessness* of a life taken. Lorraine cried until her head pounded and her eyes dried out, and all energy seeped from her pores into the worn carpet.

Finally she rolled over and lay still, spent. Her eyes fixed upon the far wall, unseeing.

Something shifted inside her.

At the center of her soul where hope used to live, a black dot appeared. It grew bigger. Deeper. Eating toward the outside. The hope that had guided Lorraine's life began to crumble into the pit and disappear. In her mind's eye she could see the pieces breaking off the edge like shale, falling, falling until the darkness swallowed them up. Until nothing was left but a bare, unstable rim.

From the bottom of that black hole she felt the throb of a new suffocating spirit.

Fear.

For a long time Lorraine couldn't move. When she pushed to her feet, exhausted and shell-shocked, she found herself wandering the room aimlessly. At some point she turned on the TV, keeping the volume low, and flipped through channels, searching for local news.

". . . this morning . . ." A blonde female reporter stood between the two AC Storage buildings. Behind her, yellow crime-scene tape stretched in front of Lorraine's apartment. Someone in street clothes ducked beneath the tape and entered the front door. Lorraine's fingers curled into her palms. That was her and Martin's home. Tammy's home. How dare strangers so casually walk in and out.

A strand of hair blew onto the reporter's cheek. She brushed it away. Such a normal motion. How could she act so calm on this terrible, deathly day?

". . . In a strange twist, we've learned that the victim, Martin Giordano, was an assistant manager at Atlantic City Trust Bank, which was robbed last night of a record seven million dollars. Police investigating the two cases aren't talking, but one source within the department did say there is conjecture of a connection. Did the four robbers come to believe Giordano recognized one or more of them? Or is this just an unfortunate and tragic coincidence?"

Lorraine blinked at the TV, her dulled brain trying to sort through the words. At least the "connection" the police wondered about didn't include Martin's involvement in the crime. Or if it did, they weren't saying it.

Martin had said nothing to her last night about recognizing one of the robbers. That couldn't be it.

*"If he finds you here we're going to lose a lot of money."*

Had Martin *helped* those robbers? But if so and they didn't trust him, her question to Detective Tuckney remained. Why didn't they shoot him before they left the bank?

". . . questioned by the police," the reporter continued. "Meanwhile the victim's wife and daughter are at an undisclosed location for at least tonight."

Lorraine stared at the screen. They knew that already? That she and Tammy weren't going home tonight?

The news switched to another topic. Bitterness rose in Lorraine. That's all the time her wonderful husband deserved? Two lousy minutes?

She sank onto the edge of the bed. A phrase from the story echoed through her

203

mind. *One source within the department . . .*
*One source within the department . . .*

Lorraine sat up straighter. Reporters had sources on the police force. Why couldn't the Mafia?

She thought about it. They did. Of course they did. With everything the Mafia controlled, surely they paid dirty cops to give them inside information. What if one of those paid sources told them what Martin had said in his interview last night? What if Martin *had* recognized one of those men and just didn't want to tell her about it? Maybe that's why the man came by this morning. Martin was trying to assure the robbers he wouldn't talk. He'd do that to protect her and Tammy.

That was it. Had to be.

Lorraine buried her face in her hands. "Martin, I'm sorry. I'm so sorry for doubting you."

*"If he finds you here we're going to lose a lot of money."*

"No." She shook her head. Martin had just been scared for her and Tammy. He wasn't talking straight.

*"I just want Tammy to get well."*

Anger at her own traitorous thoughts shoved Lorraine off the bed. She swept hair from her eyes. Enough of this. She'd go crazy spending the rest of the day in this motel room, with nothing to do but think. She should go out and take care of the horrible business that awaited her. She needed to stop by the bank and talk to someone about picking up Martin's final paycheck. She had to find a funeral home and casket for Martin that she could afford. Detective Tuckney said it might be a few days before Martin was released after the autopsy, but she should get this much over with.

Because maybe, just maybe, cleaning her husband's blood off the floor wouldn't be the worst of her tasks. What if that voice inside her head was right? What if she and Tammy were no longer safe in this town?

*"He'll kill us all . . ."*

But where would she find the energy to do these tasks now? The mere thought turned her limbs to water.

Tammy stirred on the bed. Lorraine watched her daughter, feeling so helpless. She didn't want Tammy to wake up. She didn't want to answer the questions and dry the tears.

*"I just want Tammy to get well."*

Tammy's eyelids rose, her gaze still blank from sleep. She sighed and uncurled the fist at her neck, then slid the hand down to her belly. One leg straightened. Her chin tucked down, and she blinked at Lorraine. "Hi, Mommy."

The little voice brought fresh tears to Lorraine's eyes. "Hi, sweetie. How do you feel?"

A huffy breath. "Better."

"I'm glad."

Tammy looked around the room. "Where're we?"

"The motel. Remember I brought you here to sleep?"

"But why can't we go home?"

"Because . . ."

"Where's Daddy?"

"He's . . ." Lorraine sat on the edge of the bed, summoning courage, but all she felt was exhaustion. Her throat tightened. "He's at work."

"But he got hurt. Wasn't he hurt?"

Lorraine nodded.

Her daughter's eyes rounded, and the bottom lip pooched out. "Will he get better?" Tammy whispered.

An ache spread in Lorraine's chest. She searched her brain for something to say. Not a lie, but not the truth. Not yet. She pressed her lips in a sick smile. "Come here, honey."

Tammy sat up, and Lorraine drew her into both arms, resting her chin on the warm head. Her daughter snuggled in, trusting in her so completely. Lorraine's eyes squeezed shut.

"Mommy?"

"Hm?"

"I want my bear."

Lorraine thought of the scene on TV. The yellow crime tape, strangers going in and out of her apartment. And here they were — homeless. Tammy had lost her daddy. And now she couldn't even have the stuffed animal that comforted her most.

"Okay, sweetie. I have to go out and do a few things. On the way we'll stop by the apartment and get Belinda."

# TWENTY-NINE

The back of Kaycee's neck crawled as she pulled into a parking spot in front of Studio Creations on Main. She stared at the darkened, bagged photo on the passenger seat floor. After Mark's phone call she cringed at the thought of touching it. She didn't want to think what she was thinking. Never would she forgive herself for this.

Leaning over, she picked it up with thumb and forefinger and slid it into her purse.

She got out and locked her car — something she rarely did on Main Street. But then most of the time, at least in warm months, she walked the two blocks here.

Her eyes pulled toward the railroad tracks and the continuation of East Main beyond. Some distance down that way Hannah had last been seen.

"A young man called," Mark had told Kaycee on the phone. "He was coming up Main toward the tracks last night around ten. Said he saw a girl on the sidewalk, pulling a suitcase."

"And he didn't *stop*? He didn't ask her what she doing out by herself?"

"He's twenty-one years old, Kaycee. He didn't really think much about it. Just figured she was going somewhere close to spend the night or something."

Right, at ten o'clock on a school night.

But that young man wasn't to blame for this. Kaycee Raye was. Hannah *had* been headed toward her house. And what had she found when she got there? Emptiness. Darkness. Courageous Kaycee had run off to her girlfriend's.

Did Hannah think she'd simply refused to open the door? The thought turned Kaycee's insides. She was always home at night, Hannah knew that. She imagined Hannah ringing the bell again and again, crying and begging for Kaycee's help after she'd made it all that way in the dark. How rejected she must have felt — on top of the rejection she'd already endured.

But what if Hannah never made it at all? A young girl alone at night, walking a main road through town. She could so easily have been picked up and snatched away. A right turn at the next stoplight, and the abductor would be on Highway 29 headed toward

Lexington. From there, the interstate.

Hannah could be anywhere.

Or what if she *had* made it to Kaycee's — and *they* were there?

Shuddering, Kaycee slung the handle of her purse over her shoulder.

She felt the watcher's eyes drill into her as she turned to walk across the street. She cast a penetrating look up Main. At a long diagonal across the road, a car was turning out of the gravel parking lot for Scotts Station, the white wood B&B facing the intersection of South Maple. The car headed in the opposite direction, passing the Front Room next to the B&B. The owner of the Front Room sold gifts and small antique items in the front area of the house, while she and her husband lived in the rest. Every time Kaycee had gone inside she'd found sweet tea waiting for customers, plus some kind of homemade dessert bars.

In front of a yellow wood apartment building on the other side of the Scotts Station parking lot, two elderly men sat on one of the matching benches lining the sidewalk. One of them raised his hand in a greeting. Kaycee waved back.

Her gaze raked past them, down the familiar storefronts. AdOne Media; White Casting, the jewelers; a doctor's office. Next to that stretched the green awning of the drugstore, which housed Tastebuds, the old-fashioned soda fountain she frequented three or four times a week. Tastebuds also made the best pizza Kaycee had ever eaten, with some of the most creative ingredients. And those vanilla sodas. Something about them made her smile, even on the worst of days.

Kaycee's stomach rumbled. She'd had nothing but coffee today, and that wasn't good. Fear and lack of sleep already made her weak enough. But the mere thought of eating now — even a Tastebuds pizza — turned her stomach.

Past the drugstore lay Clay's Barbershop, Union Station Texas-style Barbeque, and Jody's Beauty Salon, followed by the white stone building that hosted City Hall and the police station. Kaycee jaywalked at an angle across the street and headed for the building.

"Don't leave before I get there," she'd told Mark. "I need to talk to you."

She pulled open the glass door and stepped into the small entry area housing the Pepsi and Ale-8-One machines. The police department ran the machines, using the proceeds for such thank-you events as a dinner for officers and their spouses at

Christmas, an outing on the lake in summer. Ale-8-One — A Late One — made in Winchester, Kentucky, had become Kaycee's favorite soft drink since she moved to Wilmore. Before ordering a Tastebuds pizza, she'd stop by here to buy a bottle. It tasted like ginger ale, only deeper, better.

Bitterness rose in her chest as she knocked on the door to the station. This downtown block, once so comforting with its sights and smells and tastes, now loomed with horrifying unseen threats.

Emma Wooley let Kaycee inside. The administrative secretary hurried back to her desk to answer the phone. Emma was a large woman in her late fifties with a quick smile and sparkling brown eyes. After raising six kids and now grandmother to seven, she often declared nothing that happened on her job could surprise her.

Three stacks of colored flyers sat on Emma's desk. Kaycee slid one from the top. Hannah smiled up from her most recent school photo. She was wearing her favorite pink shirt. Even then she looked unhappy. The smile didn't reach her eyes.

Kaycee's throat squeezed. She touched Hannah's forehead, then pressed the flyer to her heart.

"Kaycee." Mark Burnett stood up from

the back area crammed with five desks and waved her over. One hand pressed a phone receiver against his chest. He looked worn, with circles under his deep-set eyes. This was supposed to be his time to sleep. At a nearby desk Officer Rich Hurlton, a salt-and-pepper haired man with a lined face, who reminded Kaycee of Harrison Ford, focused intently on a computer monitor.

Kaycee stuck a hand in her hair. Un-washed this morning, its kinky curls were even puffier than usual. And she wore no makeup. She had to look like something the cat dragged in.

Carrying the flyer, she walked toward Mark, passing the chief's empty office on her right. Although his door was closed she could picture his steel gray desk topped with wood laminate, the white paint and blue-green wallpaper. At the rear of the office sat six screens, running live video from cameras placed around Wilmore. Four times in the past year Kaycee had faced the chief across his desk, nervously claiming she'd seen someone in her backyard, or watching her from the street. Each time he'd taken her back to have a look around.

*Video.*

"Okay, thanks," Mark said into his phone. He replaced the receiver. "Hi."

213

"Hi."

They surveyed each other. Kaycee felt the lingering bittersweet of his thoughtless words at the chief's party, followed by his apology last night. As for the camera in her kitchen, Mark hadn't believed she'd really seen it. Maybe now he would.

She glanced at Rich. "He's looking at video?"

"Yeah. We can type in the date and time for any camera in Wilmore. We got way more cameras than what's on the six screens in Chief's office. If Hannah walked up this street last night, we'll know."

*If.*

"Where are the other officers?"

"Chief's at the elementary school, talking to everyone who knows Hannah. I'll call him if we find something on the video. The others are still going door-to-door at the Parksleys' neighborhood and searching the area. There's that eighteen acres out there with the gutted house. Weeds as tall as I am. Plus Bohicket Road runs into the lane that goes down by the campground. Got gulch area and lots of brush not far from that road."

Kaycee licked her lips. "But we know Hannah made it out of her neighborhood. And she didn't go toward the campground."

Mark winced. "We don't know what happened after that."

His tone said so much more. That he wanted to tell her everything would be okay, they'd find Hannah safe. But he could no longer promise it.

Kaycee sank down in the chair opposite Mark's desk. Flecks of steel dredged through her veins. She couldn't think about this. Hannah was alive and well out there somewhere. Kaycee looked away from Mark, her focus landing on the door that led to the back entrance and down to the lower level. The basement. She'd ventured down those bare wooden steps once, clutching the matching handrail and feeling the stutter of her heart. Chief Davis had taken her down to see the DARE car, a 1968 Ford Galaxy 500, like the last vehicle on *Mayberry RFD.* But she could hardly admire the car. With no windows, that basement terrified her. The floor was concrete, wooden posts rising up to attach to long, low ceiling beams like scaffolding in a deep, dark mine. Leaning up against one wall were the disassembled steel framework pieces of the old holding cell used years ago, called the "lion's cage." To the right of the DARE car the alarmed and locked evidence room held boxes of items from criminal cases. Another windowless room on the left side of the car, also locked, held supplies. At the walk-out rear of the basement were long double doors that opened up for the DARE car to drive through. Kaycee had vowed she'd never go down there again, not as long as she fought claustrophobia. Just think how dark and horrifying that place would be at night.

What if Hannah was in some place like that?

Heat flushed through Kaycee. Mandy's worst fear had come true, now so had her own. What if the worst had happened to Hannah too?

Kaycee's lungs swelled until they ballooned against her ribs.

"You okay?" Mark's voice sounded far away.

Kaycee tried to nod. Panic bloomed through her stomach. She could barely breathe. Her fingers curled around the edge of her chair. *Jesus, Jesus, Jesus.* It was the only word she could pray.

Mark laid a hand on her arm.

Kaycee's gaze roved to his face. He was bent over her, concern etching lines in his forehead. She raked in air. Slowly the panic receded.

"You okay?" He pulled his hand away and

straightened.

"I . . . yeah." She blinked hard.

Rich was eyeing her. The video on his screen stood frozen.

Kaycee's cheeks flushed. "I'm sorry. I'm okay. Really. Just . . . Hannah and everything."

"I know." Mark's voice sounded the most empathetic she'd ever heard it. Kaycee looked up at him, and their eyes locked.

He moved first. "Want some water?"

"Yes, thanks."

She leaned back in the chair, eyes averted from Rich. His chair squeaked, followed by the sound of clicking as he resumed watching the video.

Mark returned with a plastic cup of water. Kaycee drank it down and placed the cup on the desk. "Thanks. I'm really sorry."

"No problem." He walked around his desk and sat down. "So. You said you had something to tell me."

Great. After that little display this would not be the best timing.

Kaycee straightened her back. "This morning on my computer I saw that dead man again. He blipped on in place of my desktop for a couple seconds, then disappeared. On the bottom of that picture was written one word. Exposure."

Mark surveyed her. "Why didn't you tell me this?"

At least he wasn't insisting she'd gone off the deep end. "You were looking for Hannah. That was more important."

He shook his head. "Exposure. What does that mean?"

"One of my recent columns was titled that. I'm wondering if this is the work of some crazy 'Who's There?' readers." She didn't want to tell Mark about her dream and how details from it had played out in the second photo. If Tricia hadn't believed her, neither would he.

Kaycee picked up her purse and pulled out the bagged photo — her one piece of evidence, what was left of it. "Then when I got in my car to come down here, I found this stuck in the visor." She held it out to him, face up. "It's the same photo — the dead man, with a bullet hole in his jaw and one in his head. But this one has blood on it."

*"Blood?"*

"Then minutes after I found it, the picture faded to this black."

She flicked a look at Rich. He had stopped clicking through a tape to listen. Mark followed her eyes. Rich shifted in his chair and resumed his task.

Mark took the bagged photo from her hand and stared at it.

He flipped the picture to see the back, then turned it right side up. Lines etched in his forehead. Slowly he raised darkened eyes to hers. "This was a picture of that dead man?" Mark's words resonated, a doubting Thomas now facing evidence. "The third you've seen."

Kaycee nodded. "It's why I . . . almost lost it there for a minute."

He held her eyes, speechless. Kaycee bit her lip. "The thing is, Mark, Hannah's gone. And they — whoever's doing this to me — are here. For real. Lurking, hiding. They obviously were around my house last night. I didn't imagine that camera. And the minute I left to come here, they got back into my kitchen to whisk it away. If Hannah made it to my house, and I wasn't there, but *they* were . . ."

Kaycee couldn't bring herself to say the rest. Mark inhaled a long, silent breath. At the same time their eyes lowered to the blood on the photo.

# THIRTY

"There she is."

Rich's voice made Kaycee jump. Her gaze snapped up from the blackened picture.

Mark rose. "You see Hannah?"

"Yeah. I'll freeze it." Rich hit a button then pointed toward the bottom left of the screen.

Kaycee dropped her purse on the floor and hurried to Rich as Mark came around his desk. They leaned down and peered at the frozen shot on the monitor. The camera was apparently mounted in the parking lot between the police station and railroad tracks, taking in a diagonal shot up East Main and mostly focused on storefronts across the street. Near the left edge was Rice Street, running parallel to the tracks, and the Rail-Side Museum. At far left ran the railroad tracks, disappearing at a slant into the side of the screen.

Just this side of those tracks in the darkness, faintly lit by a streetlamp's circle of light, was Hannah.

"Oh." Kaycee's pulse skipped.

The nine-year-old had just crossed the tracks on the other side of the street near the museum. One foot posed in front of the other, mid-stride. She clutched a small suitcase in both hands.

Mark gestured with his chin. "Play it."

Rich pushed the button and the picture slid into action.

In silent motion Hannah put down the suitcase and pulled it away from the tracks. Her shoulders were hunched, her head swiveling, as if searching the night for ghosts. She looked so small and alone. Kaycee longed to reach into the monitor and pull her out. Tell her everything was going to be okay.

Abruptly Hannah stopped. Her head turned right.

"She's looking this direction," Mark said.

Hannah veered left and headed up Rice Street.

Kaycee's mouth creaked open. "Why would she go *that* way?"

"The station." Rich shook his head. "I think she didn't want to pass by here."

In tense silence they watched her back as she continued up Rice Street. On her left ran the tracks.

Thirty seconds later she twisted to look behind her. At the edge of the screen red lights began to flash.

"A train's coming," Kaycee whispered.

Hannah drew in her shoulders as if she wanted to melt into the pavement. The train shot from the bottom left of the screen and up the tracks. So silent on the film. But at night in the darkness, and so close — the sound must have terrified her.

Hannah slapped her hands over her ears.

The trains passing through Wilmore were long. As this one sped by, car after endless car, Hannah hunched over, ears covered. Finally her small form straightened. The train continued to pass. Hannah grabbed the handle of her suitcase and scurried up Rice Street. They saw her under the light of a street lamp, but the next one wasn't working. Hannah's form dimmed.

Fingers pressed to her mouth, Kaycee watched the girl until she faded into blackness.

# THIRTY-ONE

The first thing Lorraine did was stop by the apartment to pick up Belinda.

As she turned her van into AC Storage, Lorraine clamped a lid on her emotions for Tammy's sake — and partly for her own. She could so easily lose it right here, right now. She knew she teetered on the edge of that chasm in her soul. Get too close and she'd fall in. And there'd be no climbing out.

She chose not to park in their usual place around the corner from the apartment. That area was too close to the yellow crime-scene tape. And next to her spot sat Martin's Pontiac. Lorraine couldn't bear to look at it.

She pulled up beside the end of a storage building.

"What those people doing at our house, Mommy?" Tammy screwed up her face. A crime-scene technician wearing gloves disappeared into the apartment. A uniformed officer holding a clipboard stood guard just outside the taped-off area.

"They're looking for things."

"Like what?"

"Things to clean."

The answer made no sense, but Tammy seemed to accept it.

Throat dry, Lorraine unbuckled her seatbelt and patted Tammy on the arm. "Stay here, okay? I'm just going to walk over and ask someone to bring out Belinda."

Tammy nodded, her brows knit together, as if she understood the grimness of the situation.

The crime-scene tape fluttered in a slight breeze as Lorraine approached. Its yellow color stood out starkly against the gray of the office-apartment building and the sun-washed concrete. The young officer locked eyes with her as she drew to a halt. She didn't recognize him from that morning.

"May I help you?"

"I want . . . that's my apartment."

"Yes, ma'am. I'm sorry."

She nodded. "My little girl needs her stuffed bear. It should be on her bed. It's light brown and about so big." She held one hand above the other a foot apart. "Real soft."

"Okay."

He walked to the door and opened it. Stuck his head inside. Lorraine heard his low voice, although she couldn't make out the words. Beyond the doorway she could see movement. What could those people possibly be doing in there for so long?

How strange it was to see her own home and not be allowed inside. Lorraine pulled her arms across her chest. She felt like a refugee. A lost orphan.

The officer backed out of the threshold and closed the door. He held Belinda by one arm.

"Here you go." He offered the bear to her with a small, sad smile.

"Thank you." She clutched the bear in both hands.

"Does your daughter have a name for it?"

"Belinda. I don't even know where she got that name. Must have heard it somewhere."

He tilted his head. "Kids pick up more things than you'd expect."

Lorraine shot him a look, but his expression belied no ulterior message.

Her gaze pulled back to the apartment. She envisioned the scene inside. The horrible job that awaited her.

A small seed of hope sprouted.

She ran her tongue over her lips. "When

225

the people are done in there, will they clean up . . . everything?"

Remorse flicked over his face. "No ma'am. Afraid not."

She ducked her chin in a nod and turned away.

Back in the car she held out Belinda. Tammy grabbed the bear and hugged it tightly, her eyes squinching shut with bliss.

On the way to the bank Lorraine stopped at McDonald's. Tammy wanted a Kids Meal. Lorraine managed to swallow three bites of a hamburger.

When they reached the bank Tammy brought Belinda inside with her.

In no time Lorraine and Tammy found themselves surrounded by Martin's coworkers. Two assistant managers left customers at their desks to greet her and extend their condolences. Even the tellers stepped out from behind their windows when they could. Neither of the two women who'd been held up with Martin were at work. "We gave them the day off," a senior manager with a name pin reading Sandy Tourner told Lorraine. Sandy was in her forties with sleek dark hair and a perfectly fitting black business suit. Lorraine felt grimy and unkempt in the jeans and top she'd managed to throw on after the 911 responders screeched up to her door.

"Martin was a hero." Sandy placed a hand on Lorraine's arm. "Olga and Shelley both told me all he did. How he got them out of the vault and untied them. They said they owe their lives to him."

*They owe their lives to him.* The words sank down inside Lorraine. Yes. *Yes.* Martin deserved to be remembered that way. For his own sake and for his daughter's. It didn't matter what she suspected. The truth didn't matter. The only thing Martin had left now was his reputation.

Her gaze on Tammy, Lorraine made a silent vow to never say anything that could harm the memory of Martin Giordano.

Sandy promised she would cut Martin's final paycheck as soon as possible and personally see that it was deposited into their checking account. One less thing for Lorraine to worry about. "And please let us know when the funeral will be."

"Yes. I will."

Lorraine left the bank on wooden legs, Tammy's fingers entwined in hers.

One final stop. Before leaving the motel Lorraine had located a funeral home from the Yellow Pages. Her mind on hold, her heart dried up, she went through the motions of choosing a casket and making the arrangements for a service. Tammy sat next to her on a chair, swinging her legs and talking to Belinda.

Back in the motel Lorraine crawled onto the bed, not an ounce of energy left. How was she supposed to take care of Tammy now? How were they going to survive?

Tammy smiled and talked to Belinda. She was obviously feeling better. "Mommy." She nudged her mother on the arm. "Let's play a game."

As Lorraine forced herself to sit up, a voice echoed in her brain. The newspaper reporter at her apartment that morning, yelling a question: *"I heard you were home during the murder, Mrs. Giordano . . ."*

She tensed, her fingers digging into the side of the bed.

"Mommy, whassa matter?"

Lorraine blinked at Tammy. "Nothing, nothing. Just . . . let me go to the bathroom first." She fled into the tiny room and shut the door. There she sat on the closed toilet lid, staring at the floor.

*"I heard you were home . . ."*

The TV reporter hadn't mentioned that when Lorraine watched the news — maybe because the woman only had a minute or two to tell the story. But tomorrow's newspaper article would be full of every detail its reporters had gathered today.

Lorraine lowered her head in her hands, a sick feeling worming its way through her stomach. Forget whether or not Martin's murderer had informants on the Atlantic City police force. All that man had to do tomorrow was read the paper. He'd *know* she'd been home when her husband was killed. What if he thought she'd seen him through a bedroom window?

If he'd stormed over in broad daylight to kill Martin, what would stop him from coming back for her?

# THIRTY-TWO

Chief Davis arrived at the station soon after Mark called him with the news. Minutes before he drove up, Kaycee had been pacing on the sidewalk out front, hands fisted and her lungs unable to get enough air. Every shot of that video screamed in her mind. Over and over she envisioned Hannah on Rice Street, pulling that little suitcase. Sucked into the night.

Kaycee stared with burning eyes past the red boxcar museum on Rice. She wanted to turn back time. If only she could place herself right here last night, ready and waiting to intercept Hannah.

The weight of being watched fell heavily on Kaycee's shoulders. She swiveled to look up Main Street. A woman was entering the office of the Good News organization. Two people were coming out of the nearby Jessamine Creek Berry Company. On Kaycee's side of the street a mother with toddler in tow headed for the drug store. No one paid Kaycee any heed.

Where were her tormentors? Had they taken Hannah?

Chief Davis pulled into the parking area and slid from his car. Kaycee watched him approach, dark imaginings tumbling through her head.

"Kaycee." He nodded to her without slowing. "Come on inside." He swung open the glass door to the building.

Kaycee scurried after him, casting final glances up the street.

In the police station, she, Mark, and the chief gathered around the desk where Rich sat. Once more Rich ran the film of Hannah turning up Rice Street. Kaycee watched with hands clasped beneath her chin, unable to tear her eyes away. Chief Davis looked on in silence.

When the sequence ended he inhaled deeply. "You looked further on in the tape?" he asked Rich.

"Yeah, while you were getting here. Haven't seen her appear again."

"Any vehicles come down from Rice Street soon after that?"

"No."

"How about turning onto Main from South Maple?"

Rice Street curved right and became Walters Lane, which ended at South Maple in front of Kaycee's house. Someone could have picked up Hannah, come down South Maple, and turned onto East Main, either right or left. As Kaycee remembered, at least one of the screens she'd seen in Chief Davis's office displayed Main Street farther up, toward the Subway sandwich shop on the corner of South Lexington — Highway 29 — and Fitch's IGA behind it. Perhaps other cameras showed Highway 29 both to the right and left of the Main intersection.

"A few. We didn't see any sign of her in those cars, but I got their license plates. I'll run them down. I've done a slow fast forward for the next hour on the camera aimed at Rice Street."

"Switch over and do an hour on the South Maple intersection."

"Okay." Rich turned back to his work.

"She could have made it to my house." Kaycee could barely speak above a whisper. "Maybe she waited there a long time, hoping I'd come home . . ."

Chief Davis nodded. "Keep watching the tapes, Rich." He turned to Mark. "Where's that picture with the blood?"

"Here." Mark walked over to his desk and picked up the bagged photo. He gave it to the chief.

Narrowing his eyes, Chief Davis studied it. He turned it over to see the back, then returned it face up. "Kaycee, I need to hear everything you told Mark. Let's go in my office."

Ever calm, that voice of his. Kaycee heard no judgment in his tone. Even so, the words ripped through her. She should have told him about the picture on her desktop that morning. If she'd made this possible connection to Hannah's disappearance sooner, maybe these last hours wouldn't have been wasted. Wordlessly she picked her purse off the chair near Mark's desk and followed the chief into his office.

The chief sat down at his desk, Mark and Kaycee taking chairs on the other side. Behind the chief the six screens ran live video. He leaned forward, fingers laced, and focused on Kaycee. "I'm listening."

She started at the beginning with the previous evening, since the chief still hadn't had time to read all of Mark's report. Then she told him about the desktop picture, and finally, the blackened photo now lying on his desk. As with Mark, she didn't mention her dream and its dark yellow floor come true. Or how she'd smelled blood while going up her stairs — *before* it smeared on

233

her fingers from the third photo.

The chief asked her a string of questions about last night and this morning. He wanted details on all three pictures she'd seen. He found it significant that the blood on this third photo had not dried by the time she found the picture, meaning it couldn't have been on there long.

"Where's your car?" he asked Kaycee.

"Across the street. I drove it here."

"Is it locked?"

She nodded.

"Would you leave me the key? We'll need to dust it for prints. We'll also need to dust certain parts of your house and take a look at your computer —"

Rich stuck his head in the door. "Nothing coming from South Maple over the next hour."

Chief absorbed the news. "Okay. Keep looking on both intersections. I'm going to go ahead and call in a volunteer tracking team. The dog can start where we last saw Hannah."

Search and rescue. Kaycee's last bit of hope that Hannah was hiding somewhere gusted away, a milkweed on the wind. Kaycee's tone flattened. "How long until a team can get here?"

"Depends on who's available. Numerous

volunteers live around Wilmore. I'll start with them and work my way out." Chief Davis reached for the phone, shooting a look at Mark. "When I'm done with this call I want us to take a walk up Rice Street. Then I'll deal with this blood sample."

Mark nodded and rose. Kaycee pulled the car key from her purse and placed it on the chief's desk, then followed Mark from the office. They stood by Emma's work area, at the moment empty. Kaycee averted her eyes from the heartrending sight of Hannah's sad face gazing up from the stacked flyers. "When you walk up Rice Street I want to come with you."

Mark pulled in a deep, tired breath. "If Chief says it's okay."

She looked away. "What will he do with the blood?"

Mark's hands fell to his waist, one resting on his weapon. Why did policemen stand like that so often? Like they were going to draw the gun any minute. "We'll send it to the lab."

"Where's that?"

"Frankfort."

The capital of Kentucky, about an hour's drive away. "To do a DNA test to see if it's Hannah's?"

"That takes weeks. But it won't take long

235

to see if it's human blood, and if the type matches Hannah's."

What if it did? Kaycee's knees weakened. Her gaze rose past Mark's shoulder to Rich, who sat staring at the monitor. She could hear the chief on the phone. Sounded like he'd gotten through to some track-dog team.

"If it matches Hannah's . . ." Kaycee's throat closed up. She lifted a hand, palm out, and shook her head.

Mark touched her shoulder. Her skin tingled beneath his fingers. "Whatever happens, Kaycee, you're not to blame for this."

"But I am. If somebody's out to get me, and got Hannah instead . . ."

"We don't know that. There are still way too many unanswered questions. And even if it turns out to be true, that's not your doing."

It would be *because* of her, and that was enough. Hannah's face on the flyers pulled at Kaycee's eyes. She'd thought being watched in her own home was her worst fear come true. That wouldn't come close to feeling responsible if something had happened to Hannah.

Kaycee's mouth trembled. "You were right, Mark," she whispered. "I should never have written my columns. They started all this."

"Listen to me; we don't *know* that."

She pressed her lips together hard and closed her eyes. After a shaky moment she cocked her head in an unconvinced nod.

In his office Chief Davis said thanks to someone on the phone. Kaycee heard the clatter of a replaced receiver. He strode through his door and headed for Rich at the monitor. "Anything new?"

"Not yet."

He scratched his eyebrow. "I got Seth Wheeler and his hound on the way. They'll be here in half an hour." The chief handed Rich Kaycee's key. "Would you get somebody on to dusting Kaycee's Cruiser for prints? It's across the street. Tell them to pay special attention to the driver's door and visor. The tech also needs to go to her house. We'll need to do doors and the kitchen area there. And the office. Plus we're going to have to find someone to look at her computer system. For right now Mark and I are going to take a walk up Rice Street."

Rich had grabbed a pen and paper and was jotting notes. "Sure."

"Thanks." Chief Davis swiveled on his heel to approach Mark. "All right, let's see

237

if we can find anything out there."

"Please let me come with you," Kaycee said. What else would she do? She couldn't drive her car anywhere, and presumably she couldn't go back into her house until a tech was with her to dust for prints.

The chief considered her for a moment. "Okay."

Emma returned to her desk as the three of them filed out. Chief Davis told her where they were headed. As they stepped out of the building into sunlight, a new petrifying thought launched through Kaycee's head. If she'd smelled blood while climbing the stairs — *before* it smeared on her fingers — what about the screams and footsteps she'd heard? Maybe she was sensing them ahead of time too.

What terrible thing was yet to happen?

# THIRTY-THREE

On Rice Street they saw nothing. Mark, Chief Davis, and Kaycee spread out across the road, speaking little, heads down. Kaycee was on the left, Mark in the middle, Chief Davis on the right. "Look for anything," the chief told Kaycee. "A button, a thread. Anything."

Kaycee's neck tired of straining downward, and a headache set in. She trudged along, the sense of being watched so severe she wanted to curl into a ball. Were *they* out there, sneaking behind buildings, watching as the three of them sought a single clue?

Was that blood on the photo Hannah's?

Three times of their own volition, Kaycee's right fingers raised to her nose. She swore she could still detect a faint metallic-sweet scent of blood.

As they rounded the corner onto Walters Lane, the other senses from Kaycee's dream flooded her head. Screams, the running footsteps, a dark and closed space. Her limbs trembled. She took deep, steadying breaths and drew her arms tight across her chest.

In her peripheral vision Kaycee saw the stately gray Potters Inn B&B slide by on her right. Beyond it, Mark spotted something in the middle of the street. "Here." He bent over low. "Looks like blood."

Kaycee's stomach fell to her toes. She stumbled over, heartbeat on hold, a buzz in her head. Chief hurried to the spot and squatted down.

The area was only about three inches long and smeared. Color — brownish red. If it was blood, it had long since dried. A few small pebbles were also stained.

"Look here." The chief pointed to another spot about a diagonal foot away.

They stared at it. Kaycee couldn't speak.

"Maybe she fell." Mark held out his right hand, palm down. "She went down on a knee and threw out a hand to catch herself. The skin would be scraped in both places."

"If she was wearing shorts." The chief looked to Kaycee. "But she had jeans on in the video."

Mark cupped his jaw, surveying the first area. "Maybe they tore."

"We need to secure the street. But let's

see what else we can find." Chief Davis pushed upright. "Kaycee, please move over to the grass."

Kaycee obeyed as the two men quickly searched a little farther up the road and past its edges onto dirt and grass. They saw nothing unusual. The chief told Mark to run back and get his vehicle. "Put tape at the bottom of Rice until Seth gets here."

Mark took off, arms pumping. Kaycee watched his retreating back in a fog of disbelief. This couldn't be happening. Blood here on the road. Blood on the photo.

A car pulled out of Bethel Pointe and turned left, in their direction. Chief Davis strode toward it, hands out and fingers spread. The driver slowed to a stop. Kaycee remained frozen, vaguely hearing the chief ask the man to turn around and go the other way.

Her eyes cut back to the dark stain on the road. She was looking at a potential crime scene.

Mark returned in his car. Chief Davis told Kaycee to walk alongside the road up to her house. She needed to leave the area.

From South Maple, Kaycee watched as the two men strung a second line of yellow crime-scene tape just feet beyond her. Now all of Walters Lane and Rice Street was secured. Looking down Walters, Kaycee could see residents gathering at the Bethel Pointe entrance, other neighbors craning necks from their lawns and porches. Vaguely, she wondered what would happen if any of them needed to drive somewhere.

Officer Ed Freeling was called to guard the tape where she stood. He was in his late forties, a rotund man with a balding spot at the back of his head. In one hand he held a clipboard. Anyone having to go in or out of the area would be noted, Ed told Kaycee. The officer stationed at the bottom of Rice Street would do the same.

"How long?" she asked.

He lifted a shoulder. "Until we're sure we got everything we need. At least till the dog comes through."

They watched together as the chief squatted by the stained pavement. Using a flathead screwdriver, he loosened red-brown flakes and gathered them up. These, plus the small stained pebbles, were carefully placed in an evidence bag, sealed, and labeled. Chief Davis and Mark then searched within the area at a meticulous pace, looking for more blood, footprints, whatever they might find.

Time blurred. Neighbors gathered near Kaycee, asking Officer Freeling what was going on. Mrs. Foley was not among them. She'd consider it gauche to be so obvious. Kaycee glanced toward her living room window and saw the woman peeking out.

The people around Kaycee whispered and shook their heads. A child vanished — in Wilmore. The town had never seen such a thing. Kaycee heard the talk and could only draw away. This was *her* fault, and the knowledge was going to break her apart. If she'd just stayed home last night. If she'd fought her downward spiral after Mandy's death better, the sight of some dead man's photo in her kitchen wouldn't have thrown her for such a loop.

Mark *had* been right about her columns, no matter how he'd tried to backtrack. Fear had become her identity, even her livelihood. Maybe after fighting it all these years, she didn't know how to let go.

"No more." Kaycee said the words aloud. A young woman who'd walked over from Jessamine Village frowned at her. Kaycee's cheeks heated. Shoving the strap of her purse further up her shoulder, she swiveled and walked up the steps to her porch. She stared at the front door, knowing she should wait for the tech before going inside. Not that she wanted to enter that invaded house anyway.

Tears bit her eyes. Kaycee dug her fingers into the back of her neck and let her head tip up. "God." Her voice cracked. "You've got to help me through this."

Her chin lowered. She stared at her toes, wondering what to do, where to go. Her mind only half registered the sound of a car driving up the street. Its engine cut suddenly. A door slammed. Kaycee looked around to see Ryan Parksley jumping from the passenger seat of a police vehicle. Officer Sam Walsh, whom Kaycee only knew in passing, was getting out of the driver's side. Ryan gawked at the crime-scene tape and the officer guarding it, then turned toward Kaycee, as if wondering who to talk to first.

"Hi, Ryan." Kaycee walked down her porch steps.

He made his way over with the gait of someone lost. Ryan was in his mid-thirties, solidly built, with hair and eyes the color of his daughter's. Now he looked more like sixty. His expression mixed hope and dread. Lines etched his forehead, and his eyes were dull.

"We left Gail at home." His voice sounded rough, like an old man's. "Just in case Hannah shows up."

Kaycee nodded.

He gestured over his shoulder toward

Walters Lane. "They said she'd been down there. An officer took a piece of clothing."

For the track dog. Kaycee glanced at Sam Walsh as he sidled over to talk to Ed. "Yes. We saw her on the video. We just don't know how far she got."

Ryan's throat convulsed in a swallow. His lips pulled downward, fingers flexing in and out. He opened his mouth but no words came.

Kaycee's heart lurched. "They're going to find her, Ryan."

His head bobbed, even as his shoulders slumped. "Yeah. They will." He turned halfway to stare at the yellow crime-scene tape, tongue poking out to lick his lips. Disbelief rippled across his profile.

Wordlessly, he wandered toward the two officers.

Kaycee backtracked up her porch steps and hovered there, wedged between two nightmares. In time she saw Seth and his hound advancing up Walters Lane. Kaycee ran down her sidewalk and across the street to join the onlookers near the yellow tape. She pushed in to stand at Ryan's side.

Nose to the pavement, the dog sniffed its way along with much excitement, dragging Seth in a trot.

The hound led its owner right to the

blood stain.

*It's Hannah's!*

Kaycee's hands gripped each other so hard she thought her fingers would snap.

Ryan moaned.

Some thirty feet beyond the stain, on the left side of the road — Seth's dog lost the scent.

# THIRTY-FOUR

After the hound lost Hannah's trail, Chief Davis, Mark, Ryan, and Officer Sam Walsh gathered for a quick meeting on Kaycee's porch. They had numerous things to discuss. Ryan slumped against a white pillar with one hand thrust in his hair, his face slick with sweat. He stared at his feet, barely blinking. Guilt gripped Kaycee as she watched him. This was what real fear looked like. Her petty frights were nothing.

Chief told her and Ryan that the evidence bag of blood from the street, plus the photo she had found, would soon be on their way to the Frankfort lab. They hoped to hear by tomorrow afternoon if the blood was human and the types were the same. Hannah's type was O, the most common. Even if the blood in both evidence bags was O, there was still a big chance one or the other wasn't hers.

Ryan frowned, as if his brain just registered the conversation. "What photo?"

Gently, Chief Davis explained the events at Kaycee's house. Kaycee let him do the talking. By the time he finished explaining, Ryan's mouth hung open. He stared at Kaycee, his eyes darkened. "Why didn't you tell me this?"

"I — I didn't think they were linked."

"How could you *not* think that?"

"Because —"

"Mr. Parksley —" Chief Davis raised a hand.

"No. I want to hear it from *her.* You're my daughter's best friend, Kaycee. She thinks the world of you." Ryan's words thickened. "Less than an hour after you visited last night, she ran away to *come here.* And you don't think what happens with you is *'linked'?*"

Kaycee shrank back. "I didn't want to bother the police with my problems, I just wanted them to look for Hannah —"

"It's a little too *late,* don't you think?"

"Ryan." Chief laid a hand on his arm.

Ryan shook it off and stepped toward Kaycee. His cheeks flushed. "Why did Hannah walk all that way in the dark to come here? Tell me that. What've you been filling her ears with? Is she crying to you about my marrying Gail so soon, and you're just

248

going, yeah, yeah, poor thing, your dad's such a louse? You standing there, judging me?" Ryan's lip curled. He swung his head from her to the three officers, a dead man come to life. "You're all judging me! You got no idea what I've been through. No *idea!*"

"Ryan." Sam gripped his shoulder. Ryan pivoted away. He wrenched himself two steps toward the street and hung there, breathing hard. Peering toward the spot where Hannah vanished.

Kaycee's eyes stung. She raked a despairing glance at Mark and saw a compassion that tightened her throat. He shook his head — *You didn't deserve that.*

Ryan dug his fingers into his scalp, his spine folding over. His legs seemed to crumble out from under him. Sam jumped to his side and caught him before he toppled. Ryan hung on like a drowning man thrown a lifeline and broke into sobs.

The sound tore Kaycee's heart in two. Turning away, she covered her face and cried.

A presence materialized beside her. "It's okay, Kaycee." Mark's voice. "It's okay."

But it wasn't. Nothing was okay. Still, she nodded and gulped back the tears.

After a minute Ryan quieted. He drew

himself up, wiping both cheeks with the back of one hand. "Sorry." His voice sounded raw.

"No need to apologize." Chief Davis looked worn. He had two children of his own. Kaycee knew the pressure on him to bring Hannah home safely must be crushing.

The five of them looked at each other, the air heavy with unspoken thoughts. Defensiveness wafted from Ryan, as if he knew he'd tipped his hand to his own guilt.

He stuttered a sigh. "What do we do now?"

Chief stood with one hand on his hip. He looked to Kaycee. "We'll get someone in your house to dust for prints soon. And we'll get your car back to you. Meanwhile we've got to decide what to do with you tonight. I suggest you stay with your friend again. We'll keep watch on your house, see if we can catch anyone lurking around." He pinched the bridge of his nose. "Ryan, we really don't know if these events are linked to Hannah's disappearance, but we need to act on the assumption they are. Which means trying to catch who's doing this is of utmost importance, even as we take all the other steps to find Hannah."

Ryan nodded. His mouth opened then

shut, as if he didn't trust himself to speak. He wouldn't look at Kaycee.

"I'm staying here." The words popped from Kaycee.

Chief Davis pulled in the corners of his mouth. "That might be pretty frightening."

"Doesn't matter how frightening it is." Kaycee's words sharpened. "I *have* to stay here. Most of the stuff has happened inside my house. How are you going to know what's going on in there by just driving by now and then? And we have to remember whoever's doing this is aiming it at *me*. If it has anything to do with Hannah, it's probably only because she got in the way." Kaycee's voice cracked. She swallowed hard. "I have to do this. I left last night, and look what happened. I'm *not* leaving tonight."

Ryan surveyed her for a moment, then looked away.

Mark rubbed the back of his neck. Lack of sleep drew ridges around his mouth. "I don't know that it would've made any difference if you were home."

"I'm not leaving, Mark. I'm not walking away from this."

Chief Davis looked from Kaycee to Ryan and back. Sighing, he turned to gaze down Walters Lane. The crime-scene tape bounced in a slight breeze. Ed stood behind it, legs apart, holding his clipboard and looking their direction. Kaycee could practically see the wheels of decision turning in the chief's head. So many details to handle, with a finite amount of officers. And despite his patience, Kaycee sensed his drive to get moving. Any further searching on foot for Hannah would be far more difficult after dark.

He cleared his throat. "There is a benefit to you staying. If you're here, that may draw these suspects out. Then we can move in. But your safety comes first. I'll put two officers on your house tonight."

"I'll do it," Mark said.

"You haven't slept."

"Let me go sleep now. I'll come back on duty at nine or ten, whenever you want."

Kaycee threw Mark a look of gratitude. "But that would mean less officers looking for Hannah."

The chief shook his head. "No it won't. Soon as I get back to the station I'll be calling the State Police for help with this case. There's too much for us to handle. We'll need more officers — plus volunteers — to help in grid searches. I might request the State Police to provide the second officer to watch this place tonight. I'm thinking one officer in the black barn to cover the left side of your property and one in Mrs. Foley's house to cover the right."

*Mrs. Foley, great.* Kaycee pushed hair off her face. "Mrs. Foley might not want to cooperate. When I found that picture in my car I went a little crazy. And she saw it."

"I'll talk to her," Chief said.

Panic spiraled through Kaycee's chest. This plan, her staying here tonight — it could really happen.

"This is workable, if you think you can handle it." Chief Davis must be reading her mind. "Officer Burnett and the second man will be only a minute away if you need them. With lights off in Mrs. Foley's first level, Mark can move from front to back to see out windows, and that barn's dark at night. Plenty bowed slats to look through. Keep your cell phone with you at all times, and the officers will have theirs. I'll remain on duty all night as well, and I won't be far away."

"Okay, but . . ." This was going to sound so paranoid. "Whoever these people are, they're watching." Kaycee whisked nervous fingers up and down the bottom of her purse strap. "If they see Mark going into Mrs. Foley's house . . ."

If Chief Davis thought she was being crazy, he didn't show it. His "velvet touch" at work. "Mark, dress in civilian clothes and wear a hat. Park across the street in your own personal car. Carry your weapon and laptop in a small suitcase. You're a guest visiting for the night."

"Okay."

"As for the other guy, we'll station him as unobtrusively as possible, also in plain-clothes."

Kaycee glanced from Mark to the chief. She was suddenly having trouble processing oxygen. "So . . . what exactly do we expect to happen?"

The chief spread his hands. "None of this is predictable. But with three episodes at your house in less than twenty-four hours, it's not unlikely whoever's bothering you will come around again. This time we'll get them. And let's hope they can lead us to Hannah."

*Let's hope.*

"You okay with this?" Chief raised his eyebrows. "The alternative is to go stay with your friend."

Kaycee thought of the dream her watchers had somehow caused her to have at Tricia's house. The "wrong number" call there asking for Belinda, a haunting name that had to be connected to all this. "If I'm not here, they'll know. They . . . see things. They *know.*"

"Oh, brother," Ryan muttered in disgust. He turned toward the crime-scene tape, hands at his temples. His eyes closed, and the cynicism drained from his features, replaced with abject pain. "This sounds so crazy," he whispered. "But just . . . make it work. Bring Hannah back."

*Yes, God, please.* But it only worked if they showed up. Which would be beyond terrifying.

The meeting broke up. Sam and Ryan wandered back to Sam's vehicle to return to Ryan's house — and wait. The chief crossed the side yard to knock on Mrs. Foley's door. Kaycee could imagine their conversation. The old woman would play like she was being put upon while privately basking in her incredible fortune. She'd get to help a police officer snoop.

Mark lingered on Kaycee's porch. She surveyed him, vulnerability swirling in her chest. Ryan Parksley's words still bit deep.

Mark cleared his throat. "About last night. I'm sorry I didn't believe you."

Kaycee focused on her feet. Once again he'd surprised her. There was so much more depth to this man than he was willing to show. She wanted to reach down inside him, pull it out. "After four false alarms, why should you?"

Silence ticked by. She could feel his eyes upon her. For once she didn't mind being watched.

Mark put a finger beneath her chin and nudged her to look him in the eye. "Guess what."

Something whispered down the length of her, like silk. "What?"

"I read your column every week."

She swallowed. "The one that only 'stirs up people's fears'?"

Instantly she wanted the words back. Why had she said that? Like she had to get in a dig.

Mark tilted his head as if considering his response. "Sometimes," he said, "maybe it hits a little too close to home."

Abruptly he turned and headed down her porch steps, leaving Kaycee to stare after him, half wondering if the moment had happened at all.

# Thirty-Five

Lorraine and Tammy sat on the bed, propped up with pillows, watching *Sesame Street*. That is, Tammy watched. Lorraine's thoughts tumbled elsewhere. Tammy's legs splayed apart, her right foot jerking back and forth. Belinda lay in her arms. With one finger Tammy absently rubbed the bear's velvety nose.

Questions, always the questions. They snaked through Lorraine's head, writhing from the bank robbery to Martin's words that morning to hiding in the closet. Could she have done something different? Could she somehow have kept her husband alive?

*"Please tell me this isn't about the bank robbery."*

Lorraine knew Martin's reactions too well. She'd always been able to read him. As he'd stared at that mouse in the toilet — was that just yesterday? — she'd seen his consternation. She'd had to tell him what to do, how

257

to be the hero. Sometimes Martin's dreams outran his head. He wanted so much for her and Tammy and was afraid he couldn't always come through for them.

*"We're going to lose a lot of money."*

He'd done it, hadn't he? He'd helped those robbers in exchange for a cut of the money. The man who killed him was supposed to come over and give Martin his share. That man told Martin to get her out of the apartment because he didn't want her to see his face. But she wouldn't listen.

Maybe the man never planned to give Martin any money in the first place. Her husband was set up to die like some worthless dog.

Tears burned Lorraine's eyes.

Was all the money sitting in that storage unit this very minute?

The motel phone rang. The sound seared through Lorraine's nerves, and she jumped. Exhaling, she picked up the receiver from the table by the bed. Detective Tuckney was on the line.

"I wanted you to know they're done with your apartment."

"Already?"

"I know it's earlier than I told you. Sorry about the misinformation. We can't always judge the timing."

258

Lorraine's focus hung on the TV as Cookie Monster counted by twos in his grating singsong. Now what should she do? She felt trapped between two worlds. This room was merely a waiting station. Her apartment was reality.

Reality was a dangerous place.

"Mrs. Giordano?"

"How bad is it?"

"How bad is what?"

"The blood. On the floor. I mean, do they leave a lot after . . . whatever they do?"

Detective Tuckney made an empathetic sound in his throat. "They take samples, but that's all. The room will be pretty much like when you left it. There is a lot of blood in the hall. There's also some spatter on the walls."

Lorraine gripped the phone. *Sesame Street* switched to Big Bird talking to a group of kids on the steps in front of a blue house. A sudden thought hit. If Lorraine had any chance of finding someone to watch Tammy while she cleaned, it was now, at the end of the preschool day.

Besides, how could she be in that apartment tomorrow, after the morning newspaper hit the streets?

"You don't have to clean it up yourself, if that's what you're thinking, Mrs. Giordano.

There are specialized companies you can hire to do that kind of work."

"How much do they cost?"

"Unfortunately a lot. A hundred or more dollars per hour."

Lorraine gave a little snort. "Oh, good. I can afford that."

"*You* don't have to pay for it; that's the responsibility of the property owner."

Would Mr. Houger do that? And would he pay for her to stay another night or two at the motel in the meantime? She couldn't even afford that much. Lorraine would bet against the motel bill for sure. She'd only met Mr. Houger once — when he'd hired her. He was a busy man, with a hardness in his lined face. The owner of many commercial properties, he'd let her know, as if that made him superior. She hadn't liked him, but she and Martin needed a place to live. They'd seen it as a part of building their dream. Live in that grungy apartment free for a while, and they'd have more to save toward a house.

"Look." Detective Tuckney sounded apologetic. "Cleaning up after something like this happens isn't so simple. If you see one spot of blood on a carpet, that could mean a foot-wide circle of it underneath on the floorboard. Also, blood and body tissue are considered biohazards and potentially infectious. When special cleaning teams come in, they know how to properly dispose of all the materials they used to clean. For that reason alone, most importantly for your own emotional welfare, this isn't a job you should even think about undertaking yourself."

Blood and body tissue. Lorraine couldn't believe they were having this conversation. "Okay. I'll call Mr. Houger." She rubbed her forehead. "Do you know any more about . . . anything?"

"We're working on all the evidence we have. And we'll keep working. The autopsy is scheduled for tomorrow."

What was she supposed to do tonight? How was she supposed to sleep *tonight?*

"I met with a funeral home," her mouth said. "You wanted that information so they'd know where to take Martin?" Her mind flashed a picture of his bloodied face. Could they clean him up for an open casket? He had two holes in his head.

"Yeah, I'll take that information right now if you like."

Lorraine pushed off the bed and reached into her purse for the card from the funeral home. She read the address and phone to the detective. "I'll probably go back home

261

just long enough to pick up some things. If I can find someone to watch Tammy."

*And then what, Lorraine?* What about tomorrow, and the next day, and the next? Where would she and Tammy live? How could they feel safe anywhere in Atlantic City?

She should whisk her daughter away. Move anywhere — to a town in another state. Start a new life.

But she had no money to do that.

"All right," the detective replied. "You've got my number if you need it. And I'll be checking in with you as needed."

"Okay. Thanks."

Lorraine hung up the phone and put her head in her hands.

Minutes later she called the preschool. She kept her back to Tammy, speaking in low tones. The director had heard the news of Martin's murder and told Lorraine again and again how sorry she was. And how was Tammy? Lorraine's automatic responses slipped out as if some other person spoke them. How odd her mind felt, as though fog wrapped itself around every thought. She needed to think clearly. But clarity seemed so far away.

One of the preschool teachers, a young woman about eighteen, said she could watch Tammy for the evening at her parents' home. Lorraine could bring Tammy in half an hour. "And don't worry about dinner — I'll feed her," Michelle said.

Lorraine's shoulders sagged in relief. That would make Tammy happy. Michelle was one of her favorite teachers. "Thanks so much."

Tammy giggled at the TV. Lorraine glanced over her shoulder to see Oscar the Grouch popping into his trashcan. She turned back, putting a hand over her mouth to further muffle her voice. "And Michelle? She doesn't know yet. I just . . . haven't figured out how to tell her."

"Okay." Michelle's voice weighted with sadness. "I understand."

Lorraine put off the call to Mr. Houger. She'd do that from the apartment, when Tammy wasn't around.

Tammy was ecstatic to visit Michelle at her house. "What color's her bedroom, Mommy?" The little girl's eyes shone as Lorraine buckled her into the car.

"I don't know. You make sure to tell me."

Handing her over to Michelle, Lorraine promised it would only be a couple of hours before she returned.

"Don't worry. We'll be having fun." Michelle smiled down at Tammy and squeezed her hand. "Right?"

Tammy grinned. "Uh-huh."

Grief cut through Lorraine. She didn't want Tammy to lose that happiness. She didn't want Tammy to know her daddy wasn't coming back.

At five forty-five Lorraine drove alone to her apartment, nervous and trembling. Even though the news reported she was staying away for the night, she couldn't feel safe. She went around the block twice, down Huff Street, around and up Starling, craning her neck at the north and south entrances to check out the lot. She saw no one.

Lorraine pulled into her regular parking space around the corner from the front door and stared at Martin's Pontiac. It looked so normal. As if he might come out any minute and drive off.

She wrenched her gaze away.

The yellow crime-scene tape was gone, and the police and technicians. All the storage units across the concrete seemed so eerily quiet. She could almost tell herself none of this had happened. It was morning on a healthy day for Tammy. Lorraine had just taken her to preschool and was returning. Martin was working at the bank.

As she got out of the van, Lorraine slid her gaze toward rental unit number seven.

She hid her purse underneath the front seat and locked the van. Slipping its key into her jean pocket, she walked around the corner to her front door. As she stood at the threshold to her apartment, she *felt* that storage unit behind her. Its contents throbbed under the late afternoon sun.

Lorraine inserted her key into the lock of her home. Her jaw flexed. For a moment she stood, one palm on the doorpost, her forehead resting against the wood. She imagined Martin inside, sitting on the frayed couch, watching television. *"Hi, honey. Where've you been?"*

What kind of life would she give her daughter? All she could see was darkness and fear.

Lorraine had never been much of a praying person, but she prayed now — for the strength to go on and to raise her daughter. When her eyes reopened, one final thought hovered, even though it may not be one God approved of. Vengeance. Martin's killer needed to *pay.*

She turned around and stared at unit seven.

A minute later, gathering what courage she could find, Lorraine stepped inside the apartment.

# Thirty-Six

At four-thirty Kaycee, shaky with hunger, was headed for Tastebuds inside the drugstore. She'd ridden down to East Main in the back of Mark's car, the chief in the passenger seat. By the time she was done eating, a tech should be ready to dust her house for fingerprints.

Flyers of Hannah now plastered the Main Street storefronts. The sight of one in the drugstore window brought Kaycee to a standstill. She hung there, staring at the poster.

"She must have been picked up in a car at this spot," Seth had told Chief Davis as his hound paced aimlessly on Walters Lane. "Her scent just vanishes."

Kaycee opened the door and stepped inside the drugstore.

The familiar smell of pizza wafted as she crossed the black-and-white checked floor toward Tastebuds. Behind the red counter

Liz, the owner, was sliding a pizza onto a white plate. Two customers — looked like college students — sat on a couple of the eight red-topped stools. Three of the four booths, with their old-fashioned pull-down red seats, were occupied.

A child had been abducted — and life went on.

Kaycee sank onto the stool nearest the end and propped her feet on the footrest.

"Oh, Kaycee." Liz hustled over and peered at her. The countless times Kaycee and Hannah had sat at this very counter were reflected in Liz's worried expression. "How are you?"

Kaycee smiled wanly. "I've had better days."

"We all have." Liz sighed. "What you need's a soda." Without waiting for a reply, she turned to whip up Kaycee's favorite feel-good concoction, flavor — vanilla. Woodenly, Kaycee watched as Liz scooped real ice cream into a large glass, added vanilla syrup and finished it off with the fizzy liquid that made it a true old-fashioned. She placed it in front of Kaycee with a straw and long-handled spoon. Kaycee bent her head and took a long sip. She closed her eyes. Comfort.

Liz pressed a hand over hers. "I heard

267

what happened with the track dog. We're praying, you know that. The whole town's praying."

"Thanks."

She squeezed Kaycee's fingers, then drew away. "Which one today?"

No need to check the menu. Kaycee knew each Tastebuds pizza by heart. Hannah had always been enthralled at the fact that she could recite every ingredient. Besides the typical pepperoni and sausage, Liz had concocted specialties of her own. Spinach pizza, Portabello, the Chicken Caesar, the Cheeseburger pizza, and the Barbeque Chicken. The Waldorf had garlic, apples, walnuts, gorgonzola, bacon, and Tastebud's ubiquitous four cheeses. The Taco pizza included salsa, beef, black olives, jalapenos, tortilla chips, and sour cream.

For the first time, not one of them appealed to Kaycee. But she really needed to eat.

"I'll take the Cheeseburger." Liz knew to hold the dill pickles.

"You didn't bring in an Ale-8-One today."

"Didn't even think about it. I'll just take water."

Staring at the gray countertop, Kaycee spooned down her soda while Liz made the pizza.

Night was coming. Hannah was still missing. Her watchers were out there, lurking. And Kaycee would have to go home.

Time blurred. The smell of beef, red onion, and tomatoes filled the air as Liz slid Kaycee's pizza before her. "There you go, hon."

"Thanks." Kaycee looked out the window. The sun would set around eight-fifteen. The thought of herself at home, alone — even with two officers nearby — filled her with dread.

Robotlike, Kaycee ate the pizza. Halfway through, she'd had enough, but she forced herself to eat more. Who knew when she would eat again? It was going to be a long night.

Stomach full, Kaycee headed back down East Main to the police station. She knocked on the door, and Rich let her inside.

"Find anything more on the video?" she asked.

He shook his head. "We got two officers going door-to-door through Jessamine Village right now. And they looked in that barn again. So far — nothing."

As Seth had said, Hannah reached a spot on Walters Lane — and simply vanished. She was either hidden somewhere in the area or she'd been driven away.

A scene flashed in Kaycee's mind. Hannah, bound in the trunk of a car. A dark, closed place. Like the place Kaycee had been trapped in her dream. In that dream she'd seen through someone else's eyes.

Could those eyes have been Hannah's?

Kaycee pressed a hand to her forehead, as if to force the horrific thought away.

"Officer Statler dusted your car," Rich said. "He's down in the basement. He'll be up in a minute, ready to go to your house."

The basement. Kaycee shivered. Another dark, closed space.

"Okay." She wandered up toward Emma's work area. The secretary had already left for the day. The stack of flyers on her desk had now dwindled to half a dozen. Kaycee picked one up and stared into Hannah's eyes. They looked frightened, pleading.

"We're going to find you, honey," Kaycee whispered.

Even before she finished forming the words a whirlwind of screams and running feet careened through her head.

# THIRTY-SEVEN

Nico hunched over a steak and potatoes in his kitchen. From the TV in the next room he heard canned laughter from some comedy. Noise to keep him company, not that he was really listening. Nico had spent the day in his house, nearly climbing the walls. Stupid Bear, ordering him to stay here. What was the point? If the cops thought he had anything to do with Giordano's murder, this was the first place they'd look.

In the back of his mind, Nico knew the score. Bear didn't trust him anymore.

Nico snorted as he cut off a huge bite of steak. He chewed the rare meat, barely tasting it, glaring out a sliding glass door into his backyard. He pictured Bear's hand trailing down his scar. Nico supposed he should count himself lucky. At least he had a chance. Deliver that money before dawn, and maybe he'd live to see another day.

The phone rang. Nico snatched up the

receiver from the counter, steak still in his mouth. "Hello."

"The cops are outta Giordano's place." Dom's voice.

Nico swallowed. "Everybody?"

"That's what I hear."

"Any talk who did the murder?"

"Didn't hear none of that. I don't think they gotta clue."

"Okay, Dom. Thanks."

"No problem."

Nico finished his steak before calling Bear with the news that Giordano's place was clear.

"All right. Take the boxes down to the Harding warehouse by the wharf. Put it in the storage area at the back. Bring me a million in hundred dollar bills early tomorrow morning."

Bear wouldn't keep all of the million, Nico knew. Well over half would be kicked up to the boss. "It's done."

"I hear the cops got no leads on Giordano."

Nico's gut twisted. Bear had someone else reporting to him on this? Was Dom informing Denny, not even his own captain? Maybe Denny had his own soldiers on it. Either way, Bear's message came through loud and clear. He hadn't relied only on

Nico's boys.

"Yeah. True."

The underboss paused, letting his unspoken words sink in deeper. "See you in the morning."

Bear's house. The million-dollar drop-off would force Nico to prove he'd removed the money from the storage unit. At least Bear hadn't ordered him to take Denny along with him. That would have signaled the nail in Nico's coffin.

On the other hand Denny could be waiting for him at the warehouse.

"I'll be there."

# THIRTY-EIGHT

In the apartment Lorraine could barely breathe. The smell hit her as soon as she walked in the door. Coppery mixed with sweet — and something utterly horrible.

Death?

Her mind turned inward. She wasn't here. Not really. She wasn't smelling her husband's blood, seeing the stained hallway flooring from the corners of her eyes.

She looked toward the kitchen — and saw red spots on the wall.

The black chasm within her yawned open. Terror and grief wrapped skeletal fingers around Lorraine's throat. She couldn't stay in this place. Not for a minute. Never again for a night. No matter how much professionals cleaned, even if every bit of carpet and floor and every piece of furniture was replaced — none of that could erase what had happened here.

*Get what you need and get out!*

274

Heart drumming, Lorraine edged toward the hall, both hands drawn to her chest. Part of her wanted to wail out her pain. Part of her wanted to scream with rage. But she did neither. Once she started she wouldn't stop.

At the edge of the living room carpet she stared at the stained floor. The bright red she remembered had muted to rust. Tears squeezed from her eyes. For a crazy moment she nearly dropped to her knees and raked her fingers through the gore. Yes, it was blood, but it was *Martin's* blood, and right now it was all she had left of him —

*Stop it, Lorraine.*

Holding her breath she lifted one shaking foot and made a wide step over the blood.

In her bedroom she pulled a small suitcase from the closet and threw in two changes of clothes. She hurried into the bathroom to snatch up toiletries. Then she carried the suitcase into Tammy's room and threw it on the bed. In went two pairs of pants, underwear, and two tops. Tammy's hairbrush and an old pair of pajamas. The pink pair lay in the corner where Lorraine had thrown them this morning, stained with patches of red.

Lorraine yanked the zipper shut and lugged the suitcase from the room.

At the end of the hallway, clutching the

suitcase with both hands, she pressed against one wall and skirted around the stain on the floor. After peeking through a window to check the lot, she rushed out the door and slammed it behind her without looking back.

Spent, she sagged against the doorpost and breathed.

As she carried the suitcase to her van, Lorraine's eyes pulled toward storage unit seven.

With the bag stowed in the passenger seat, Lorraine found herself staring at the unit again. She narrowed her eyes, biting one side of her cheek. *Had* those robbers stashed that money in there? Then come back to kill her husband?

She could call Detective Tuckney right now and tell him her suspicions. But that would only drag Martin into the robbery. No way would the detective think the money being hidden on this property was a coincidence. Besides, right now she could at least hope Martin's killer wouldn't come back for her. If she talked, her life wouldn't be worth two cents. Then what would happen to Tammy?

A series of insane thoughts catapulted through Lorraine's mind. Slowly her head pulled back.

Her gaze raked toward the office.

An unseen hand pulled Lorraine across the concrete toward unit seven. She looked up and down the street running along the far side of the lot but saw no sign of someone parked and watching. At the unit, glancing around again, she moved in close to examine the lock. She lifted it up in her palm. It was a strong padlock. The best.

Her gaze rested on the door's hasp.

Lorraine strode back to the van and snatched her purse from under the front seat. She pulled out the key to the office and returned the bag.

As she entered the dim office, Lorraine told herself this was as far as her crazy idea would go. Tomorrow she would come to her senses.

The cabinet door squeaked as she opened it.

Mr. Houger's long-handled, powerful bolt cutter sat on the bottom shelf. She should use it, he'd told her, only when a renter defaulted long enough on payment that the contents of his storage unit could legally be put up for sale. In that case an auctioneer would come in, people bidding on the contents of the unit as a whole. Some auctioneers brought their own bolt cutters for the padlock. Others expected him to furnish it. Mr. Houger showed her how to work the tool, its long handles providing leverage to move the blades together. "Takes some power," he said, "but it works. Most padlocks are less strong than the hasps on our doors. But if the padlock's impossible to break this way, go for the hasp."

Lorraine didn't tell him she'd used a bolt cutter before. In high school one of her friends lost the key to a padlock she'd used to chain up her bike. Her father had a bolt cutter, but he was at work. Lorraine had managed to break through the lock.

She lifted Mr. Houger's tool from the cabinet, plus a pair of thick gloves lying beside it.

At the office door she poked her head out and looked around, heart beating in her ears.

Holding the items close to her body, Lorraine pulled the door shut. She hurried to the van and opened up the expansive, empty back. From every direction eyes seemed to follow her. But she saw no one.

*"This guy's in the mob . . ."*

Lorraine laid the items on the floor of the van and closed it up.

Her hands trembled as she started the engine. Pulling out of the parking space, she stopped for a long, aching look at Martin's abandoned car.

She drove back to Michelle's house to pick up Tammy, telling herself how stupid she was. She'd never go through with this. Not in a million years.

Even so, her rebellious mind sifted through details of a plan.

■ ■ ■ ■

# PART 3

■ ■ ■ ■

Do not take counsel of your fears.

George Patton

# THIRTY-NINE

Nearly midnight. Clouds had clustered in, gobbling up the moon and stars.

Restless and nerve-ridden, Kaycee huddled in her den on the old brown couch she'd inherited from her mother. Both arms were wrapped around her drawn-up knees. She stared unseeing at some rerun of a legal drama on TV. Every room in the house blazed with light. The porch lamps in front and back were on. All blinds and curtains were drawn.

Hours ago she'd watched as Officer Statler dusted her front and back doorways, the kitchen table, and her office desk. Of course he lifted fingerprints. But how many would be her own? In her heart Kaycee knew her watchers would not be so careless as to leave such evidence behind. They were far too cunning for that.

Heart skidding and palms moist, Kaycee then had walked through the house with

Officer Statler, checking every room. All clear, he pronounced, but she didn't believe it. As she watched him drive away, the living room seemed to close in on her, vibrating with unseen evil. For a wild moment she pictured alien eyes in the framework of the walls, watching.

*We see you.*

This plan was crazy. If they were watching, they'd know full well who Mrs. Foley's visitor was. The civilian clothes and baseball cap wouldn't throw them at all. Plus, they'd know another officer was hiding in the black barn. These people were all-seeing, omniscient. They even messed with her dreams.

What would happen if they didn't show up tonight? How many nights would she have to go through this?

Kaycee snatched up the remote and hit the channel button. A crime show blitzed on. Great, just what she needed.

Mark had called Kaycee's cell an hour ago as she paced her kitchen. "Just want you to know I'm here and set up." He spoke in low tones with a certain hesitation, as if his concentration lay elsewhere.

"Where are you?"

"In the kitchen, watching your backyard. I can see this side of your house from here, but not the front door. Officer Nelson's got that and his side of your place covered."

Officer Nelson, from the State Police. He also carried a cell phone — on vibrate. Police radios were too loud.

"Where is . . . she?" Kaycee didn't want to say too much. What if they'd rigged her house and were listening right now?

If Mark caught her paranoia, he didn't let on. "Upstairs in her bedroom. The chief asked her to stay up there."

Anger flashed through Kaycee. Maybe by now the old woman finally believed Hannah was in trouble. "She's actually doing what she's told?"

"Ah, she's not so bad. Just set in her ways. I got a great aunt like that."

"Aunt Battery Acid?"

He chuckled.

"I was in her living room once," Kaycee said. "She's got so many colors in there it probably glows in the dark."

"Close to it."

Silence. She could hear him breathing.

"How you doing, Kaycee?"

"Fabulous. I'm thinking about taking up espionage for a living."

"No room for fear in that."

"Hey, after tonight, I could do anything."

"Stand in a hive of bumblebees?"

*Yikes.* "Sure, why not?"

"Walk across High Bridge?"

A railroad bridge not too far outside Wilmore, stretching across the Kentucky River Palisades — once the highest of its kind in the world. People told horror stories of getting caught up there when a train went by — mere feet from the railing. The thought of that bridge's dizzying height, train or no train, sent Kaycee's stomach dropping. "Going up there hasn't been allowed for years, Mr. Policeman."

"It's the willingness that counts."

"I thought you were supposed to be watching out for me, not trying to make me panic."

"You don't sound panicked."

"Easy for you to say."

They fell silent again.

"Everybody's got fears, you know," Mark said. "You're just more honest about yours. Most people don't have the courage to be that honest."

Kaycee blinked. It was one of the nicest things anyone could say to her. She'd never thought of her honesty as courage. She'd never thought of a single bone in her body as courageous.

"Thank you for saying that."

"You're welcome."

Kaycee stared at the kitchen table where

the camera had sat. "Why'd the chief want you to bring . . . that certain thing with you?"

"Uh, my laptop?"

"Yeah."

"You know those cameras around town? We can review any film from our own computers."

Kaycee processed the information. "Oh."

Another pause. Kaycee floundered for something to say. She didn't want to hang up. Never had she realized how good Mark's voice sounded.

"Kaycee, when this is all over, I'm taking you out. To celebrate."

She blinked in surprise as her heart did a little dance. Had he even had one date since his fiancée left him three years ago? Rumor had it the answer was no. "Let's hope we have something to celebrate."

"We will."

"Where will we go?"

"Kings Island. I'm taking you on the biggest rollercoaster they've got."

Kaycee's eyes closed. "You rat."

"Okay, maybe I'll think of something else."

*Please,* Kaycee thought but couldn't form the word.

Mark cleared his throat. "I should go. You got me on speed dial, right?"

"Yeah, but only if I need you. I've got Tricia standing by. She's promised to talk on the phone all night if I want."

"That's what a friend's for."

Long after they hung up, Kaycee's thoughts hovered on the conversation. *"Most folks don't have the courage."* And he'd asked her out. No, not asked, *told* her. Mark Burnett wanted to take her out!

If she survived the night.

Time ticked on. The tingle of the conversation faded, and Kaycee was left alone with her fear. Every minute seemed a lifetime.

Where was Hannah on this dark night? Was she even alive?

*God, save her.*

Kaycee had called Tricia and tried to talk but couldn't find much to say. The last thing she wanted to discuss was her terror, and spilling the beans on her date with Mark just might jinx it. Who knew, maybe it would never happen.

Now hours later Kaycee hunched on her couch, limbs atremble, and watched the crime drama, barely registering.

A loud creak sounded in the office.

Kaycee whipped her head around. She froze, muscles tight, eyes probing the visible part of the room. Her desk and computer, the arm chair, the door to the hallway off her kitchen. Some detective on the TV was droning on about mitochondrial DNA. She punched the mute button on the remote, then listened. She heard nothing but the whoosh-whoosh of her own pulse in her ears.

It was nothing. Her old house always creaked.

Kaycee's fingers curled around her cell phone. She slipped off the couch and straightened, head cocked. Slowly she approached the arched office doorway, neck craned to gaze around it to the left.

Empty.

She walked to her desk and stared at the black screen of her monitor. Biting her cheek, she surveyed what she could see of the hall. They couldn't possibly be in here. For all her paranoia, she knew that. Two officers had all four sides and every entrance to her house covered.

She sidled into the hallway. Peeked in the laundry room and bathroom. Then forced herself into the kitchen. The dining area. Living room. Back to the den.

*There, see, Miss Courage?*

Kaycee sat back down on the couch. On the TV a dark-haired actress in a white lab coat was silently positioning a thread on a microscope slide. Kaycee put her phone

289

down on the table and picked up the remote.

Her skin prickled from the heat of unseen eyes.

"No one is here," she said aloud.

She checked her watch. Not even twelve-thirty. This night would last an eternity.

Her nerves writhed.

The silence would swallow her. Kaycee pressed the mute button again, and TV voices kicked to life. Feverishly, she channel-surfed, looking for something light to occupy her mind. She blipped through the History Channel, a cell phone commercial, cable news, a car ad, an *I Love Lucy* rerun —

And a full-screen shot of the dead man in vivid color, his eyes half open, lying on the dark yellow floor.

# FORTY

Lorraine lay in the motel bed, staring up through the darkness. Dim light from a streetlamp filtered through the curtains, splotching the ceiling with vague patterns. Cars passed on the street. A dog barked. Lorraine had listened to latecomers pass in the hall and enter their rooms. Finally the motel settled into quiet. But sleep had not come. Like the world outside, her thoughts refused to still. Memories, fear of the future, emptiness, and grief jumbled in her head. And the crazy plan. The idea that would not die.

Beside her, Tammy sighed the even breaths of sleep. Such innocence. Such peace.

What would they do in the morning? And the next day, and the next?

Lorraine had never called Mr. Houger about cleaning up the apartment. While she was there, she'd forgotten. Then how to have the conversation at the motel with

Tammy in the room? She closed her eyes. But those were just excuses, weren't they? Deep inside a voice whispered that making sure the apartment was cleaned would no longer be her problem.

Over and over Lorraine had sifted through her choices. She could return to the apartment with Tammy after it was cleaned and resume their lives — without Martin. Somehow she'd have to live each day and endure each night with the fear that any moment Martin's killer would come back to silence her. Maybe he'd kill Tammy too. Maybe he'd let Tammy live — to wake up alone and find her mother bloodied and dead.

Lorraine's fingers dug into the bedcovers. It was too awful to imagine. And to think after all that killing, those evil men would be living it up, spending their millions.

Choice two: she could tell the police what she knew to be true. Martin had been involved in the robbery. The money may even be sitting in storage unit seven. They'd investigate the renter of the unit. Maybe break in and check it out. If the money was there, or if it wasn't, Martin's name would be dragged through the mud. Word would leak that he'd been linked to the Mafia. All those people at the bank who'd treated Lorraine and Tammy so nicely, who'd called

Martin a hero? They'd turn on him. Plus, she and Tammy would *really* be in danger. The police would have to protect them. How long would they do that?

And how did she know she could even trust the police? Who on that force might be reporting everything to those Mafia men, including where she was hidden? Lorraine tried to tell herself she'd seen too many movies. But was she willing to bet her daughter's life on that?

Tammy sighed in her sleep and turned over. Lorraine gazed at her through the darkness, just making out the back of her head, the tangled hair. Her heart constricted. Above all else, more important than anything in this world, she would protect her daughter.

Choice three: carry out her own vengeance and run.

But the price she would pay. Leaving Martin's body behind, not even able to attend his funeral. Forever living with her secrets . . .

Restlessness vibrated through Lorraine. She slipped out of bed and padded to the bathroom. Leaving the door ajar she flicked the light switch. Tammy wouldn't wake up. The little girl slept soundly at night. Lorraine's eyes squinted, blinking at the floor until they adapted to the light.

Resting her hands on the sink, she stared at herself in the mirror. Could she do it?

If she didn't, what then? Choice one or two? She'd rejected both of them.

Maybe the money wasn't in the storage unit at all. The two men, one tall, one short, their black clothes, the timing, their hurried movements — all coincidence.

If the money wasn't there, she would have no vengeance for her husband's blood. With no vengeance she couldn't bring herself to run and hide without even seeing him buried.

She'd be right back where she was now, facing the first two choices.

But in her gut she *knew.* The money was in that unit. The Mafia had stolen it. And with Martin dead and unable to testify against them, they were going to get away with it.

Lorraine held her own eyes in the mirror, looking down, down into her soul, to the black hole that kept on growing. For a long minute . . . she stared.

She pictured her husband lying in his casket. No family to mourn him. Her heart cracked.

"Martin," she whispered. "Forgive me."

She swiveled and strode from the bath-room to dress.

# FORTY-ONE

Kaycee cried out at the sight of the dead man on her TV screen. Her hand jerked. The remote flew from her fingers.

She gaped at the picture, heart flailing.

For one glorious second her mind flashed a stunning explanation of everything that had plagued her. This was a shot from some crime drama she'd watched before. The footsteps and screams, the dark place — they'd come next . . .

The picture on the screen didn't move. This was no TV show. Just the dead man.

Kaycee doubled over and threw an arm over her eyes.

"— this medication isn't for everyone. Talk to your doctor . . ."

Her head snapped up. An ad for a prescription cholesterol pill played on the screen.

She froze, breath backing up in her throat. The dead man — he'd been there. Right?

Maybe only for two seconds, but she'd *seen* him.

The TV switched to a dog food commercial.

Kaycee sprang to her feet and snatched the remote from the floor. She jabbed a button, backing up one channel. No dead man. Backed up another. And another. Then surfed forward, back to the dog food ad, on past that, one, two, three, four channels. With each push of the button tension tightened like a turned screw in her chest. Five channels, six. Seven, eight. No dead man. Nine, ten, eleven. Not anywhere. *Come on, come on, I know I saw it!* Twelve, thirteen. No frozen bloody scene. Just commercials and shows and TV as she'd always known it.

Kaycee punched off the television and hurled the remote to the floor. It bounced off the hardwood, its battery cover popping off and skittering to rest at the base of a chair.

She fell onto the couch and thrust her head in her hands. Kaycee could barely breathe. How could these people get into her TV reception? You could hack a computer, put a camera on a table and a picture in a car. But her TV pulled in cable. How did they *do* that?

Terror washed over Kaycee in cold waves, trailing screams and running footsteps. The smell of blood flooded her nostrils, stronger than before. Kaycee yanked her head up. Where was that smell coming from, *where?*

She jumped up, searched the cushion where she'd sat. No blood. She pulled it off the couch and flipped it over. Nothing. With a gasp she shoved it back and grabbed the second. Seeing it clean, she snatched the third. When all three cushions were back in place, she ran both hands down her jeans, checked the backs of her legs. Felt around her T-shirt. No blood.

She still smelled it. It was here, right *here.*

Footsteps sounded. Shouts. Kaycee whirled left and right, every pore prickling. Where were they?

Panic stabbed her, bright and sharp. Kaycee ran. Past the staircase, through the living room. Small cries spilled from her mouth, her feet with minds of their own. Her wild eyes cut left and right, looking for blood, for a camera, a dead man. Kaycee barreled through the dining area, chased by screams. Into the kitchen. She banged into the table and bounced off, shaken. Darkness clouded her brain and snatched air from her lungs. She tumbled into the hall, rounded the corner to her office. Through the arched doorway back into the den.

No one was there. No dead man, no blood. Yet still she heard the screams. And that smell!

*We see you.*

Kaycee flung herself to a front window and edged back a curtain. Scanned what she could see of the porch.

No one.

*What's happening to me?*

Maybe she had gone crazy. Maybe all of this was in her head — a far worse paranoia than her mother ever faced.

*Mark.* Kaycee whirled toward the couch and her phone. No matter that he'd think she was losing her sanity, she needed to tell him —

The blood smell vanished. The screams and footsteps stopped.

All energy drained from Kaycee. Like a puppet with its strings cut, she fell onto the couch. Sinking onto her stomach, she buried her face in a cushion and begged God to heal her ravaged mind.

"Got to you, didn't I," a male voice sneered.

# FORTY-TWO

Midnight.

Lorraine drove through the darkened streets, back straight and hands gripping the steering wheel. In the passenger seat Tammy leaned against the locked door, head lolling. She was still in her pajamas. Belinda lay tucked in beside her. Lorraine had first carried their small suitcase and her purse from the motel room, stowing them just behind her seat in the van. Then she carried Tammy and her stuffed bear out. Tammy woke up as Lorraine belted her into the seat. But she'd fallen back asleep by the time Lorraine pulled out of the motel parking lot.

Lorraine halted at a stoplight. She'd gone insane, bringing her daughter along on such a mission in the middle of the night. At every block after that she nearly turned around. Then, suddenly, the north entrance of AC Storage loomed on her right.

She slowed, gazing down the concrete between the two long buildings. Past the lot on the other side she could see Huff Street. Two tall lamps lit the wide area between the buildings, one near each end. Unit number seven, in the middle of the building to her right, lay in dimmer light.

The place was empty.

She could stop this madness right now.

Two gunshots echoed in her mind. She pictured Martin's frozen face, his blood smearing the floor.

Lorraine didn't know much about the Mafia. But she did know its members worked in layers, one man reporting to another. And some powerful "don" sat at the top. Whoever led the robbery and killed Martin would have to report to that leader. Imagine what would happen to the man when he claimed the money, all seven million dollars of it, had just up and disappeared . . .

Lorraine turned into AC Storage.

As she rolled past units, the memories kept flashing in her head. Tears bit her eyes. No turning back now. She'd come this far; she'd go through with it. No time to second-guess or hesitate. Just *do.*

Dry-throated, she drove down to the apartment and stopped in front of the door, leaving the engine running. She pulled the front door key from her pocket and went inside, holding her breath against the smell of blood. Screams and muffled gunshots echoed in her head. Without turning on a light, she fumbled her way toward the kitchen, making a wide arc around the top of the bedroom hallway.

From a cabinet she pulled out a flashlight. She opened a drawer, felt around inside, and took out a screwdriver.

Back in the van she placed the screwdriver inside the console and closed it, leaving the flashlight on top. She drove to unit seven, reversing to within a foot of its roll-up door, turned off the van and cut the headlights.

She glanced at Tammy. Still asleep. Lorraine picked up the flashlight and slipped out of the van.

Opening up the rear, she laid down the flashlight and pulled on the heavy gloves. She drew out the bolt cutter.

A car passed the Starling entrance. Lorraine froze, pulse whooshing in her ears. She shot a look toward the driver, seeing only the vague bulk of the person. But he (she?) didn't even turn his head.

Lorraine glanced at Huff Street. Empty. From where she stood she couldn't see the southern Huff Street entrance some distance beyond the office. The end of building two blocked her view. If someone turned into that entrance, she wouldn't know until she saw the wash of headlights coming. By then it would be too late.

She turned toward the padlock. *Here goes.*

Her hands felt awkward in the heavy gloves. She wished for a second person to hold the padlock out of the way while she positioned the bolt cutter on the hasp. Alone, she had to nudge the lock aside with the blades. It shouldn't have been that hard, but her arms were shaking. The padlock kept slipping back. In the dim light it was hard to see. She tried once . . . twice. Three times. Four. Her mouth creaked open, breath coming in short little bursts. This was *stupid.* If she couldn't even do this much . . .

On the fifth try the blades closed around the hasp. Lorraine's forehead itched with sweat.

She grasped the ends of the long handles and squeezed.

Lorraine knew this would take a few minutes. And it would require every ounce of strength she possessed, even though her arms were strong. She still carried Tammy a lot, and the little girl weighed close to forty pounds. Lorraine's high school friend's padlock hadn't been as thick as this hasp. But then, neither had the bolt cutter been as powerful.

The blades didn't move. She might as well have been trying to cut through a boulder.

She pushed harder.

Her arm muscles burned. She ignored them.

Scenes of the men loading the storage unit last night flashed in her head. She'd never seen what they'd put inside. But Martin said the robbers had left the bank with fifteen duffel bags of money, separated by denomination.

The hasp was holding. Lorraine loosened her grip on the bolt cutter and rested her hands, panting. After two deep breaths she squeezed again.

If she didn't find those duffel bags inside, she'd drive straight to the police. Tonight.

*And let on that Martin was involved, Lorraine?*

The blades wouldn't move. She gritted her teeth.

So she couldn't tell the police anything Martin had said. Nothing about losing money or the Mafia. But she could beg them to hide her and Tammy.

Sweat trickled down Lorraine's temple. The nerves in her arm flared all the way to her shoulders. She pushed harder.

She'd tell the police how frightened she was for her and Tammy's safety. Maybe she could lie and say someone had been skulking around her motel door. She thought they were being followed . . .

Lorraine's arms were going to break. Her back muscles screamed. She eased up on the bolt cutter handles and leaned her forehead against the unit door, sucking in oxygen.

This was impossible.

Lorraine looked right toward Starling, left toward Huff. The streets were empty. But any minute her husband's murderer could appear. What if they decided to move out the money in the middle of the night?

Terror and rage sped through Lorraine. She didn't want to die here. But neither did she want to leave seven million dollars for the man who shot her husband. And it was here, wasn't it? She could smell it.

A low grunt rattled in her throat. She would *do* this.

Gathering her strength, Lorraine wrapped her hands around the bolt cutter handles and squeezed with all her might. Cords tightened on her neck. She pressed her eyes shut, tears pushing through her lashes.

Between the bolt cutter blades she felt

movement. Lorraine held her breath and pushed even harder. Heat coursed through her face. Her arms shook like an epileptic's. Any minute now her head would explode.

The hasp wouldn't give. *Come on, come on . . .*

Another second, maybe two. That's all the strength she had —

*Crack.* The hasp snapped. Her arms jerked. The end of the bolt cutter thwacked against the unit door.

Lorraine dropped the tool and stumbled back, chest heaving. The bolt cutter clattered as it hit the ground.

Twisting her head left and right, she checked the streets.

She drew an arm across her forehead, swiping perspiration from her eyes. She snatched up the bolt cutter and heaved it into the van. Her gloved fingers could hardly function as she pulled the broken hasp and attached padlock off the door. She tossed them into the van as well.

Gasping, she bent down to pull up the unit door. Even that was hard for her exhausted muscles. The door rolled up with a grinding whir that echoed through the night. Surely it could be heard a mile away.

Lorraine's mouth felt like desert-scorched cotton. She looked toward Huff and Starling streets. No cars.

A dry, closed smell wafted out of the unit. Little light filtered inside. Lorraine squinted into the dimness but couldn't make out the shapes in the center. She grabbed the flashlight from the van, knowing what she would find. Already her next moves flashed in her head.

*For you, Martin.*

She aimed the flashlight into the unit.

Boxes.

Lorraine jerked backward. Rectangular boxes, about twice as long as they were high. No duffel bags.

No money.

A half moan, half hysterical laugh burst from her mouth. She backpedaled to the van and leaned against it, all remaining energy draining away. Arguments ping-ponged through her brain. If the money wasn't there, then Martin was innocent.

Not true. He *was* involved. They just hadn't put the money here.

But if she'd read this part so wrongly . . .

*Lorraine. You know.*

Now what? She'd broken through some innocent renter's door.

She could still run for her and Tammy's protection. But not now. Not before attending her own husband's funeral.

Her gaze fixed on the boxes. She counted them. Twelve.

Could those twelve boxes hold fifteen duffel bags' worth of money?

Lorraine strode over and set the flashlight upright on the floor, aiming its beam toward the ceiling. She picked up a box. It was heavy in her weakened arms. Maybe close to Tammy's weight. She set it down and picked up another. Exactly the same weight. And solidly packed. No rattling.

She put the box down and squatted, examining the tape around it.

Lorraine ran to the van and fetched the box cutter. Positioning the blade along the top edge of one box, she dragged the tool through the packing tape. Then she hustled around to open the other side. She lay down the cutter, grabbed one half of the box top in each hand, and pulled. The tape running down the middle popped open.

She knelt on the hard floor, not even sure what she wanted to see. If only she could know Martin had been completely innocent.

Holding her breath, Lorraine folded back the four box flaps.

# FORTY-THREE

In slow motion, as if her neck was weighted with stones, Kaycee lifted her head.

A man stood before her. Dressed in black pants, a long black T-shirt. Hard-faced, cold-eyed. Dark hair fading to gray. Her cell phone lay in his left hand. His right thumb slid back and forth against his fingers as though itching for evil. One side of his mouth lifted in a satisfied smirk.

"Heard you on the telephone to your girlfriend this afternoon. I consider it a compliment you call me 'they.' As if I've managed the work of multiple men."

Kaycee's mind crumbled.

He raised his eyebrows, mimicking concern. "I understand you've been having some strange experiences." His speech sounded refined, almost stilted. He glared at her with a mixture of victory and contempt.

No words would form. No breath.

The man smiled. Kaycee's soul curled inward. "You hearing things? Seeing a dead man wherever you go?"

Her vision blurred. This was a nightmare. Not real.

"For a columnist who spills her guts, you don't talk much." He stepped toward her.

She shrank against the couch. "Wh— what do you want?"

"Ah. She speaks."

Suddenly aware of her vulnerable position, Kaycee sat up. Her brain shouted fight-or-flight responses — scream, run, *hit* him. She couldn't move.

"Get up." His tone could cut steel.

She shook her head.

His expression flattened. "That cop in the barn won't help you. I shot him twice. In the jaw and in the head." A wicked smile spread his lips, a knowing look at her horror glinting in his eyes. "That's right. Just like in the picture."

Kaycee stared at him, her thoughts a million broken pieces. The blood she'd smelled had come true — on her own fingers. Now the dead man — the state policeman?

The floor of the barn — was it old bare wood, now dark-yellowed with age?

She whimpered. "How? *Why?*"

His gaze rose. He focused on the wall

behind her as if seeing a movie unfold. "Your columns led me here, you know. For this past year I've been studying the fascinating depths of the mind." His eyes blinked back to her, gleaming with vindication. "Apparently my education has proved effective."

The words barely registered. Kaycee could only think one word: *Mark.* If this man knew about the state policeman, he knew about Mark. Her mouth sagged open. She dug her fingers into the front of the couch, a vision of Mark shot dead blazing in her mind.

The man surveyed her smugly, as though reading the horrible question she dared not ask.

"So you see how it is. Everyone who was supposed to protect you is gone." He set her cell phone on the side table and lifted the bottom of his T-shirt. The top of a gun stuck out of his pants' waistband. "Now you will come with me."

"Why?" Kaycee's voice held no life. "You're going to kill me anyway. Might as well do it here."

"I could have killed you a hundred times if that's what I wanted."

"What *do* you want?"

"You haven't asked my name."

She gaped at him.

"It's Rodney. As for what I want, my

exercise in the mind is not yet over. I still need something from you."

"Take it, it's yours."

"Unfortunately it's not that simple."

Kaycee stared dully at the floor. Didn't matter. Nothing mattered. The constant fear of her life now stood in the flesh. In her living room. He'd killed two men because of her, one of them Mark. He'd probably killed Mrs. Foley too. *Mark.* Kaycee couldn't think of that, couldn't bear it.

If she survived this night, what would be left of her?

"You have no choice but to come with me, Kaycee. Without sound, with no resistance."

Mark. Dead. Because of *her.* Tears clawed her eyes.

"Why should I?"

"Because Hannah is waiting for you."

# FORTY-FOUR

The flashlight beam shone on hundred dollar bills. Stacks of them.

The box flaps slipped from Lorraine's hand and closed. She rocked back on her knees, heart thudding.

For a long second her brain blanked to whiteness.

Lorraine set the flashlight on its end and reached for the flaps again, spreading them apart. She snatched up a tightly bound stack of bills and feathered the ends with her gloved thumb. Then explored the lower layers in the box with the flashlight. More hundred dollar stacks.

*Separated by denomination,* Martin had told her. They'd repacked the bills into these boxes in the same way.

Reality screamed down on her head. *They.* The Mafia. And all this money. This was *real.* She had to get out of here.

Lorraine leapt to her feet and grabbed up

the open box. She lumbered to the van with weighted steps and heaved it inside. With both hands she pushed it back as far as she could. Sweeping aside the bolt cutter, she climbed into the van and shoved the box up toward the driver's seat, right behind her suitcase and purse.

She threw a glance at Tammy. Still sleeping.

Lorraine reversed out of the van, her knees slapping against the thin rubber flooring. On her feet she hesitated, then ripped off the heavy gloves and tossed them to the ground. It would be easier working without them. She twisted back into the storage unit for a second box.

Back and forth she went, waddling out of the unit, arms loaded, then running back for more. In her head she counted the boxes. One . . . two . . . three . . . She pushed each one toward the front of the van. Kneeling inside, she had to stack the boxes in two layers. Without the leverage of her legs, they pulled at her arms like lead.

By the time the fifth box was loaded, Lorraine was exhausted. Her pace slowed.

As she backed out of the van after the eighth one, a pickup truck passed on Huff Street. Lorraine carved to a stop, chest heaving.

The truck drove on.

For interminable seconds she hung there, eyes glued to the pavement in front of the apartment. Watching for the wash of head-lights. In one minute she could be dead, Tammy left here in the dark all alone. What had she been *thinking?* Her grief had clouded her head.

No lights came.

Lorraine whirled back inside the unit.

She snatched up the flashlight and aimed it at her watch. Twelve forty-five. Every minute she stayed tempted fate. Maybe the robbers would stay away from this place for days. Maybe not.

Lorraine picked up the ninth box — and her hands gave out. The box slipped side-ways from her fingers. One end landed on her right toes.

Breath hissed between her teeth. She yanked her foot from beneath the box, and it whumped on its top to the floor. Lorraine bent over, whimpers spilling from her throat. She pressed a hand against the throbbing toes, blinking back tears.

"Mommy!" Tammy's frightened wail rose from the van. "Mommy!"

*No.*

Lorraine jerked up and hobbled toward the passenger side door. Flinging it open, she pulled Tammy into a hug. "It's okay, it's okay."

Tammy clung to her. "Where *were* you?" Her voice was thick from sleep.

"Just behind the van. I'm close, sweetie. Always close."

Tammy's chest convulsed. She raised her head. "What're you doing? Why're we here?"

Lorraine smoothed her daughter's hair. Her gaze flicked over Tammy's head and out the driver's window toward Starling Street. They needed to *leave.* "I'm just putting some things in the back, that's all. You need to go back to sleep."

"Stay here."

Fear chewed Lorraine's nerves. She fought to keep her voice even. "Tammy, I'll be just a few feet away, I promise. I need to load some more stuff. You know, like when we go to the grocery store?"

"We're not at the store."

"I know. Please, Tammy, just . . . Can you go back to sleep? Here's Belinda." Lorraine pushed the bear into her little girl's arms.

"I wanna help."

"You can't help. Just stay here."

"But —"

"*No,* Tammy." Panic edged Lorraine's voice. What was she doing out here? Now her daughter was awake, and her toes pulsed with pain, and she had four more boxes to load.

Tammy started to cry. Lorraine's eyes slipped shut. Now she'd done it. Why hadn't she kept her tone calm?

She pressed her palms against Tammy's cheeks, feeling moisture beneath her fingertips. Lorraine's heart rat-tatted, and her ankles shook. "Look at me." She forced a little smile. "Your mommy's right here. I'm just going to finish loading the van, then I'll get back in my seat. But you need to stay here. You need to wait. Okay?"

Tammy's big eyes blinked, her mouth trembling. She hugged Belinda to her chest. "Okay."

Relief flooded Lorraine. "That's my girl." She backed up and started to shut the door.

"No, leave it open!"

Lorraine's arms halted, her mouth opening to say no.

"Okay. I'll leave it like this. Halfway."

Before Tammy could protest, she turned and ran, limping, toward the storage unit.

Her toes throbbed as she moved the ninth box. The van was nearly filled. Tammy stayed quiet. Even if she called out now, Lorraine couldn't stop. A terrified voice in her brain screamed for her to get out of here.

Her arms could barely carry the tenth box. By the eleventh her wrists threatened to give out. Teethed clenched, she dropped it into the back of the van with a heavy thud. She pushed it to the right, even with the two stacked boxes on the left. The last box would have to be lifted on top of this one.

Lorraine's legs wobbled. Shoving her fists onto the floor of the van, she slumped over and pulled in air. She couldn't manage that final box. No way.

The memories flooded back — Martin's frozen face, his blood on the floor. In her mind's eye she pictured his killer's corpse, twice as bloody. The other three robbers — also dead. She imagined the rage within the Mafia family as they searched for money they'd never find.

Lorraine's mouth twisted. She pushed up straight, every muscle in her body flaring.

*For you, Martin.*

She turned and reentered the storage unit.

Her arms could not handle the last box. She shoved it with one foot across the floor and out to the van. There she bent down, took a deep breath, and willed herself to lift it. Her back strained as she struggled to edge one corner above the floor of the van. That done, she rested for a moment, holding the box's other end and gulping air.

Lorraine eyed the eleventh box, envisioning this one on top. *You can do this.*

A final wave of power flushed through her. Grimacing, Lorraine lifted her burden one more time and raised it inch by inch until its bottom cleared the eleventh box. With two hands she pushed it into place.

Puffing, she stood back and blinked in amazement at the loaded van. The doors would just close.

Lorraine glanced toward Huff and Starling streets, then reached down to pick up the gloves. Putting them on, she hurried inside the unit to fetch her flashlight and the bolt cutter. She threw them into the van on top of a box. Lorraine pulled down the unit door, wincing at the sound it made. She tore off the gloves and tossed them into the van. Nerves humming, she closed up the rear.

Almost there.

Lorraine ran to the driver's door and yanked it open. She flung herself into the seat, slammed the door, and started the engine. Only then did she notice the passenger door hanging ajar. Tammy had wriggled toward the console, her head flopped in Lorraine's direction, Belinda on the seat to her right. Lorraine thrust a hand on the console and heaved over her daughter toward the door. Tammy shifted beneath her weight and mumbled. Lorraine leaned farther, left hand reaching for the door handle.

"Nnnn." Tammy tried to push her off.

Lorraine stretched her arm out but couldn't touch the door. Tammy fought. Lorraine ignored her. She jerked her right hand from the console to the far side of Tammy's seat and lunged for the door.

Belinda rolled off the seat to the ground.

"No!" Tammy cried.

Lorraine's fingers closed on the handle. She yanked the door closed.

"Belinda!" Tammy reached for the door handle.

"Stop!" Lorraine caught her arms. "I'll get her."

Movement past the two storage buildings caught Lorraine's eye. Her gaze cut toward it.

Light. Washing the concrete. Someone had turned in off Huff Street.

# FORTY-FIVE

They left through Kaycee's dining room door that opened onto the wrap-around section of the porch. It was already unlocked. Rodney smirked at her. "Locks never stopped me. But you know that."

He closed the door and pushed her off the porch onto grass. "Over there. Toward the barn."

Terror bubbled in Kaycee's lungs. That barn was dark. With a dead man in it. "I know Hannah's not in there. That barn was searched."

"Keep your voice down. We're going around the fence to the back."

He gripped her arm hard and pulled her forward. As they neared the fence he veered right. Kaycee stumbled along, trying not to fall. *God, just let me get to Hannah.*

They hit an area of trees bordering the backyard of a house on South Walnut. Rodney yanked Kaycee left, all the way down until South Walnut dead-ended. A dark-colored SUV sat waiting. Rodney shoved her into the backseat.

"Lie down."

She obeyed.

He ran around to the driver's side, jumped in, and started the car.

Gripping the edge of the seat, Kaycee lifted her head a few inches. She focused her gaze high, angled through the window, intent on watching where they were headed. All she could see was trees and telephone poles going by. The car drove a block, maybe two, and turned left.

*East Linden.* Kaycee pictured the street in her mind.

A short distance, a stop. A second left turn.

*South Lexington — Highway 29.*

Kaycee sat up.

"Get down!"

"You see anybody on the streets?" She turned around and looked back toward the stoplight at the East Main intersection. "This is Wilmore."

"Do you want Hannah to live?"

Kaycee lay down.

No more turns. They were headed out of Wilmore toward High Bridge. She felt the car climb a hill. They stopped. Kaycee twisted her head up and saw a stoplight. *Lowry Lane.* On the edge of town.

Rodney drove on, past all streetlights into darkness.

Kaycee pressed her face into the seat. This road was long and rural, passing wooded areas and curving toward the Kentucky River. So many hiding places. They'd never find her and Hannah.

The car slowed. *Already?* Kaycee stretched her neck up and peered around the front seat through the windshield. Rodney turned right, the headlights washing over a sign that read Shanty Hill Road.

*Shanty Hill.* A narrow hilly road, practically one lane. Kaycee had driven down it once. She'd seen an occasional house, and some distance down on the right, a sign for the Asbury College Equine Center. College students boarded their horses there and studied Equine Management. The program was run by the mayor of Wilmore.

In daylight Shanty Hill was a pretty road. Now after midnight, blackness claimed the countryside in thick, smothering velvet.

Kaycee's breath snagged. She shrank down to the seat and held on.

They curved sharply to the left. Kaycee remembered that hairpin turn. It was past the Equine Center. She counted about thirty seconds. The car slowed and turned left. Gravel popped under the tires.

A driveway.

The popping ceased. The SUV hitched and bumped. Seconds drew out, a minute, and still they drove. Kaycee visualized an unused rutted road snaking into the woods. Far from people and help.

Without warning the screams and running footsteps from her dream rose in her brain. The shrinking, stifling sense of a dark, closed space.

Panic wrapped around Kaycee's throat. Rodney had made her dream about whatever horror he had planned, hadn't he? *I still need something from you . . .*

They rounded a curve. Long seconds later the car stopped. She couldn't move.

Rodney slid from behind the wheel and opened the back door. He snatched up a handful of Kaycee's hair and yanked hard. "Get out."

# FORTY-SIX

*Headlights.*

Lorraine had only seconds. She threw the van into gear and surged left toward Starling.

"No!" Tammy writhed in her seat. "Belinda!"

"We'll get her, we'll get her!"

Lorraine's back was rammed straight, her fingers like claws around the steering wheel. She had no time to disappear down Starling. At the corner of building two she cut to the right and drove behind the units. Her headlights were off, illumination from the nearest tall lamp receding behind her. She strained to see in the growing dimness. No wash of light was visible from the vehicle at the other end of the lot. Lorraine could only hope that as she passed this side of the building, it passed the other.

Tammy smacked her window and wailed for Belinda. The sounds hissed in Lorraine's ears. "Be quiet!"

The little girl only cried louder.

At the next corner Lorraine braked hard. Tammy slid forward in her seat, caught by her seatbelt.

"Mommy, stop it!"

Lorraine edged the van forward. Leaning as far toward the windshield as possible, she peered to the right down the long side of the building. No car. No lights. The Huff entrance, at the other end of the lot and to the left, was empty. Whoever turned in had passed building two. The driver would now be between the parallel storage buildings.

"I want Belinda!" Tammy threw herself across the console as far as the belt would let her, little hands pummeling Lorraine's shoulder. Surely she was loud enough to be heard. Lorraine wanted to clamp both hands over her mouth.

"Be quiet, Tammy!"

She swerved around the corner and sped down the length of building two.

At the bottom she slid to another stop. Tammy pitched forward again. Her seatbelt caught with a snap. She let out a wail.

Lorraine rolled forward until she could see around the corner.

No one there.

It was him. Had to be. Martin's killer,

maybe some of the other robbers, skulking in the night to unit seven to clean out their millions.

Lorraine threw a wild look toward the Huff entrance. She could make it without being seen — as long as those men stayed up by unit seven. She wanted to roll down her window and listen in the darkness, but Tammy shrieked on. One crack of the window, and they'd hear her.

Lorraine's chest tightened. By now they would be finding the broken hasp. They'd see Belinda.

"Mommyyy!"

Gritting her teeth, Lorraine whipped the wheel toward the entrance and hit the gas.

Every second seemed a lifetime. She wanted to screech out of there but couldn't risk being heard. The van was old, but at least its engine ran quietly.

She checked in the rearview mirror, seeing only the long stretch of concrete leading up to the apartment. It would be the last glimpse of the life she'd had with Martin.

The Huff entrance jumped into view on her right. Barely slowing to check traffic, she darted into the road.

Lorraine accelerated to the next block, then swerved in a right turn. Her muscles hardened to granite. Any minute she expected a car to materialize behind her, shots to ring out.

At the next block she veered left.

Then right again. Then left.

She kept up the jagged pattern, her mind clamped down, all thoughts on hold.

Tammy cried herself out and lay back in her seat, panting. "You *didn't* get *Belinda.*" Her voice trembled with exhaustion and bitterness. "You lied to me, you said you'd get her, but you *didn't.*"

Lorraine's throat ached. What had she done to her daughter this night? What would they do for the rest of their lives?

"I'm so sorry. I'll buy you another bear."

"I don't *want* another bear."

At the edge of town Lorraine spotted a sign for the freeway. She sped up the on ramp, not knowing, not caring which way they were headed.

Not until a few exits had passed did she see they were traveling south.

# FORTY-SEVEN

Kaycee half fell from the SUV, her pulse a hard, steady grind. By the roots of her hair Rodney pulled her up. Needles dug through her scalp. She gasped and staggered, getting her bearings. Through the blackness she could barely make out trees all around her. Vague dual tracks ribboned behind the car's wheels, soon disappearing into the night. Before her slumped an abandoned cabin with sagging porch and soulless windows.

Rodney dug his fingers into her arm. She flinched. "Where's Hannah?"

"Inside."

"There's no lights in there." The thought of a young girl in the dark by herself made Kaycee want to shriek. Was Hannah tied up? Hurt?

Rodney pushed Kaycee's back. "Go."

She tripped up the two porch steps and went down on one knee. Rodney lugged her upright. At the battered entrance he fished in his pocket for a key.

When he pulled the door open its hinges moaned.

They stepped into greater darkness, dispelled only from a wedge of light oozing beneath a closed door on the left. Kaycee blinked, her eyes adjusting. They stood in a sullen and tangled room, a ragged couch, table and chairs at angles, a bookcase of broken, emptied shelves. A bare bulb hung from the ceiling. To the back on the right lay a semblance of a kitchen. The place smelled of must and dirt and a thick heaviness.

Rodney walked toward the closed door. "Hannah."

A pause. The silence vibrated in Kaycee's ears.

"Yeah?"

Kaycee's breath caught in her throat. The familiar voice sounded so small and frightened. She flung herself toward the room, palms flat on the barrier between her and the girl. "Hannah!"

"Kaycee?"

Uneven footsteps, a creak in the floor. A thump hit the other side of the wood. "Kaycee! I want to go *home.*" Hannah burst into tears.

Rodney grabbed Kaycee's elbow and

pulled her back. She swiveled around and launched a fist at his face. He caught her wrist and bent her arm downward. Pain shot through the joint.

"Aah!" Kaycee aimed a knee at his groin. He jerked to his right, slapped both hands on her shoulders and shoved her against the wall. Her head rebounded with a stunning thud. Both eyelids fluttered.

Rodney jumped back and whipped out his gun. The thing had the longest barrel she'd ever seen. *A silencer?*

"Hit me again, and I'll shoot your arm." His words spat venom. "I'll still get what I want out of you, but you'll wish you'd done it without the pain."

Kaycee glared at him, chest heaving and teeth clenched. Hatred like she'd never known swirled acid through her veins. "There was blood in the road where she disappeared. Is it hers?"

Hannah's sobs wheezed from the room. "Kayceeeee."

The girl was so close, just a few inches of wood away. The thought snatched air from Kaycee's lungs. She reached out a shaking hand and pressed it against the door. "I'll get you . . . out of there, Hannah. Promise."

Her head throbbed. Both knees jellied. Kaycee fought to keep upright.

Rodney grunted with disgust. "She fell and scraped her knee. I haven't touched her. Only *you* can keep it that way."

The jelly liquefied. Kaycee slid down the wall to the floor.

"Hannah!" Rodney smacked the door. The girl gulped mid-sob. "Tell her what I told you."

Kaycee tilted her head up. Barely lit from the crack of light beneath the door, Rodney's face looked like calcified wood, the lines in his forehead cut deep, bleak shadows for eyes. He held the gun ready, finger on the trigger and pointed at the door.

The hatred eddied and sizzled. What would be left of Hannah's spirit after the horror this monster had put her through? As if she hadn't already lost enough.

"Hannah!" Rodney kicked the door. Kaycee jumped.

"Give him what he wants!" Hannah screamed. "Give him what he wants, and he'll let me go home!"

Hood-eyed, Rodney smirked at Kaycee. Rage injected her limbs with energy. "I will, Hannah. I will." She pressed both hands against the floor and pushed to her feet.

Rodney's lips coiled into a smile — and Kaycee knew his promises were lies. She stared straight into his heartless eyes — and from a lifetime ago Mark's voice echoed in her head. *"Most people don't have the courage . . ."*

A strange, sudden calm radiated through Kaycee. This man had stalked her because of her columns, her vulnerability. What did *he* fear?

Kaycee licked her lips, her gaze still locked with his. "Hannah, just relax now, okay? Everything's gonna be fine."

More lies. The truth? Rodney had already killed two policemen and maybe Mrs. Foley. He'd kidnapped two people. Now she'd seen his face. So had Hannah. They could identify him. Rodney had everything to lose and nothing to gain by letting them go.

Once he got whatever it was he wanted, he'd kill them both.

# FORTY-EIGHT

Nico stared at the broken hasp in disbelief. He twisted around, his gaze cutting to the stuffed animal he'd seen lying on the concrete as he pulled up.

No. *No!*

He folded over and grabbed the storage-door handle. Yanked it up. The door rolled open with a *skreek.*

Nico peered into the dimness, seeing no shapes. Nothing.

He whipped a slim flashlight from his pocket and thrust it on. Shone the beam into the unit.

Empty.

Nico spat curses. His knees turned to water, and he sat down heavily. The flashlight smacked against the concrete.

Mind reeling, he stared at the four blank walls.

Had Bear done this? Had he sent Denny and his men here for the money? If so, this was a setup. Nico's life would end tonight with a bullet to his head.

Snatching up the flashlight, he dragged to his feet. He stumbled over to the stuffed animal lying on its face. Nico picked it up and turned it over. A teddy bear. His mouth tightened. Was this some sarcastic message from the underboss?

What else could it be?

Nico swiveled around, searching the lot for a dark figure. Who'd be the one to whack him? Denny? Dom?

No one was there.

Bear wouldn't play games like this. If he wanted Nico whacked, the deed would be done by now. Denny or somebody would have been in that storage unit, waiting for him to roll up the door.

Nico gaped again at the bear in his hands. A sudden insane thought popped into his head. Slowly his eyes lifted to glare at Martin Giordano's apartment.

But Giordano hadn't known the money was here. He *hadn't known.* So how could his wife?

Nico threw the bear down and strode across the concrete.

This was foolish. Desperate hope. Giordano's wife wouldn't be in that apartment. News reports said she was hiding somewhere tonight. The apartment wouldn't even be cleaned up yet. And if she had taken the money, home was the last place she'd go. But pure vengeance drove Nico. He so wanted to catch her sleeping in bed, the kid too. He would strangle them both with his bare hands.

Nico passed unit eight, nine, ten, his heart picking up speed, anger drilling his spine. By unit eleven he was running.

He slid to a stop outside the apartment, rocked back on one foot, and kicked the door with all his might. Wood crunched. He kicked again. The door flew open.

Nico stormed inside.

Arms out, feeling his way in the dimness, he tore across the small living room, flashlight turned off. At the top of the hall his foot slipped. He righted himself and switched on the flashlight. *Blood. Footprint.*

Nico didn't care. Rage blazed inside him, burning away all caution. He just wanted to find Martin's wife. By some pretzel twist of fate she'd be here. She *had* to be.

He rounded the corner into the first bedroom and stabbed the bed with a beam of light. It was unmade and empty. He jumped across to the other side, checking the floor behind it. He looked in the closet. Nobody.

Cursing, he left the bedroom and ran to the second. He looked over every inch of it. Then the bathroom.

They were gone. With *his* money.

How could she have done this? How could some stupid *woman* outsmart him like this?

Nico drew a shaking hand across his forehead. His life was over. A bullet to the head would be merciful. Bear would wrench him limb from limb.

He stumbled from the apartment on weak legs.

Back on the pavement, he grasped his head in his hands, the flashlight hard against one temple. He couldn't go to the warehouse empty-handed. Couldn't go home.

Had she taken the money to the police?

That made no sense. She'd have told the police it was here. They'd inform the FBI. G-men would be swarming this place.

Nico dropped his arms to his sides and stared up the concrete at the stuffed animal.

How long ago had she been here? How much lead time did she have?

She'd have to be traveling in a large vehicle. A car could never hold all those boxes.

His blood boiled, fueled by panic. Nico closed his eyes, forcing himself to go over the names of his friends on the Atlantic City police force. Who was working nightshift? How long until he could get a license plate?

Spewing curses, Nico set off running toward the van.

# FORTY-NINE

With one fluid motion Rodney slid his long-barreled gun back into his waistband.

He flipped a wall switch, and the bare bulb above their heads flushed on. Kaycee squinted in the sudden light. For a moment he surveyed her with relish, a lion considering its prey. He walked over to a dusty square table and pulled it beneath the bulb, its legs sputtering across the bare wood floor. "Get a chair." He gestured with his chin as he pulled one up to the table for himself.

Robotlike, Kaycee obeyed. The old wooden chair was light. She slid a look toward the closed door. Hannah had quieted.

"Sit down."

She lowered herself to the chair. Her ankles shook.

Rodney ran his tongue between his lips. He remained standing beside his chair, arms folded. "On the phone you talked to Tricia about dreaming of the dead man. You heard screams and footsteps. You saw a dark yellow floor." His words were clipped, terse.

The sense of those eyes upon her — in her own home. Kaycee's skin flushed. "How did you know?"

"I tapped your phone."

"Why?"

His expression blackened. "Answer the question!"

"Wh— what question?"

"You heard screams and footsteps."

"Yes."

"Just in the dream? Or also while you were awake?"

"I — both."

His mouth flattened in a cold smile. "And you 'saw' a dark yellow floor under the dead man. *Before* you saw it in the picture on your monitor."

Kaycee's fingers curled around the front of her seat. "How'd you get that picture on my computer?"

Rodney shot her a withering look. "Do you think I am incapable? I've studied technology for years. I've planned this. It's nothing for me to get in and out of your house with a motion-sensored camera. I only added a few seconds' delay to it. As for hacking into a computer, that's rudimentary. The TV was harder, but far from impossible. I have special toys that can interrupt a signal. And yes, I can develop a photo so it fades in sunlight." He slapped both palms on the table and leaned toward her. "I'm your 'they,' remember? Your worst fear come true. I live in your walls. I see what you do and hear what you say. You've sensed me since you were a child. Known me practically all your life. So why now do my abilities surprise you?"

Kaycee's neck arched back until it started to cramp. "I . . . you've been watching me, for real, since I was a child?"

He shook his head, as if disgusted with her slowness. "Only in the last year since I found you."

"You've lived in this cabin for a year?"

"Do you think I'm that tasteless? No, no, I've saved this lovely abode just for you."

A year he'd been watching her. The knowledge jarred her bones. A year ago Mandy had died, and Kaycee's own downward spiral began . . .

Understanding glimmered. "Those times I went to the police in Wilmore. When I thought I saw somebody . . ."

He gave her an evil smile. "Part of my plan to make you look crazy. They *don't* believe

341

you, you know."

Maybe not before. They did now.

But now was too late.

Slowly Rodney straightened, leaving two smeared handprints in the dust. "Now, if you don't mind, I'd like to proceed." He swiped his palms together to clean them. "I want to hear about everything you've been sensing."

So he could make sure all those fears came true?

Kaycee's mouth dried out. She needed water.

Rodney yanked up his T-shirt and reached for his gun. "Tell me if you want Hannah to live!"

She jerked. "Yes, I saw the dark yellow floor. I felt a dark, closed space where I could barely breathe. I heard screams and footsteps and saw bright light. And I smelled blood."

Kaycee's words cut off. She eyed Rodney's hand on the gun.

He drew it away. "Anything else?"

She shook her head.

He swung toward the kitchen, reached in a tilted cabinet, and withdrew a large manila envelope. His movements thrummed with dark, excited glee. At the table he pulled out the envelope's contents and slapped them down.

Eight-by-ten color photos. The top one was the first one she'd seen of the dead man. The close-up. Kaycee recoiled.

Rodney thumped a forefinger on the dead man's face. "Who is he?"

Kaycee looked away, sick. "The policeman in the barn. *You* killed him."

Rodney made an impatient sound in his throat and flicked the picture off the stack. The next photo showed the man on the blood-smeared dark yellow floor. Rodney jabbed at it. "That look like a barn floor to you?"

Kaycee's shoulders drew up. "I don't know."

He flicked away the picture to reveal a third. The same man, looking into the camera very much alive. "Who *is* this?"

"I *told* you. Why do you keep asking me, what do you want me to say?"

"You want to help your little friend in there?"

"Yes!"

"Then *think!*" He picked up the top photo and smacked it down to the side. With both hands he spread all the remaining pictures except one, which he left hidden. "Look at them."

Kaycee's vision blurred. She knew what

343

the final hidden photo would show. Mark, dead.

"Look!"

"I am!" Kaycee hitched a breath and wiped her eyes.

"Here." He smacked his fingers on the close-up face of a young woman. Blue eyes, long strawberry blonde hair.

Kaycee stared at it, her mind on the unseen photo. "Who is she?"

"You don't know?"

"I've never seen her before."

"Look again."

"I don't *know* her!"

*"Give him what he wants, and he'll let me go home."* She couldn't help Hannah. They were trapped. Kaycee felt sweat pop out on her forehead. Why was he doing this?

Rodney hit the second photo. "This one." The same man and woman, standing side by side, smiling.

"The policeman and his wife?"

An angry vein throbbed in the side of Rodney's neck. "This one."

Some dingy-looking apartment living room. An old couch, cheap curtains. "I don't know this place." Kaycee's voice flattened. "Please. I don't know it."

"I have one more to show you." Rodney raised his eyebrows, his face a mask of contempt. Kaycee dug her heels into the floor. "Close your eyes."

Her lids slipped shut. Kaycee's chin lowered, silent sobs battering her chest for release. She heard the soft whisk of one slick paper against another.

"You will know who this is."

*Oh, dear God.* Kaycee pressed the back of a hand against her mouth.

"Now look."

Muscles like steel, Kaycee opened her eyes.

Her heart wrenched. Not Mark's dead face.

It was a little girl with long unruly red curls. She'd never seen herself so young. "That's me," she whispered.

Something foreboding and deathly clanked in Kaycee's head, as if the ancient cover of a deep well shook loose its rusty chains.

"What do you know, she gets one right." Rodney lifted a leg around his chair and sat. He listed over the table with expectation, pushing the picture toward her. "Looky here, it's little you, just turned four. It's time you two met. Time you learned your real name. Kaycee Raye? No." He tapped the photo one, two, three times.

"Tammy Giordano."

# FIFTY

*Tammy. Tammy.*

The name glistened like water drops at the bottom of that dark, dried well.

*Tammy Giordano.*

Kaycee's startled gaze rose to Rodney's face. He turned his head, considering her askance. "You remember, don't you."

She swallowed, her eyes dropping to the picture of the woman. In her brain a pale light flashed. She leaned closer to the photo, examining the eyes, the lips. "That's my *mother.*"

"Yes."

"But my mother had dark hair."

"Only as far back as you remember. She dyed it to hide her identity."

Kaycee stared at him, uncomprehending.

"Think, Tammy. Did you ever see pictures of your mom before you were in elementary school? Pictures of her childhood, your

346

parents' wedding? Even *one* photo of your father?"

The well opened up before her. Black, deeper than ever imagined. How had she not known it was there? Kaycee's eyes widened. She shook her head.

The picture of the couple pulled at her gaze. Her mother — and the man.

"M— my father?"

"Yes."

Kaycee drank in the handsome face, the dark hair. Sudden longing swept through her. The father she had never known —

But he was the dead man.

Kaycee gasped. No. None of this was right. "My father died when I was a baby. He was in a car accident."

Rodney separated his lips with a small popping sound. He picked up the manila envelope and stuck his hand inside. "I have one more picture." He looked pleased with himself. Out came an eight-by-ten of her father and her — at the same age she was in the other picture. Kaycee shook her head. "No —"

"Your father died when you were four."

"No. When I was a baby. My mom told me. And he *wasn't* shot!"

"Your mother told you lots of things."

"But I don't even *remember* him!"

347

"You did then." He pointed to Kaycee's picture. "Until your mother — Lorraine Giordano — changed your life and your name and your memories. Until she filled your head with lies."

"Why? Why would she do that?"

Rodney's fingers scrabbled through the stacked photos. He yanked out the close-up of the dead man. "See this? *I* did it. I shot him when you were four."

Kaycee jumped up, knocking into the table. She stumbled sideways. "You're lying."

Rodney leapt to his feet and ran around the table. He caught her by the neck and shoved his face in hers. "I. Shot. Him. You were there, you and your lying mother. She hid you in a closet. Remember that? Remember, Tammy? The darkness. The heat." With one hand he snatched up the picture of the dead man and the blood-smeared floor. Shook it before Kaycee's eyes. She tried to jerk away, but he held her neck with a rocklike grip. "You *saw* this with your own eyes, Tammy — when your mother let you out of the closet. You saw your daddy dead on the floor. You threw yourself at him, got his blood on your hands, your clothes. I saw it all in the police report. That pig's blood I smeared on the picture in your car is nothing. In your head it's your father's blood you're smelling!'

A sob burst from Kaycee. She wrenched her head away. "No. *No!*"

Rodney let her go. She fell sideways, wobbled, then sank to her knees. *No,* she yelled silently, but she knew the truth. A gush of water, newly tapped, poured into the well within her. Her mother had lied to her. All these years, nothing but lies.

The water rose — and Kaycee felt the darkness of the closet. Her little hands beating against her mother's chest. *"Let me go!"*

Vaguely Kaycee registered Hannah calling her name from beyond the door.

"Shut up!" Rodney spat toward Hannah. He strode to Kaycee's side and leaned over her. "You're so close. I've given you everything you need. Now *remember.*"

Kaycee covered her face with her hands. The well filled more, and she heard her panicked footsteps running. *"Daddy!"* Horror shot through Kaycee. She doubled over, head sinking. The dead man's gruesome face flashed in her mind — Tammy's mind. Kaycee felt her four-year-old knees hit the floor, saw her pudgy fingers reaching for her daddy's face. They came away red, and they smelled tinny and sweet . . .

Kaycee's muscles lost all strength. She

lurched sideways and fell, grinding a cheek against dirty wood. Her limbs curled into a ball. The smell of blood filled her head, and she shut down her nostrils, sucking air through her mouth, but it did no good. Kaycee groaned from deep within her stomach. Hands closed around Tammy, and her mother caught her up and ran, her shaking body bouncing up and down against her mother's chest, and a door opened, and sunlight poured in, and her mother ran outside, screaming, and she was screaming, and they tipped back their heads and lengthened their throats and shrieked louder, and somebody shouted, and a man came running, and the sky broke into pieces and hurtled to the ground . . .

Kaycee clawed the dusty wooden floor of the cabin and sobbed.

# FIFTY-ONE

"Get up, Tammy." Rodney shoved a foot against Kaycee's leg. "We're not done."

She lay on her side, shallow-panting, tears spent. The well had filled, and the memories bobbed on the surface, taunting.

Hannah had fallen silent.

"I said get up." Rodney kicked her in the thigh. Pain shot through her muscle. Kaycee gasped. With effort she pushed herself to a sitting position.

Rodney dragged a chair over to her and sat. He leaned toward her, anticipation curling one side of his mouth. "You see it now." It wasn't a question.

Kaycee narrowed her eyes, hating the man. "Why did you kill him?"

"He helped me steal seven million dollars from the bank where he worked. He knew too much."

She stared blankly, her emotions saturated. His crazy words would not soak in.

"Why Hannah?"

"She got in the way. But how convenient when she came up that road. More persuasion for you."

"You knew who she was?"

He smirked. "I know everything about your life, Tammy. I know you were a sick little girl in Atlantic City. So ill your father was willing to rob a bank to help you get well."

Kaycee couldn't reply. She couldn't remember being sick.

"For twenty-six years to this very month I've hunted you and your mother. She was good at hiding. Kept on the move. I'd nearly given up — and then you started writing your columns. Spilling all the details of the paranoia you learned from Monica Raye. Oh, the stories you told of constantly moving as a child, friends forever left behind. No relatives. Her untimely death. The circumstances seemed right, your age was right. I looked up your picture" — he smiled a chilling smile — "and then I knew. It was too late to catch Lorraine Giordano. But I could catch *you.*"

The well water swirled and eddied. Any more from this man and Kaycee would fall in and drown. Her mother, always watching, flicking glances in the rearview mirror.

She hadn't been sick. She'd had a *reason*.

*"I'm sorry for passing it on to you, Kaycee. I tried to make a better life for you."*

Kaycee thrust her fingers into her scalp. Her chest sagged.

"Tell me where the money is." Rodney pushed his thumb against the base of her neck.

"What money?"

"The seven million! Your mother stole it from me."

"You're out of your mind."

"She took it, Tammy. Remember? You were with her. She fled Atlantic City that night."

"My mother would never steal from anybody!"

"She did it to get me back for killing your father. Left me as good as dead."

"I —"

"Where'd she hide it?"

Kaycee emitted a bitter laugh. He'd tortured her with memories, killed two policemen, kidnapped Hannah — for this ridiculous story? "I don't know what you're talking about!"

Rodney jumped up and grabbed her arms. Yanked her to her feet. His face flushed deep red, his eyes specks of coal. "Don't you laugh, don't you *dare* laugh." He pushed her backward and slammed her against a wall. Breath gushed from her throat. "You have no idea what I lost. I chased your mother that night — and could never go back. I lost my home, my family. My *life*." He snarled at Kaycee, his voice like flint. "She chose to run, but Joel 'Nico' Nicorelli didn't. For twenty-six years I've looked over my shoulder. You know what it's like to hide from La Cosa Nostra, Tammy? I had to change my name, my accent, the way I walked. I had to become somebody else, inside and out. You owe me. So you tell me where that money is, or Hannah will never leave here."

"If she took the money, she spent it."

"I've read every column you've written. You and your mother lived simply."

It was true. Kaycee's mouth snapped shut.

"You'll remember! I've made you remember everything else." Rodney jerked her from the wall and into the kitchen. "Here." He rammed her against a cabinet, then flipped her around. "Open it."

Kaycee lifted a shaking arm. Her fingers slipped off the handle. She tried again. The door creaked open.

Inside sat a tattered brown teddy bear. The sight sent her reeling.

*Belinda.*

Heat flooded Kaycee. Why had she thought that name? She shrank from the stuffed animal, then toward it, her hand lifting it out. She pressed its softness against her chest. Terror and comfort and joy and grief sloshed inside the well, spilling new memories over the top.

*"I want Belinda!"*

*"We'll get her, we'll get her."*

Rodney whipped Kaycee to face him. "You dropped it. That night."

Her throat swelled shut. She couldn't breathe. This man's story was for real.

"Where'd you go after that?"

Kaycee shook her head.

"You know! Your mother drove a big Ford van. Close your eyes, see it. Did you drive all night? Did she unload those boxes on the way to some new town?"

"I — I don't remember."

"Yes, you do."

"No, I *don't*."

Rodney's teeth clenched. "I will *make* you remember."

He dragged her away from the cabinets, toward the closed-off room. Belinda slipped from her hands. She heard Hannah crying. At the door Rodney held on to both of her wrists with one hand and shoved his other into a pocket. He brought out a key and unlocked the door. Flung it open.

Hannah sat on a bare mattressed bed, her face tear-stained and eyes puffy. She wore the long-sleeved blue shirt Kaycee remembered, a sweatshirt wadded and thrown into one corner. The knees of her jeans were torn, a dark red scrape across one palm.

Kaycee fought against Rodney's strong grasp. "Hannah —"

"Shut up, Tammy." He pulled her into the room and scowled a look at the girl. "Get out."

Hannah's eyes widened in terror.

"Get out!"

She limp-ran from the bedroom.

One corner of the room thrust inward about four feet square, with a door. Rodney smacked a wall switch, and the bare bulb overhead snapped off. He shut the bedroom door. Instant darkness fell, softened only by light filtering underneath. He hauled Kaycee toward the walled off corner and threw its door open.

She couldn't see it, but she knew. A closet.

"No!" Kaycee's lungs congealed. She would die in there. Her legs tried to pedal backwards, her arms wrenching free and flailing wild punches at Rodney. He ducked and caught them again. "A closet, Tammy. Just like the one you and your mother hid in. Your mind is ripe now. In there, you'll remember. When you do, I'll let you out."

"No, *please,* don't make me —"

Rodney threw her inside and slammed the door. Kaycee thudded against the back wall and collapsed in darkness.

# FIFTY-TWO

The unseen walls closed in. White-hot claustrophobia clawed Kaycee's throat. Her mouth sagged open, air stutter-creaking down her windpipe. Not enough, never enough. She was going to *die.*

Kaycee threw herself forward, hands scrabbling for the door. Her fingers bumped over the frame, seeking a knob.

Nothing. Just bare wood.

Kaycee kicked it. Beat her fists against it. "Lemme *out!*" The small of her back caved in, pushing her stomach up against her lungs. No room to breathe, no oxygen in the air. She keened like a mad woman and flung herself against the door. "Lemme oooutt!"

She gasped and gulped, kicked and pummeled, her limbs out of control, mind shrieking. For how long she didn't know, only that it lasted a lifetime. Each second she would surely suffocate. Each second she didn't, only for her terror to swell. Her torso shrank, her hands and legs shortening. Kaycee's cries rose in pitch like a little girl's. "Lemme go! Mommeeee!"

Kaycee screamed until her throat was raw. Beat until her fists throbbed. Her chest swelled and shrank like creaking bellows. Her side ached. Still she yelled and begged and pounded until her energy waned. Her beating fists slowed, her legs too heavy to kick. In her brain the fear shrieked on, but her limbs lost their ability to fight.

Kaycee sank to the floor, groaning.

A distant sound filtered to her ears. She raised her head. A child crying.

*Hannah.*

The panic beat back, a receding wave on battered shore. Kaycee leaned her head against the wall, trapped and helpless. A new, bright terror arose. If she died in here, no one could save Hannah.

From far away and days gone by came Tricia's voice. *"You have to pray every day. You have to pray against the fear."*

Both hands fisted and pressed against Kaycee's face. For the first time in her life she fully understood what Tricia meant. Asking for God's help here, now, was the only thing she had left.

"Please, God, *please.* Save me and Hannah."

*Mark.*

Kaycee pictured his face, heard his voice. *"When this is over, I'm taking you out."*

She folded over and sobbed.

Minutes ticked by, long and black. Hot. The well memories swelled. Fresh terror fluttered wings against Kaycee's chest.

No. *No.*

She listened. Silence drummed in her ears. Where was Hannah? What was Rodney doing to her? Kaycee held her breath, straining to hear.

She had to get *out* of here.

Not until she remembered . . .

Could she?

Kaycee blinked at the blackness, willing herself to focus on that night. Losing Belinda. Crying for her bear . . .

The well water shifted — and she saw her mother at the wheel of the van, back ramrod straight.

*Yes, yes, come on!*

Little Tammy's eyes drooped with sleep. Her head lolled against the passenger seat . . . and the memory faded.

Kaycee fought to get it back. It wouldn't come.

Where had they gone that night? Kaycee's

360

first memory of a specific town wasn't until she started kindergarten at five and a half. Maybe they wandered like gypsies till then. How terrified she must have been as a four-year-old without a home, with a new name. What her mother must have done to chase the memories from her head.

*"She stole that money to get back at me . . ."*
*"I tried to make a better life for you . . ."*

Kaycee shifted her legs — and new fear fibrillated her limbs. She clamped her jaw. In another minute the claustrophobia would come rushing back. This time it would kill her. She focused hard on remembering, but nothing more came. Only a dark hole where her early childhood had been.

Why should Rodney believe she would ever remember where the money was? Even if she could conjure the scene in her mind, after all these years she may not be able to name the place. The man was crazy. As obsessed with the millions as she'd become with her own fears —

A trapdoor opened in Kaycee's stomach. The walls closed in. New panic surged up her spine. Kaycee shoved to her feet and hurtled herself against a wall. A second time, a third.

Deep in her brain a voice shouted no, no! She had to save Hannah.

Kaycee gulped two deep breaths and kicked what she thought was the door.

"Rodney! Nico! I remember!"

Silence.

"Nico!"

Muffled noise. Footsteps approached. Light filtered in from beneath the door. Kaycee fixed upon it as if she'd never seen such a blessed sight. But now she saw the closet walls, the closed space. Her chest burst open —

A metal sound. The lock clicked and the door flung back. Light bounced into Kaycee's eyes. She squinted, one hand flinging up.

Rodney looked her up and down with contempt. She could imagine her splotchy face, the wild curls. This man detested her for her fears.

Kaycee pushed hair off her cheeks, chest heaving. She *had* to get hold of herself. Center.

"Where is it?" he demanded.

Such arrogance on his face. Kaycee swallowed. "Not till I see Hannah."

Rodney's jaw flexed. He turned his head slightly toward the door, gaze fixed on Kaycee. "Hey! Come here!"

Timid steps. Hannah edged across the threshold, her face pale and chin tucked in.

Kaycee's heart leapt. "Hannah, you okay?"

The girl's gaze cut to Rodney as if seeking permission to speak. He broke eye contact with Kaycee and glowered at Hannah. Her head shrank down between her shoulders.

Anger at her victimization exploded in Kaycee. She barreled out of the closet and into Rodney's chest.

He stumbled backward, arms flailing. His hand caught Kaycee's wrist. One thing about fear and rage — they knew how to shoot adrenaline. She plowed the man back with all her might. He tripped, floundered sideways, and fell, pulling her down with him.

Hannah screamed. Kaycee heard other screaming — and realized it was her own.

She thrust up on one knee and threw a wild punch at Rodney's face. His nose crunched. Blood spurted on her hands. He cried out in fury, slapped both hands against her shoulders, and pushed. She tumbled off. Her temple thudded against the floor.

Rodney sprang up, blood running down his mouth, his chin. He hulked around to face her, right hand shoved under his T-shirt for his gun.

Kaycee shook her head hard to clear it. Rodney's fingers grazed the top of his weapon. She rocked back on her spine, drew up both legs like a spring-load, and shot her heels straight into his left knee. It snapped backward. He yelled and collapsed.

Strength borne of terror pushed Kaycee to her feet. Pain scrunched Rodney's face, his eyes murderous. He would kill her now, forget the money. Or make her watch while he shot Hannah. For an eternal second she hovered, not knowing what to do. Rodney's uninjured leg dug against the floor, scuttling him around to face her in a jagged half circle. Both hands fumbled for his weapon. Blood smeared down his cheek, over the wood. The smell rose in Kaycee's nostrils. Her stomach flipped. In her mind she saw her daddy's frozen, bullet-holed face, his blood streaked against dark yellow . . .

Panic blossomed in her chest. Kaycee pivoted and fled.

She tore across the room, thinking *no, no, get the gun!,* knowing she'd be shot if she tried. She raced across the threshold and flat-footed to a stop, head swiveling. Hannah hunched to her right, fingers to her mouth, still as stone. Kaycee grabbed her arm. "Come on!"

They ran for the front door. Kaycee yanked it open and pushed Hannah onto the sagging porch. Weak light spilled from the cabin's darkened windows. The night stretched beyond, so very dark. She saw the SUV in the driveway.

Were the keys inside?

Uneven, hard footsteps shook the porch floor. Kaycee swiveled. Rodney lurched from the bedroom, purple-faced, gun in hand.

Kaycee slammed the front door.

She caught Hannah's shoulder and jerked her sideways. A muted *crack* sounded. A bullet hit the door.

Hannah wailed. Kaycee hauled her toward the side of the porch. They jumped down a foot into dimness and sped for the woods.

# FIFTY-THREE

Kaycee and Hannah stumbled through blackness, around thick trees, branches whipping their bodies, their faces. Hannah ran with an awkward gait. "My knees." Her voice hitched. "I scraped them bad." The close air tanged with dampness and wood. Kaycee pulled Hannah along, panting, not letting her slow. *Run, run, run,* her mind shrieked, but the more they ran the greater her fear. Where was Rodney?

On they staggered. Hannah fell twice, Kaycee once. They helped each other up, grunting. Hannah couldn't stop crying.

How far had they gone? What direction? In her mind Kaycee could see the near ninety-degree turn of Shanty Hill. The long rutted trail they'd driven to the cabin had taken them back toward Highway 29, parallel to Shanty Hill above that hairpin turn. But how far? She and Hannah had leapt off the porch to the side and run straight. But then what? Had they gone in circles?

The trees thinned. They burst out into a small open area. A stingy crescent moon dribbled light. Kaycee whipped her head around, seeking a house, a road. Nothing but more woods.

Two green eyes low to the ground stared at them, unblinking.

Hannah yelped. Kaycee jerked her back into the trees. They ran. Hannah clutched Kaycee's hand. "Wh-what was that?"

"I don't know. A cat."

They bore left, skirting the meadow. Hannah was slowing. "I . . . can't go . . . any more."

"Can't stop yet."

Kaycee slipped and went down on one knee on something hard. Pain shot into her joint. She whooshed out air and forced herself up, limping.

Time stretched on, the forest never ending. No houses, no help. No road. Where were they?

Hannah cried harder. The guttural sounds filled the night. "Shh," Kaycee squeezed her fingers.

"I c-can't go any m-more." She sank to the ground.

Kaycee sat down beside her and drew her close. "Hannah, shh. You have to be quiet."

Hannah buried her face in Kaycee's neck and choked her tears into silent gulps.

Kaycee felt a tree trunk at her back. She shifted and leaned against it, exhausted.

They breathed and rested. For how long? Were they far enough away from the cabin? Hannah stopped crying. Finally they huddled, shivering.

How much night remained? They had to find help before the dawn betrayed them.

Noise in the distance. Kaycee froze, head cocked.

A crackle of underbrush. A second and third.

Rodney.

Hannah sucked in a breath and whimpered. Kaycee slid an arm around her shoulder and drew her in. She put her mouth to Hannah's ear. "Shh. Don't move."

The snapping grew closer. Kaycee's muscles tamped down. Should they run? He'd hear them.

She couldn't have wounded him as badly as she thought. He might move faster than she could push Hannah. And he had a gun.

The sounds kept coming. Kaycee tilted her head, gauging. They were a little to her right. Twenty feet? Ten?

The noise stopped. Kaycee could hear Rodney's thick breathing.

Hannah ducked her head farther, shuddering. Kaycee's arm around her shook. Her heart rammed, her body craving oxygen. She pulled in air through her nose, willing absolute silence.

Time spun out. Rodney's clothes rustled. *Oh, God, please, God . . .*

Hannah's fingers dug into Kaycee's side.

"I smell you," Rodney said.

Sudden light beamed through the darkness. Kaycee stiffened. It cruised away from them to the right. The left. Underbrush crunched. Kaycee could make out Rodney's left arm, holding the flashlight. His right hand clutched the gun. The beam arched around, spanning over trees, a bush, a fallen dead trunk, sweeping toward them, twenty feet away . . . fifteen . . . ten.

Kaycee's breathing stopped.

Hannah lifted her head, saw the light. She squeaked.

The beam swung to her face.

She slapped a hand over her eyes.

Rodney wheezed a long, mocking laugh. "Well, well."

He made his way toward them, chuckling, so proud of himself. Kaycee watched him come, one leg dragging. This thief and murderer, killer of her daddy and policemen, kidnapper of children. The man who filled her mother's life with terror.

Kaycee's mouth hardened. Something within her shifted, then snapped. Like ice floe her fear broke off and drifted away.

She eased her arm from around Hannah's shoulders. Slid both palms to the ground. The muscles in her legs quivered, gathering energy.

Rodney stopped three feet away. Kaycee could see blood smeared on his face. "Did you really think you could run from me, Tammy?"

"You never caught my mother."

His jaw flexed. "Where's the money?"

"She sank the boxes in the Atlantic Ocean."

Rodney's head pulled back. "You're lying."

Kaycee glared at him.

His gun moved to aim at Hannah. "Try again."

"Okay, okay, just kidding!" Kaycee raised both hands. "They're in some cave at a rocky beach on the ocean. Not too far from where we lived. Maybe I could find it . . ."

He stared at her, assessing. "If you're lying, she's dead."

"Would I lie to you?"

He backed away two steps. "Get up. Slowly."

Hannah shrank against Kaycee's side. Kaycee pushed to her feet, helping the girl up. "I don't know how to get back to the cabin."

Rodney gestured with his head to the right. "That way."

Even with a gun at their backs, the return trek seemed so short. They *had* gone in circles. Directed by the flashlight, Kaycee helped Hannah in as straight a line as possible, over fallen logs, through thick forest. Along the way, she prayed.

They stepped from woods to a sudden clearing. There sat the cabin, dim light filtering from a dirty side window.

"In the car. You're driving."

"All the way to New Jersey?" Obsessed was too tame a word for this guy.

"I've hunted you for twenty-six years. Nothing is stopping me now."

They headed over soft wild grass toward the SUV. Rodney opened the back door for Hannah to crawl in. She collapsed on the seat. He shut the door.

Rodney moved to set the flashlight on its side on the car hood, beam aimed slightly away from his body. He switched the gun to his left hand, aiming at Kaycee's face. His right hand slid into his pants pocket. Out came the car keys. He held them toward her. She reached to take them —

Sudden light from down the driveway swathed the forest behind her. Kaycee registered the sound of a car engine.

Rodney's head swiveled toward the light. Survival reflex flared through Kaycee. This was her chance. She rammed her outstretched hand against the long gun, knocked its aim away from her face. Her right foot rocketed into Rodney's groin.

"Unkh." He doubled over as car beams cut across their bodies. Kaycee squinted in the brightness. The keys clicked to the ground. Rodney staggered, teeth clenched, clutching his weapon with both hands.

Tires ground to a halt and a door smacked open. "Police! Drop it!" The raucous command wrenched through the air.

Rodney waved the gun toward the sound. "Drop it *now!*"

Kaycee jumped away from Rodney. Wheezing a curse, he aimed at the light —

Three shots split the night. Kaycee screamed. Hannah's muffled cries rose from the car.

Holes torched in Rodney's chest. He jerked in a death dance and thudded to the ground face down. His fingers still curved around the gun.

Running footsteps approached. Kaycee

leapt toward Rodney. "Stay back!" the policeman yelled, but her body moved as if yanked by a ghostly arm. For surely, surely this evil being would twitch to life and kill them all . . .

With a grunt, she kicked the weapon away from Rodney's fingers. It slid beneath the SUV.

The officer ran up, pushed Kaycee aside. His gun remained ready in his right hand. Bathed in light from the car beams, he knelt down and felt for a pulse in Rodney's neck. Kaycee raised an arm to block the light from her eyes. In a stunning, mind-reversing second her blinking gaze registered two things: Hannah's whitened face pressed against the car window — and the profile of a man risen from the dead.

# FIFTY-FOUR

"Mark?" The name trembled from Kaycee's tongue. She squeezed her eyes shut and reopened them, praying she wasn't imagining the sight before her.

The policeman rose and slid his gun in its holster. For the first time Kaycee noticed the hard rise and fall of his shoulders. Lingering adrenaline and fear shafted across Mark's face. He gazed at her as if shell-shocked. "He's dead."

Her brain scrambled for clarity. It wouldn't come. "So are you."

"I am?"

"Rodney said so." Kaycee swallowed. "No, maybe he didn't. But I thought . . ."

They surged toward each other. Mark pulled her close, so tightly she couldn't breathe. A silent sob racked from her chest.

"It's okay, it's okay." He smoothed her hair. "It's over."

Was it, after twenty-six years? Even now

she half expected Rodney's glaring eyes to pop open, his zombie arm to snatch up the gun . . .

Hannah cried loudly in the SUV. Mark let Kaycee go and stepped over to open the back door. Hannah spilled out into Kaycee's arms. She pulled Hannah across the rutted driveway into the grass, away from Rodney's body. There, beyond the glare of headlights from Mark's police car, they clung to each other and cried.

Mark tucked his chin down and spoke into his radio. A response crackled back. Kaycee's eyes followed his every move as he walked to the gaping door of his car and closed it. He approached Kaycee and Hannah. Gently, he laid a hand on the girl's head.

"We've been looking all over for you, Hannah. Your daddy's been so worried."

"I wanna see him." Her words muffled into Kaycee's shirt.

"You will — real soon. An officer's with your dad at your house. They're on their way."

Hannah trembled with chills. Kaycee rubbed her shoulders. Still Kaycee stared at Mark, hardly believing he stood before her. "She's got a sweatshirt in the cabin. In the bedroom."

"I'll get it." He turned away.

"And Mark. Somewhere in there is a stuffed brown bear."

"Okay."

She watched him step into the cabin of horrors and shuddered.

A moment later he returned. Hannah put on the sweatshirt and clutched Belinda to her neck. A memory surged in Kaycee's mind of herself at four, clinging to that same bear. Sudden, violent longing for her mother washed through her.

Mark put his arms around them both in a three-way hug. "We've had officers out this direction for hours, looking for you two." His voice sounded gruff. "We saw you on film from the camera at South Lexington, Kaycee. Got the license plate of the SUV."

Her throat tightened. "He made me lie down in the backseat. I sat up on purpose."

"Smart thinking. We ran the plate. Owner's name is Rodney List."

"That's him." Kaycee's eyes roved toward Rodney's still form. "But his real name's Joel Nicorelli. They called him Nico."

Mark made a sound in his throat. "He killed Officer Nelson."

Kaycee's chin dropped. She closed her eyes. An officer dead because of *her.* "How did you know I was gone?"

"Mrs. Foley was watching from her bedroom window upstairs and saw two figures at the opposite corner of your property. Couldn't tell who it was. I'd never have seen them. Officer Nelson was supposed to cover that side. I checked your house. The side door was unlocked. I couldn't believe it." Mark's arm tightened around Kaycee's back. "I'd already called the chief. He found Nelson in the barn." For a moment Mark was silent. "It's an answer to prayer we found *you.* For all we knew you could have been taken to High Bridge or beyond. We knocked on doors out on the highway for hours, but nobody had seen anything. Finally some guy down Shanty Hill said he'd seen a big car turning up toward this abandoned place —"

A car engine revved in the distance. Red lights strobed the forest, the cabin. A police vehicle surged to a stop behind Mark's car, and Chief Davis jumped out. Hannah broke away from Kaycee, face lit with anticipation, and started toward the car. A second later she slid to a halt. "Where's my dad?" she wailed.

Chief Davis ran to her and grabbed her shoulders. "Any minute, honey," he said. "Any minute."

More blood-red flashed through the night.

In quick succession two police cars bumped up the driveway. Ryan Parksley leapt from one before it stopped. "Hannah!"

"Daddyyy!"

They ran to meet each other, arms outstretched. Kaycee watched through blurred eyes, her heart tied in a knot.

Chief Davis strode toward her. "You all right?"

She nodded.

He gave Mark a grim smile. "Good work." He veered toward Nico's body, where other officers were already gathering.

Mark turned to join them, then stopped. He looked back to Kaycee. Laid a hand against her cheek.

"This *is* over now. You're going to be fine — stronger than before. You'll see."

Memories stabbed through Kaycee. Her father, dead and bloodied on a dark yellow floor. Belinda, fallen from her arms onto concrete. Her mother's nervous glances in a rearview mirror. *I tried to give you a better life . . .*

Kaycee's throat convulsed. If she fought her way back to strength it wouldn't be of her own power.

"Yeah. I will."

One side of Mark's mouth crooked upward. "And don't forget — you promised me a date."

Kaycee held his gaze until she managed a weary smile. "It's not going to be on a Kings Island rollercoaster, Mark Burnett."

■ ■ ■ ■

# PART 4

■ ■ ■ ■

Feed your faith and your fears will starve
to death.

Unknown

# FIFTY-FIVE

Kaycee stepped from the white stone police station building, a cold Ale-8-One in her hand, and gazed up East Main. May in Wilmore. On both sides of the street, cherry trees blazed pink. Another few weeks and the town would hang the large multicolored baskets of flowers from hooks on every lamppost. These would stretch from the railroad tracks up East Main, then to the right on North Lexington, all the way to the outskirts of town.

She tipped the Ale-8-One to her mouth and drank.

Today was her *monthaversary* — Mark's word. One month ago today she'd looked *them* in the face.

"One man," Mark had reminded her last night over supper in Lexington. It was their ninth date — but who was counting? "He was just a man."

Kaycee prickled. "Easy for you to say."

"Hey, I'm not saying he wasn't danger-ous." Mark held up both palms — *peace, peace.* "Downright evil. I'm glad I killed him."

She thought of Officer Nelson's wife and two children at his funeral. Hannah's night-mares. Her own father's dead face, her mother's life on the run. "Yeah. Me too."

Chief Davis had alerted the FBI regarding Rodney's claim of an Atlantic City bank robbery twenty-six years ago. Over the past four weeks of investigation the story had unfolded. A record heist at the time, un-solved until now, and the inexplicable circumstances of Martin Giordano and his wife and daughter. The families of La Cosa Nostra in Atlantic City had long since lost their power, but in the early 1980s the organization was alive and well. Rodney List — Joel "Nico" Nicorelli — had been a part of the Lucchese family. Like Mark said — just one man. With his own failures and fears.

Mark slid his hand across the table and placed it over Kaycee's. "You make peace with Mrs. Foley?"

"I'm not screaming at her anymore if that's what you mean."

"At least she knows you're not crazy. You're vindicated."

"Like she'd ever admit it."

Mark's lips curved. "How's Hannah?"

"Haven't talked to her for days now. Her dad's still mad at me. Can't blame him."

"You brought her back. Safe."

"I'm the reason she was taken in the first place."

Mark shook his head.

"I'm just giving them time." Kaycee lifted a shoulder. "That family has so much healing of their own to do. Hannah needs to be talking to her father and stepmom right now, not me. And she's getting better. They all are."

So was Kaycee. She looked over her shoulder less these days. In time she would regain the strength she'd had before Mandy's death. And one day she would conquer her paranoia completely.

Mark squeezed her fingers. They were silent for a moment.

"You write that column?" he asked.

"You know I did, Mr. Self-Satisfied."

"See. I was right."

"Yeah, well. Don't let it go to your head."

Now standing on Main, Kaycee smiled at the memory. She took another drink of Ale-8-One and started up the sidewalk. Behind her, the glass door swished. "Kaycee."

She turned around. "Hey, Chief."

"Where you headed?"

"To Tastebuds for a pizza and soda. Wanna come?"

"Can't, I'm going out to do DARE in a minute."

The DARE car — the spiffy 1968 Ford Galaxy 500. "You promised me a ride last week."

"That's why I came out. Here's your chance."

"Cool. I'll wait here; you bring it around."

He glanced toward the building. "It's just down in the basement."

Okay. Hidden agenda. He'd obviously been talking to self-appointed therapist Mark. Kaycee gave him a look. "What happened to your velvet touch?"

One side of his mouth turned up. "You coming or not?"

It was a chance to face down a fear. The basement would be lit. Chief would be with her.

It would be terrifying.

"Yeah. Yeah, I'm coming."

She followed him back inside the building and through the station. Out the rear door and to the rickety-looking wooden steps to the basement. *Oh, boy.* Kaycee hung tight to the banister on the way down.

The fear gripped her before she hit the last stair. Kaycee's knuckles whitened around the Ale-8-One bottle. Her mouth creaked open. *Breathe.*

Shoulders drawn in, she stepped onto the concrete floor. She glanced around, eyes grazing the wood and stone walls, the door to the storage area. The shiny DARE car sat in the center, backed in and facing the basement's wide double doors.

The wooden posts and low-beamed ceiling closed in. Kaycee's stomach flipped. Her right hand jerked to the base of her neck.

"You okay?" Chief asked.

She nodded stiffly, eyes bugged.

"We'll be out real soon." He hurried over to push the doors wide open. Sunlight streamed in. "Okay, in the car."

Kaycee got in the passenger seat, gripping the Ale-8-One bottle, her spine like stone. Chief started the engine and drove into the blessed afternoon.

She exhaled. One deep breath. Two. Sweat trickled down her temple.

Chief Davis put the car in park. "I'll get the doors." He gave her an encouraging nod. "Good for you, Kaycee. You did it."

She looked back through the doors at the mine-like basement. A shudder jagged between her shoulder blades. The place looked like it would eat her alive.

Kaycee managed a wan smile. "Yeah. I did it."

## WHO'S THERE?
### BY KAYCEE RAYE
# Good-bye and Hello

By now you've heard the whole story.

The media has a way of whisking the corners for the last bit of dust. Despite my efforts to crawl into a cave somewhere and hide, you've surely seen every detail on TV, read it in the papers (including the one in your hand), and devoured even more in magazines.

Contrary to certain rumors, I have no idea where the money is. I am not planning to snatch it up and disappear. Been done already. The statute of limitations may have passed for prosecution of the crime, but as far as I'm concerned, the Atlantic City Trust Bank still deserves its cash back. Some day, if my memories continue to surface, I may flash on where it is. If that happens, the bank will be the first to know.

It *is* true I almost stopped writing this column. It took a certain person to convince me it's only just begun.

What now to say to you, my loyal readers, about fear? Bees, heights, closed spaces, the dentist's drill, roller coasters — all of these things still make my gut tremble. Don't suppose that will ever stop. But I have seen my worst fear come true and lived to tell the tale. In a surprising way, the experience has set me on the path to healing.

Okay, the path looks really long. And narrow. Did I mention curvy?

Confession time. I wanted to stop writing "Who's There?" because I was afraid. Ha-ha.

Some weeks ago a certain man accused me of stirring up fear through this column just to make a few bucks. At the time I wanted to slug him. Guess what. He's the one who's now convinced me to continue "Who's There?" He got in my face recently, this time accusing me of the worst affront of all in his book — withholding the truth.

"You helped me face my own fear, Kaycee," he said. "Now write that column and tell them what *you* learned."

So here I am. What truth did I learn? Fear is everywhere. But that's only half the story. The other half?

God is bigger than fear.

Once upon a time I longed for a magic wand to make me all better. There isn't one. Day to day I still struggle. And frankly, right now there's lots of new stuff to work through. But a few nights ago I was gazing at the full moon, and an amazing thought occurred to me. God hung it. That's a lot of power. If he could do that, why in the world did I fail to believe he could help me overcome my little problems?

Apparently God also invented irony. Soon after promising him I'd write about this epiphany, I took a walk to a friend's house. I passed an empty field. Lo and behold — bumblebees.

One of these Cessnas with stingers decided on a flyby. You've seen cartoons of a bee in flight, screeching on the brakes and pulling a Uey? Happens to me every time.

The bumblebee came back around, closer. I screamed and ducked.

Don't ever let anyone tell you bees are color-blind. No way. They take one look at my bouncy red hair and go nuts. Like it's the grandest, juiciest flower they've ever laid eyes on in their entire life. Either that or they've just died and gone to heaven.

My movement scared the thing off, but not for long. In a flash it was back with a vengeance.

For all their flying power, bumblebees lack decent radar. On its final flyby the thing miscalculated and rammed into my head.

I shrieked bloody murder, and my knees gave out. The bee bounced off and buzzed away. Sorely disappointed, to be sure. The enticing flower had turned out to be hard and sweaty. And loud.

I cowered on the ground, gusting air. That's when I noticed *all* the bumblebees in that field. Back and forth they flew, and I'd have to pass every one of them. A good half would do flybys of their own.

The thought sent me shaking.

Sure, I should fight any fear that holds me back from accomplishing something I need to do. That's what fear usually does. But I *didn't* have to walk in that direction. In the recent past, even if a diamond mine waited on the other side of that field, I'd have turned around. No more.

So what did I do?

I took a deep breath, whispered a prayer for God's help . . . and set out down that sidewalk.

And that is what I hope for you.

# EPILOGUE

Some twelve hours after she'd fled Atlantic City, Lorraine Giordano found herself near Lexington, Kentucky. She needed to get off the interstate and find a place to stay. The April skies drizzled rain, the whir of the windshield wipers grinding her raw nerves. She hadn't stopped to rest except for bathroom breaks, to feed Tammy, and do what she had to do. Her emotions had drained to empty. She felt nothing. Dead.

Lorraine turned off the interstate onto Highway 68.

Hours ago in the parking lot of an all-night grocery store she'd shined her flashlight into an opened box in the back of the van. She'd never planned to use a dollar of that blood money, but now she had no choice. Lorraine lifted out three hundred in twenty dollar bills.

In the store she bought hair dye and scissors. Her long strawberry blonde tresses were now gone, replaced by dark brown hair cut blunt above her shoulders. Tammy's red curls were gone too. Lorraine had cut them all off and dyed what was left. Tammy sobbed as she felt the strangeness of her head.

"It's a new game, honey." Lorraine's heart lay sodden with guilt. "You have a new name, too. Kaycee. Isn't that cute?"

Before dawn, behind a Kmart in another town, Lorraine used her screwdriver to steal a license plate off an old car and put it on the van. She put her own plate in the glove compartment.

Now in the afternoon her fingers felt glued to the wheel, her backside as numb as her brain. Pure adrenaline and fear had kept her alert. Finally she felt her body shutting down.

The money in the back of the van thrummed and vibrated. Surely every driver could see it. Every police officer could smell it. Every time she stopped she'd wanted to get rid of the boxes. But where? That was a lot of weight to move. And how far were *they* behind her? She'd seen their headlights in the storage parking lot. They'd been close then, so very close.

Lorraine's eyes flicked to the rearview mirror.

Highway 68 wound by green, rolling hills, white fences, and horses.

"Mommy, look at their tails swish." Kaycee's voice sounded throaty from coughing. She'd slept much of the way. Now she squirmed in her seat.

"Pretty."

The road forked. A sign on the left read Highway 29. The way to Wilmore and Asbury College.

A college town. People coming and going. Lorraine bore left.

They rolled into town and fate intervened. Lorraine spotted a sign: *Furnished Two-Bedroom Home For Rent.* She followed the directions to a small white wood house. Pulling over to the curb, she stared at another sign in the front yard. *For rent — go to 203, next door.* She still needed a new name, new driver's license. She had no idea how to get a new identity. And she'd need more money.

Lorraine drove away to a quiet street and opened the back of the van. From the closest box she drew out two thousand dollars in twenties and stuffed them in her purse.

The landlord at 203 was an elderly lady, Martha Wiscom. She took one look at Lorraine's worn face and Kaycee's puffy eyes, and invited them in for a sandwich.

Before long Kaycee was sitting on her lap. Lorraine told the woman her name was Monica Stanling. She'd saved every dime to finally flee an abusive husband. Mrs. Wiscom rented her the house on the spot. Monica paid for the first month in cash.

Tired as she was, she could not rest until she'd moved every one of the twelve boxes into the house's unfinished basement. She withdrew another five thousand in bills and hid them under her mattress.

The next day while Kaycee stayed with Mrs. Wiscom, Monica drove to Cincinnati. She cruised residential streets, looking for a used car for sale. She found a gray Volvo station wagon, parked her van a block away, and walked back to buy the Volvo for two thousand dollars. In cash. She drove back to the van and got in it. She headed for a strip mall she'd seen on the next block. Behind the buildings she parked and pulled a large paring knife from her purse. She took the remaining three thousand out of her purse and put it into a brown grocery bag, leaving her wallet and driver's license behind. She dropped the purse on the floor.

Using her screwdriver she replaced the stolen license plate with the van's original one. Back in the van Monica slid the stolen plate into the grocery bag of money.

She picked up the paring knife and held it for a long time, heart scudding.

*For you, Kaycee.*

She drew the blade across her left forearm.

The blinding sting hissed air through her teeth. Instant tears bit her eyes. Monica pressed her hand over the cut, smearing blood on her palm and fingers. She swiped those fingers over the seat, pressed them into the dashboard.

From the glove box she took a dishtowel and wrapped it around her arm.

The keys remained in the ignition.

Monica got out of the van again, eyes blurred, and walked back to the Volvo. She carried the grocery bag. Halfway between Cincinnati and Wilmore she pulled the license plate out of the bag and threw it away.

For the next few weeks Monica held the cut on her arm closed with tight Band-Aids. She didn't want to explain to some doctor how she'd gotten it. The cut would eventually heal into a ropey scar.

The boxes of money sat in her basement, ticking time bombs. She had to find a way to get rid of them.

She bought a small television and watched news constantly. The Atlantic City police along with the FBI were searching for her and her daughter, as well as the seven million stolen from Trust Bank. They still weren't sure what the connection between the two crimes might be. A lock on one of the storage units where Lorraine Giordano served as manager had been cut through, her apartment's front door kicked in. A man's footprints were found in the blood on the floor. The mother and daughter apparently had been abducted. Authorities feared for their lives.

Footprints in her apartment. A busted front door. They had come for her.

Monica couldn't stop trembling.

The next day with Kaycee along she drove four hours to Nashville and stayed until she found a man who furnished her a driver's license and social security number in the name of Monica Stanling. She didn't ask how he managed it. She paid him five hundred dollars in cash.

Everywhere she went, Monica cast frightened glances over her shoulder.

She took Kaycee to the physician in Wilmore, with an office down on East Main. The doctor drew three vials of Kaycee's blood for tests. Poor Kaycee screamed and cried. The physician also gave her two "scratch" tests on her wrists, one for TB and one for some disease Monica had never heard of — histoplasmosis, a fungus on the lungs.

When the ordeal was over, Monica treated Kaycee to an old-fashioned ice cream soda at the nearby drug store. Only then did Kaycee stop crying.

Within four days the histoplasmosis wrist was red and swollen up to her elbow.

"No treatment for it," the doctor said. "But in a year or two she should be fine. Make sure she gets lots of rest in the meantime. Feed her plenty of protein. Give her all the steaks and milkshakes she wants."

After all the expensive tests in Atlantic City, it came down to one simple "scratch" by a small-town doctor. And no money needed for treatment. Day after day Martin's desperate voice echoed in Monica's ears. *"I just want Tammy to get well . . ."*

She fed Kaycee steak and took her to the drugstore for an ice cream soda three or four times a week.

One night as Monica washed dishes she heard her old name on the news. The van had been found. Bloody fingerprints inside matched her blood type. Authorities were now looking for the bodies of Lorraine and Tammy Giordano.

But *they* knew the truth.

Monica's paranoia grew. She searched for

them constantly, not even knowing what they looked like. A glance too long in her direction could send her reeling. She fought to hide her fear.

Within a month she landed a clerical job, working for the City of Wilmore's Utility Department. Kaycee attended preschool at a church when she was well enough. On sick days she stayed with Mrs. Wiscom. Monica worked hard and gained the favor of her boss. Soon she was taking on extra responsibilities.

To house supplies, the department used a locked storage room in the police station's cave-like walkout basement. Looking at the white stone front of the station, a person wouldn't even know the basement existed. The entrance around the back was fairly secluded, nothing nearby but the rear of other buildings fronting Main and the railroad tracks. The basement had a low-beamed ceiling, part stone walls and a concrete floor. Monica found the place eerie.

One day a pipe broke in the Utility Department's storage room ceiling. Water doused everything and stood two inches on the floor before maintenance stopped the flow. Monica hustled down to the room to help move out supplies.

"Man," her boss complained as they huffed boxes of who-knew-what out to the center area of the basement, which remained dry. His face was sweaty and gray. "Most of this stuff goes way back. Never even seen that rear wall, and I've worked here for twenty years."

Monica surveyed him. "You don't look so good."

"Think I'm gettin' sick."

When they were done it was almost five o'clock. Monica stood staring at the big room as workers moved in to mop up the water.

"Looks different, doesn't it." Her boss sagged against the wall.

She'd found what she needed in the basement of a police station. The irony pierced.

"Get home and go to bed," she said. "I'll return tonight and move everything back in."

"You can't do that yourself."

"Pay me double-time, and I'll show you what I can do."

He sighed. "At least wait until tomorrow. Maybe I'll be better then."

"No you won't. Besides, I have that big project starting in the morning, and you know it. I won't be able to leave my desk for days."

Her boss gave in. He handed her his keys to the basement door and storage room.

That night in her house, Monica stood over two open boxes of the stolen money, biting her cheek. One box held twenties, the other held hundred-dollar bills.

Blood money.

This would be the last time.

She pulled out a total of fifty thousand in twenties and hundreds and hid it in her closet. Savings, for when she and Kaycee had to move on.

When that day came, Monica promised herself, she'd let her daughter's beautiful red curls grow back. And she'd change their last name one more time, to cover their tracks here. Maybe to Raye. She liked the sound of that.

With the fifty thousand taken out, Monica was able to consolidate what was left in the two boxes into one. She resealed the box with packing tape. It would take two trips to drive all eleven boxes to the police-station basement. Kaycee would have to ride along.

First Monica took a black felt tip pen to the side of each box, writing in large capital letters: BANK RECORDS. KEEP.

On the concrete behind the police station, Monica left the Volvo idling as she unlocked the basement's wide double doors. She pulled them back, drove her car inside, and shut them. One night-shift policeman would be on patrol in town. Not likely he'd find her down there, if he happened by the station at all. Even if he did, she had reason to be there.

She unlocked the windowless storage room and flipped on the light switch. Back in the Volvo she cut the headlights. The basement fell into darkness lit only by the light seeping from the empty storage area.

"Mommy, I'm scared." Kaycee started to cry.

"Shh, you have to be quiet."

"It's *scary!*"

"I'll turn the light on in the car. Stay here."

Monica practically ran from car to storage room, moving the money, a horrific night from not so long ago playing in her head. Kaycee wouldn't stop crying. Monica was afraid someone would hear her. One by one she heaved the first six boxes onto the deep rearmost shelves and shoved them to the wall, the writing face out. Her nerves sizzled for her daughter, for the incredible chance she was taking. Kaycee sobbed on.

When the car was emptied, Monica returned to the house for the final load. Kaycee quieted on the way home. But when they entered the basement for a second time, she wailed all over again.

Monica's throat was dry by the time she pushed the last box of bills into place. She ran to the Volvo and her crying daughter. "It's okay, Kaycee, it's okay. Just a little while longer."

Kaycee's face was red and splotchy. What Monica had put the little girl through. She'd thought her soul would feel so much lighter without the money. But guilt over Kaycee replaced whatever weight she had lost.

For the next hour Monica hauled the now dry Utility Department supplies off the basement floor and into the room, pushing them in front of the eleven boxes. She didn't bother to go through and throw anything away. No time, and besides, she wanted as many boxes as possible to hide the ones containing her sins.

Kaycee sobbed all the way home. Monica wanted to cry too. Tonight, finally, it was over. Except now they faced the rest of their lives.

When she got out of the car her legs shook.

"Mommy, hold me." Kaycee reached out her sweet little arms. Monica picked her up and hugged her tightly. "Shh, it's okay now. Mommy's here, she's always here." She carried Kaycee into the house, sat down on the couch and rocked her.

"Tomorrow I'll take you downtown for an ice cream soda."

# A NOTE FROM THE AUTHOR

**Dear Reader**

Wilmore, Kentucky, is a real town. In fact, I grew up there. The streets in this story are real, the businesses are real. Even many of the houses. All characters are fictional.

When I began this book I promised little to my mother, who still lives in Wilmore, as to how I'd treat her beloved home. "I may or may not blow up the town," I said.

Happy, Mom?

In *Exposure* I set out to write a suspenseful tale about fear and how it binds us. Along the way Kaycee's story deepened to so much more. The consequences of our wrong choices, their fallout on subsequent generations. The irony of sin. The enigmatic workings of the mind.

And now some serious thank-yous are in order. First, my thanks to Gary and Beth Hoenicke, the true owners of Tastebuds, for allowing me to feature their brick-oven pizzas and old-fashioned soda fountain. If you're in the Wilmore area, you simply must stop by and order one of each. Tell them Kaycee sent you.

Thanks also to Wilmore Police Chief Steve Boven and Officer Mike Bandy for granting me interviews about how their department would handle some rather odd scenarios and for showing me around the station. Any deviation from their procedures was intentional fictionalizing on my part. My special gratitude to Officer Bandy, who enthusiastically told me not one but *four* possible scenarios for making the final pages of the epilogue work.

To sweet-faced little Merrick Kasper of Ohio, thanks for allowing me to keep your picture before me as inspiration for Hannah. And my gratitude to Merrick's mom, Dana, who allowed this strange woman with an even stranger request to photograph her daughter. May you both be blessed.

Many thanks to Sue Brower, my Zondervan editor, and my agent, Lee Hough of Alive Communications, for all you did for this story. And I can't leave out Bob Hudson, whose careful copy editing tightened details. Rachelle Gardner has freelanced with Zondervan to edit my last three novels, and she's been fabulous to work with.

Rachelle, thanks for your insights. *Exposure* is a better story because of you.

Most of all, my heartfelt gratitude to you, my readers, for strapping into that seatbelt one more time and rocketing through this ride with me. May you face and conquer your fears through God's power.

Brandilyn Collins